MARRIED
STRANGERS

MARRIED STRANGERS

DWAN ABRAMS

URBAN CHRISTIAN

www.urbanchristianonline.net

Urban Books, LLC
78 East Industry Court
Deer Park, NY 11729

ISBN 13: 978-1-60162-896-1
ISBN 10: 1-60162-896-X

First Mass Market Printing March 2011
First Trade Paperback Printing December 2008
Printed in the United States of America

10   9   8   7   6   5   4   3   2   1

*This is a work of fiction. Any references or similari-
ties to actual events, real people, living, or dead, or
to real locales are intended to give the novel a sense
of reality. Any similarity in other names, characters, places, and incidents is entirely coincidental.*

Distributed by Kensington Publishing Corp.
Submit Wholesale Orders to:
Kensington Publishing Corp.
C/O Penguin Group (USA) Inc.
Attention: Order Processing
405 Murray Hill Parkway
East Rutherford, NJ 07073-2316
Phone: 1-800-526-0275
Fax: 1-800-227-9604

This book is dedicated to my mother,
Gwendolyn Fields

Acknowledgments

Thanks be to God for allowing me to pursue my passion and live my dreams! Thanks to my daughter, Nia, for inspiring me to be the best person that I can be. A special thanks to Alex for all of his love and support.

I'm blessed with a mom who is an encourager and supporter. I love her dearly. To my dad, who has been more like a friend than a father, I love you.

To my best girlfriends: Aleta Barnes, Yolanda Bowen and Margherita Graham, thanks for your encouragement and unconditional love. To Diana Block and Lori Gallon, I'm so fortunate to have you in my life. Whoever would've thought that after high school we would've found our way back to each other as adults? God is good!

To all of the members of The Writers Hut and American Christian Fiction Writers—VIP Chapter, you guys are like family to me. Keep on writing. To my writer friends: Kendra Norman-Bellamy, Murray Silver, Jessica Tilles, Patricia Pope, Valerie Coleman, Vanessa Hollis, Marissa Monteilh, Angela Lewis, Francine Huff, and Monique Lawton, thanks for making me smile and supporting my endeavors. I'll continue to support yours, too. To the writers on the Urban Christian roster, keep on walking in your anointing. A special thanks to my wonderful editor, Joylynn Jossel. Thanks to my sister, Ireana, for encouraging me—more like demanding—that I turn the short story, *Favor*, which appeared in *The Midnight Clear: Stories of Love, Hope and Inspiration* anthology, into a novel. She wanted a better ending for Jonathan and Cheyenne; therefore, creating the foundation for *Married Strangers*.

To the ladies who participated in the 2008 Divas of Literature Tour, it was a pleasure touring with you. I have so much gratitude for Cordella Warren and Marisa Jones for going over and above the call of duty. Those ladies help me run my publishing company, Nevaeh Publishing, as well as review and critique my manuscripts. Thanks to my attorney, Sheila Levine. Thanks to my publicist, Rhonda Bogan, I appreciate you so much. And thanks to all of the loyal readers who continue reading my titles, as well as all of the new ones for giving me a chance.

Peace and Blessings,
Dwan Abrams

One
Rayna

Rayna's eyes welled with tears as feelings of loneliness and disappointment overtook her emotions. All of the romance and passion she envisioned would occur during her honeymoon didn't happen. She imagined that this would have been one of the happiest times of her life. Instead, she was miserable. She had already felt a sense of cognitive dissonance, better known as "buyer's remorse," after her new husband, Bryce, had promised to take her on an exotic vacation in Cancun.

Yeah right! she thought.

Here they were, two weeks before Christmas, in a log cabin at Forrest Hills Mountain Resort in Dahlonega, Georgia. It was a five-day package that Bryce's best friend, Fox, had given them for a wedding present. A friend whose nickname came as a result of not so savory sales tactics, Fox earned the nickname because, according to

Bryce, he was slicker than a snake oil salesman. Rayna found it strange that Bryce would refer to his friend in such a derogatory manner. It vexed her spirit, and she immediately remembered Proverbs 27:19: *A mirror reflects a man's face, but what he is really like is shown by the kind of friends he chooses.*

Now Rayna faced a deeper problem, the dislike of her honeymoon location. Besides the fact that Rayna was not the outdoorsy type, hiking and horseback riding never appealed to her. She and Bryce had discussed, at length, where they would spend their honeymoon ... on the beach. Rayna's fondest memories are of her vacationing in the Bahamas, Hawaii, and different beaches in Florida. There was something about the tranquil waters that made her feel at peace; almost as if she was communing with God.

Bryce had promised her they'd go to Mexico. At the last minute, he told her that he was unable to get the time off from work. He worked as a field reporter, and although he could have gotten a few days off, it wouldn't have been long enough. She was disappointed. Her heart was set on an exotic locale, not somewhere with frost on the trees and snow on the ground. She wondered whether she was catching a glimpse of what her life with Bryce would be like. Broken promises. Even with advance notice, he still wasn't able to come through for their honeymoon. The only person she blamed was herself for not getting to know her husband better before marrying him. As far as Rayna was concerned, a year of knowing Bryce hadn't been nearly enough time. Trying to deal with her regret seemed overwhelming at times.

Rayna considered herself to be spiritually intuitive. But this time, she ignored the signs. A couple of weeks before getting married, Rayna had a disturbing dream about her wedding day. In the dream, her wedding day was a fiasco. She couldn't remember all of the details, but one thing was clear—her feelings throughout the dream were unpleasant. At one point she said, "I'm marrying the wrong man." Having awoken with beads of sweat on her forehead, Rayna dismissed the dream as a case of pre-marital jitters.

Even though the log cabin was nice—hot tub, double showers, and fireplace—the problem was her new husband.

"Good morning, Mrs. Henderson," Bryce said as he kissed Rayna on the cheek.

"Morning." She stretched her arms over her head.

The way Bryce said, "Mrs. Henderson," sent shivers up her spine. To her, he sounded so macho at times. She found that whole "Me Tarzan, you Jane" thing sexy.

"You hungry?" he asked.

She looked at the clock sitting on the wooden nightstand next to the canopy bed. The LED display read 9:00 A.M. in red digits.

"We need to hurry up before they stop serving breakfast," she said.

Rayna wanted to escape out of bed and get dressed before Bryce touched her, again. His passionate desires seemed to be insatiable. Once, she asked him whether he took enhancement drugs, because even after making love, Bryce's physical disposition remained the same. Of course, he denied it. Most women would love to have a man who could last for hours. For Rayna, it didn't take all that. Not if he knew what he was doing. Unfortunately, Bryce wouldn't know how to satisfy her if she were an air traffic controller directing him from the lighthouse. She remembered hearing that sex comprised only two percent of a relationship, if it's good. *But when it's not-so-good, it's about ninety-eight percent*, she thought. Having an ungratifying sex life made it difficult for her to appreciate the good things about Bryce. Like the way he'd rub her feet whenever they sat next to each other on the couch, or the way he'd give her an all over body massage.

"Let's take communion first," Bryce suggested, revealing a devilish grin.

Communion was Bryce's way of asking for physical intimacy, and she thought it was sweet. He had this good guy, bad boy routine down to a science. Rayna looked over at him and immediately, her passions awakened. Her husband was hot. Brad Pitt and George Clooney had nothing on Bryce. He wasn't wearing a shirt and his smooth, hairless chest was toned and muscular. She noticed that his abs workout was working, because the lining of a six-pack was visible. She thought he was sexy. Too bad he couldn't deliver.

"Not right now," she grumbled.

It amazed Rayna how her husband could have so much going on—good looks, a body like a Greek Adonis, sex appeal, and a smile that could light up a room; yet, he didn't know how to straighten her hair and curl her toes, so to speak. It's not like she hadn't expressed her dissatisfaction to Bryce. He knew full well that she was frustrated; yet he wouldn't do anything to change it. Every time she wanted to try something new or different, he called her sadistic. Her feelings were crushed. More than anything, she wanted to please him, and in the process, find pleasure. His inflexibility made Rayna feel less desirable and unappreciated.

She got out of the king-sized bed, walked across the hardwood floor, and went into the double showers. Thankfully, the water running down her face camouflaged the tears streaming down her cheeks. Rayna felt as if she had made a terrible mistake by marrying Bryce. After they consummated their marriage a couple of nights ago, she went into the bathroom and cried. She wondered how two people could be so physically incompatible. She had never heard of such a thing, especially not with married couples. She wondered what she had done to deserve such an unfulfilling union. Silently, she prayed.

Lord, forgive me for my sins. Please help me deal with this marriage. Whatever sin is blocking me from being a good wife, I ask that you remove it. In Jesus' name, I pray. Amen.

As she exited the shower and wrapped her body in a towel, Bryce entered the bathroom. He embraced Rayna, and she melted. Her desire to be close to him was overwhelming; then the thought of being disappointed crept in and immediately turned her off. Not because she didn't love him, because she did. It was more because of his indifferent attitude. In their intimate times, she sensed that his thoughts were elsewhere. He wouldn't look at her, and that bothered her. She wondered whether it was because he was white, and she was black. Then she quickly dismissed that notion because Bryce didn't seem to have a racist bone in his body. His expectation of going all the way at the slightest hint of affection made her hesitant to hug or kiss him. She couldn't even rub her hand along his leg without him getting turned on.

Freeing herself from his toned arms, she looked at his disappointed face and said, "I saved you some hot water. I'm going to get dressed."

Rayna went back into the bedroom. Since it was cold outside, she slipped into a cashmere sweater, jeans, and boots. Her hair was styled in a short, curled "'do" like the actress, Halle Berry's.

Several minutes later, Bryce came from out of the shower. "You look nice," he complimented as he dried off, and changed into a gray mock neck sweater, jeans, and Timberlands.

"Thanks. So do you."

They put on their coats and gloves and left the cabin. Rayna noticed there was frost on the surrounding trees. They walked to the couples-only "Secret Garden" dining room, which happened to be a few feet away.

The hostess, dressed in a sweater and jeans, said, "Are you on your honeymoon?"

"Yes," Bryce replied, smiling. "How could you tell?"

Rayna felt like saying, "Because we're in the *couples-only* dining room," but she refrained. In Bryce's defense, they could've been dating and vacationing together, she reasoned.

"You have that glow about you," the hostess replied.

Bryce looked at Rayna lovingly, and grabbed her gloved hand.

"It's a buffet," the hostess explained, smiling. "Seat yourselves wherever you like."

Thank goodness, Rayna thought. Every time they went out to eat, Bryce always asked the waiter or waitress, "What do you recommend?" It used to bother Rayna, so she asked him why he did that. He told her that it eliminated the guesswork. "Who better to tell you about the food than the people who work at the restaurant?" Bryce replied. She understood, but never adopted that philosophy. Rayna enjoyed scanning the selections. When she would narrow her choices down to two entrées, then she would ask the waiter or waitress for their opinion. Her indecisiveness tended to bother Bryce, but she didn't care.

They sat at a table surrounded by large, panoramic windows. They took off their coats and gloves and placed them on an empty chair.

"Can I get you something to drink?" the hostess asked.

"Two hot teas with sugar and lemon," Bryce replied.

"And an orange juice," Rayna added.

After the hostess took their drink orders, they got up and each fixed themselves a plate. The food looked scrumptious and fresh. Rayna had the cheese grits, scrambled eggs and bacon. Bryce filled his plate with French toast and sausage links.

They went back to their table, and Bryce led them in prayer.

"Father, thank you for this food and fellowship. I pray that this meal is nourishing to our minds and bodies. In Jesus' name, we pray. Amen."

She mixed her eggs with the grits and crumpled bacon on top. Then she stared out the window. Trees for as far as the eyes could see . . . acres and acres of secluded woodlands. Her thoughts drifted to the first time she and Bryce met.

They were standing in line at the café in the Barnes & Noble off Cobb Parkway in Atlanta. After striking up a general conversation, Bryce paid for her latte. He seemed intelligent, not to mention handsome, with that sandy blond hair and green eyes. So, when he asked for her phone number, she gave it to him.

Rayna went home immediately afterward.

Within twenty minutes, her phone rang. It was Bryce, asking her to go out with him.

"When can I see you, again?" Bryce asked.

"How about tomorrow night?" she responded in a flirtatious tone.

"Great." He sounded excited. "Where would you like to go?"

"Pizza Hut," she laughed.

"Pizza Hut?" She could tell by the influx in his voice that he had expected her to name some fancy restaurant.

"Yes."

Besides the fact that Pizza Hut was her favorite pizza establishment, Rayna didn't want Bryce to feel as though she were trying to take advantage of him. When they met, he was dressed in a suit. Not a cheap suit either. Rayna checked his shoes and Bryce wore black Kenneth Coles. He seemed to be doing pretty well. Even still, Rayna had wanted to get to know him personally. At the time, she was not impressed by the fact that by all appearances, he could have taken her to an expensive restaurant.

The following day, he picked Rayna up at her apartment in a rental car and took her to Pizza Hut. While at the restaurant, he explained to her that he actually lived in Chicago and was in Atlanta on business. He worked as a field reporter and was chronicling a news story. He also wrote a newspaper column. His profession seemed exciting to Rayna, because she had written numerous poems and short stories.

One day, she planned to write a full-length book. Speaking with a real life reporter/writer fascinated her. As he told Rayna about his travels and how he became a writer, she hung on his every word.

"I have always been fascinated by the written word," Bryce explained. "You know, it's funny how I became a columnist." He chuckled. "A friend of mine used to write a column for the *Chicago Tribune*. She got a promotion and recommended me for her old job."

"Wow! That was a major blessing." Rayna smiled.

"I know," he laughed. "Especially since I had just graduated from college."

Rayna was not surprised to hear about Bryce's accomplishments. He seemed so eloquent, well-spoken, cultured, and poised. When they arrived at the restaurant, they talked incessantly. She felt as though she was in a therapy session, because he was so easy to talk to.

"Where are you from?" Bryce asked, looking at her.

"I grew up in Orlando, but my parents and I moved to Georgia about . . ." she rolled her eyes upward, "ten years ago." She took a bite of pepperoni pizza.

"Tell me about your family."

She held up her index finger while she chewed the pizza. After she swallowed, she said, "I'm an only child. My mom's a pharmacist, and my dad's a neurologist. What about your family?"

"I have two older brothers and two younger sisters. I'm the middle child. I spent a great deal of my childhood being raised by my grandmother."

"What happened to your parents?"

He sipped from a glass of soda, or "pop" as he called it. "My dad died of a heart attack when I was five, and I don't have a good relationship with my mother."

Curious, Rayna was taken aback. *What kind of guy doesn't get along with his mother?* she wondered.

"My brothers and sisters have the same father, and I have my own father," he explained. "As you can imagine, I was the black sheep."

"You're the middle child, yet you have a different dad?" She said it as more of a statement than a question, trying to make sure she understood him correctly.

"Yes. My mom was married, but she had an affair. I'm the result." He stared at a scratch in the wooden table before taking a sip of his sparkly drink.

Rayna cleared her throat, not really knowing what to say. His candor surprised her.

He looked at her and sucked in his cheeks as if he were sucking a lemon. "My mom's marriage suffered because of it, but they stayed together and had my twin sisters."

"Then why did you have to stay with your grandmother?" She tilted her head to the side.

He looked her in the eye and said seriously, "Because my stepdad didn't treat me the same as the other kids. He was harder on me. My mom figured that with me out of the house, the family could be put back together."

"That's terrible." She furrowed her brow.

Rayna felt sorry for him. She hadn't expected to learn such personal information about him on their first date. In a strange way, seeing Bryce in such a vulnerable state attracted her to him. She had finally met a man who was in touch with his feelings and knew how to convey them. Something in his almond shaped eyes expressed sadness. She could tell that his hurt ran deep. He was so nice that she wanted to help him.

Bryce squeezed Rayna's hand, which was resting on top of the table, and said, "What are you thinking about?"

Rayna had been so deep in thoughts of their first meeting that she hadn't even realized that the hostess had placed their drinks on the table.

"How do you know I was thinking?" she answered, smiling. "I could've been admiring the scenery."

"You might've started out doing that, but I can tell by the way your eyes shifted downward and to the right that you were remembering something."

He's so analytical, she thought. *He pays attention to everything*. That's what she got for hooking up with a brainiac. "I was thinking about us," she admitted. "I can't believe that after six months of being engaged, we're finally married."

Rayna's decision to marry Bryce was an easy one. He proposed to her three months after they met. They had been talking on the phone every day, several times per day. Maintaining a long distance relationship wasn't easy. She missed him terribly and wanted companionship. She was twenty years old and a sophomore at Mercer University. Bryce was three years her senior. They were deeply in love.

"Rayna," he said, interrupting her thoughts once again. "I love you so much," he grinned sheepishly, licking his pink lips.

"I love you, too." She gave a faint smile.

"You don't understand. I love you more than I've ever loved anybody, including my own mother. I don't know what I'd ever do without you, Rayna," Bryce declared.

Somehow, hearing Bryce say he loved her more than his mother disturbed her, because although she loved him, she didn't think it could be compared to the love she had for her parents. Never had she met anyone who could make her remotely think that she loved them more than either one of her parents. She couldn't even imagine. Then again, she thought, Bryce's relationship with his mother was strained. So was it really far-fetched for him to love someone more than her?

Even though she believed him wholeheartedly, Rayna wasn't sure how to respond to his statement. The first time Bryce ever told Rayna that he loved her was one week after they met. It caught her completely off guard. She found it peculiar, because she thought it was too soon for them to exchange those three little words that carry a whole lot of weight. She didn't say it back to him, because she didn't take saying, "I love you" lightly.

Marrying Bryce seemed to make logical sense to Rayna. He was an avid reader, had an incredible vocabulary, and was well-versed in many different things. And she couldn't deny the obvious. Bryce was fine and saved. And in Rayna's opinion, that was definitely a plus. Not to mention that he was a visionary and ambitious. One of the things Rayna admired about him was the fact that he knew a little about a wide array of subjects. He was able to discuss anything with anyone ranging from jazz music to the Greek classics to the Bible. And her parents loved him. Before deciding to commit, Rayna had a conversation with her Aunt Sylvia, which persuaded Rayna to marry Bryce.

Aunt Sylvia and Rayna had a close-knit relationship. She was Rayna's mother's younger sister, in her forties, and had never been married. Based on what she had told her aunt, like the way Bryce would call throughout the day, or send flowers, or take Rayna to nice restaurants, Sylvia was convinced that Bryce loved Rayna. What tilted the scale in Bryce's favor was when Aunt Sylvia said, "Girl, what are you dragging your feet for? Do you know how hard it is to find a man who wants to get married?"

Rayna was glad when the hostess returned and asked, "How's the food?"

"Fine," she replied. That way, she didn't have to acknowledge Bryce's declaration of loving her more than he did his own mother.

He bit into his French toast. "Delicious."

Rayna picked up her cloth napkin and wiped the powdered sugar off Bryce's full lips. His lips didn't look like the average white boy's. They weren't exactly the Mick Jagger model, but they were luscious and sexy. He smiled a dimpled smile. She could tell he appreciated the gesture. They finished their breakfast and walked back to their cabin, glove in glove. As they breathed the cold, crisp air, smoke formed every time they exhaled.

Back in the cabin, Bryce started a fire in the gas log fireplace. They took off their shoes, wrapped themselves in a colorful quilt, and cuddled in front of the blazing fire. It was quite romantic. Rayna closed her eyes, listened to the crackling noises being emitted from the fireplace, and imagined that Bryce would ravish her body and leave her feeling satisfied. Fantasizing and praying helped her get through the remaining three days of her honeymoon. Thankfully, she had her fantasies.

Two

Aja

"Just a minute," Aja yelled as she stepped over a couple of blocks making her way to the side door in the kitchen. She flung the door open and greeted Mrs. Halston with a smile. Unlocking the screen door she yelled over her shoulder, "Amari, your mother is here."

"Hey, Ms. Aja," Mrs. Halston said as she stepped inside. "How was Amari today?"

"She was good. We practiced our ABC's today. I'm trying to teach the children how to say them without singing."

"That's great. I'll work with her at home, too."

"I appreciate it."

Amari ran into the kitchen.

"Hey, baby," Mrs. Halston said as she kneeled down and gave her daughter a hug.

"Amari, didn't you have a jacket today?" Aja asked, scratching her chin. The girl nodded her head. "I thought so," Aja said, smiling. "Go and get it."

"Okay." Amari went back into the other room and retrieved her jacket. When she came back she was struggling to put it on, so Aja helped her.

"There you go, big girl," Aja said once the task was complete. "I'll see you tomorrow."

Amari reached out and wrapped her arms around Aja's waist and squeezed. Aja hugged her back.

"All right, baby," Mrs. Halston said. "You'll see Ms. Aja tomorrow. We've got to go."

The little girl seemed as if she was about to cry. Aja was used to most of the children having a difficult time going home after being with her all day. She prided herself on not only teaching the children, but playing with them and giving them healthy doses of affection and attention. Her students absolutely adored her. And the feeling was mutual.

Aja bent over and picked her up. "Don't you start crying, pretty girl," she said, looking Amari in the eye. "I'll see you tomorrow, okay?"

Amari poked out her lips, and Aja held her close. Then she put her down.

"Come on," Mrs. Halston said, holding out her hand.

Amari waved at her daycare provider before grabbing her mother's hand and saying, "Bye," in a soft tone.

"See you tomorrow," Aja said with a smile.

Mrs. Halston and Amari left, and Aja locked

the door behind them. All of the children were gone for the day, so Aja needed to clean up. She walked back into the play area and noticed that her son, Jayden, was still playing. Her part-time assistant, Iesha, was watching him.

"Iesha," she said, "do me a favor and start straightening up while I make Jayden a snack."

Iesha gave her two-thumbs up. "I got you."

Aja retreated to the kitchen and fixed Jayden peanut butter crackers and a glass of milk. "Come with me, honey," she said to Jayden as she exited the kitchen and entered the other room.

He got up and followed her up the stairs. While upstairs, she turned on his favorite cartoon, *Go Diego Go*, and set the snack on the table. Aja kissed her son on the cheek before going back downstairs to help Iesha clean up. They washed off the toys in a cleaning solution before drying them and placing them in their appropriate places. Once they finished, Iesha left, and Aja started dinner.

The spaghetti, salad, and garlic bread were finished, and Aja sat on the couch in her Tuscan-inspired living room. The walls were dark blue and the furniture, cream. Her feet were crossed at the ankles, resting atop an area rug. A week had passed since her friend, Rayna, had gone on her honeymoon, and she missed her. She figured that Rayna should be back by now. Wanting to hear all of the details, she decided to give her a call at home.

"Hello," Rayna answered.

Aja was glad to hear her voice. Since she hadn't spoken to Rayna in a week, she couldn't wait to find out the details of her getaway.

"Hey, girl, it's Aja. How was the trip?"

"It was too cold to hang out. We mostly stayed inside. One day, we had a delicious, indoor picnic basket lunch for two. Dinners were by candlelight. When we did go out, it was for short trips."

"Uh-huh. Getting your groove on," Aja teased.

She heard Rayna suck air through her teeth. "Puhleese."

"What? Did something happen?" Aja wrapped a strand of hair around her index finger.

"How about we spent the last few days of the trip arguing?" Rayna paused. "One day, we were in the car, and I was driving. He said something so trivial, I don't even remember what started the fight. I got so mad, I kicked him out of the car."

"Girl, no you didn't. You did not kick him out of the car!" She stopped twirling her hair and gasped, placing her hand over her open mouth.

"Yes, I did. He was getting on my nerves."

Laughing, Aja removed her hand from her mouth and said, "Then what happened?"

"I drove away."

"Please don't tell me you left the man standing in the cold." She squeezed her eyes shut, still laughing.

"I came back," Rayna relented.

Aja opened her eyes. "Don't feel bad. Hunter and I got into it on our honeymoon, too."

"Serious?" Rayna sounded surprised.

"Girl, yes. You'd be surprised how many people fuss and fight during their honeymoon. Everything's cool those first couple of days. After that, anything can happen." She sighed.

"Nobody ever tells you the downside. All you ever hear about are the love stories. How romantic everything is." Rayna paused and blew into the receiver. "Aja, can I ask you a question?" She sounded serious.

"Of course you can."

"Have you and Hunter ever had incompatibility issues?"

"What do you mean?"

"Like not being on the same page, physically."

"Girl, no!" She laughed loudly. "We have never had that problem. Ol' boy can throw down. He brings out the wild side of me. I told him he's never going to find anybody to do all the unconstrained stuff I do to him."

"TMI, Aja," Rayna said. "Too much information."

"Okay, seriously. What are you saying? Bryce's not taking care of business?"

"No," she said hesitantly.

"No, he's not taking care of business, or no, that's not it?"

"He's not handling business," she clarified.

"Where's he now?"

"He's at the library doing research for a story."

"I was about to say . . . we shouldn't have these types of conversations if he's at home."

"I know." She sighed. "I'm frustrated. I don't know what to do."

Aja exhaled deeply. "I wish I could help you with that one, but—"

"Anyway," Rayna interrupted, "how are things going with you and Hunter?"

"Everything's okay." She was concerned about Rayna and had some questions. Since they were close friends, Aja decided to take the direct approach and just ask her. "Didn't you sleep with Bryce before you married him?"

"I did, but I thought things would get better." She sounded disappointed.

"Girl, don't you know stuff like that don't change? If anything, it gets worse."

"I see that now," she admitted.

"Maybe y'all can watch movies, or you can teach him how to please you." Aja sounded more southern than usual. Although she was from Decatur where (as the saying went) it was greater, she didn't usually talk with a strong accent.

"He's a grown man. I can't teach him how to make love," Rayna said defensively. "Besides, he gets offended every time I try to instruct him on what to do. He says I shouldn't be so controlling. Then he resists. If I want a position other than the same ol', same ol', he calls me sadistic. It's like he gets disgusted with me."

"For real?" Aja sounded surprised.

"Yes. I don't feel like talking about this anymore. The more I talk, the more upset I get."

"You better go buy yourself some toys," Aja joked, laughing. She was trying to lighten the mood.

"Can't."

"Why not?"

"If Bryce found out, he'd take it personally. He's already complaining about feeling rejected. I don't mean to make him feel bad or hurt his feelings. Sometimes I don't even realize I'm pushing him away. It's just that I feel so terrible inside every time we're intimate. I hate feeling that way, and it comes out whenever he makes a move on me."

"That's understandable. I'd probably do the same thing if I were in your shoes."

"Did I tell you that I'm going back to school to get my MFA?"

"You're going back to school?"

Aja remembered that Rayna had mentioned returning to school, and she was glad to hear that she was going through with it.

"Yes. Bryce landed a job as an evening news anchor," she explained, voice perking up. "Since he relocated to Atlanta, he gave up his job at the Tribune. He still does freelance writing, though. With his promotion and pay raise, he'll be more than able to support us while I'm in grad school at Georgia State University."

"That's good, Rayna." Aja sincerely felt that Rayna had a good man, and she wished that her husband was as dependable as Bryce. She hoped that Rayna knew how good she had it. "The fact that he's willing to work two jobs to help support his family speaks volumes about his character. Let me tell you something; don't let sex ruin your marriage. It's obvious that Bryce loves you very much. I don't think he'd ever cheat on you, and he's ambitious. He'll take care of you. There are so many men out there who are good in the bedroom, but aren't worth squat anywhere else. They don't want to work, they lack ambition, aren't motivated, and are just plain lazy. You've got yourself a good man. You don't have to worry about him. Hang on in there."

"Thanks. Listen at you, dropping knowledge," she chuckled. "I hear you, big sis. Don't worry about me. Love you, girl."

They both laughed.

"Love you, too."

They ended the call, and before Aja could ponder her friend's problem, her cell phone rang. She retrieved the phone from her purse and checked the caller ID. It was Trevon, a guy she had met while coming out of the grocery store. He was a young thug; a straight-up hustler. He was twenty-three years old, which made him eleven years her junior. God, along with common sense, spared Aja from the appearance of a thirty-four year old.

"Hello," she answered in a seductive tone.

"What up, shawty?" he said with a southern drawl.

"Nothing. What are you up to?" She felt like a school girl. All giddy.

"Not much. Chillin'. A brother wanna know when he can get atcha."

"You know I'm married," she said in a reprimanding but playful manner. "I'll have to let you know about that."

"Don't make me wait too long." He smacked his lips. "I want to see that pretty face. You're one pretty chocolate drop. I'll bet you just as sweet, too. Ain't ya?"

Aja laughed. She couldn't believe she was entertaining this boy. Her biggest internal battle was regarding the color of her skin. She looked at her soft, chocolate-colored hands and wished they were lighter. Having grown up in the south, dark skin automatically meant being less attractive. As much as it pained her to admit it, she had often times considered bleaching her skin.

It wasn't until she voiced her insecurity to Hunter that she realized what a mistake that would've been. She remembered the disappointed look on his face when she confided in him that she thought she was too dark. His response was, "Bay, I don't know what you're talking about. Your complexion is beautiful. You're like butter pecan and sweet milk chocolate all rolled into one. When you look at women like Oprah, and supermodels like Iman and Naomi Campbell, or singers like Diana Ross and Patti LaBelle, or that actress, Kenya Moore, that doesn't make you realize how blessed you are? Black women are some of the most beautiful women on earth. Those sisters are baaad! Not a red one in the bunch, and can't nobody take anything from them."

She heard the garage door open. "I gotta go," she said in a rushed tone, heart beating fast.

"All right. I'll holla."

She hung up and turned off the phone. Cell phones, pagers, and emails were not a cheater's friend, she realized. More people than a little bit got busted by modern technology, she didn't intend to be one of them. Aja didn't consider herself to be a full-blown cheater, because she hadn't been intimate with anyone, other than her husband, since their marriage. However, she was guilty of flirting and entertaining the idea. As a Christian, she knew that lusting in her heart was a sin, too. Just because she hadn't committed the physical act, she was still committing adultery. Even still, she wasn't ready to stop. Somehow, the attention from other men gave her the validation that her husband didn't.

She heard keys fumbling at the door. Hunter entered, wearing his FedEx uniform. He worked for the respected company as a delivery guy.

Aja stood up. "Hey, boo."

He handed her the mail and kissed her on the cheek. She perused through the stack . . . bills, bills and more bills. She used to have more money before getting married, she thought. Seemed to her like the opposite should be true, but it wasn't. That's what she got for marrying for lust. Her judgment was cloudy.

When she met Hunter six years ago, he was going through a divorce, living in a low rent, one-bedroom apartment, and didn't have a car. She overlooked his circumstances, because she had a good job as a realtor. Being an independent woman, she had a four-bedroom house and drove a Benz.

After getting married, he moved in with Aja. That's when she learned that he was deep in credit card debt. When she discovered his bleak financial outlook she wished that she had taken the time to find out more about Hunter's financial portfolio before marrying him. If she had, she might've thought twice about tying the knot. Since Hunter was now her husband, Aja felt as if it was her responsibility to help him. She paid off his credit card debt and bought him a car. Then she found out he was behind on his child support payments. His ex-wife, Sunni, took him to court and garnished his wages. Aja was furious. She had no idea that her income would be considered, along with his, when the South Carolina courts determined how much his new support payments would be. The thought of her disposable income taking care of a child that wasn't hers made her feel as helpless as a butterfly trapped in a glass jar.

Eventually, Aja's real estate sales decreased, and commission wasn't as lucrative as it used to be. Forced to find a new profession, she opened up a home daycare. It did not pay nearly as much money as Aja used to make in real estate, and the kids sometimes worked her nerves, but it allowed her the opportunity to take care of her own four-year-old son, and she loved that.

"What's for dinner?" Hunter asked as he headed toward the kitchen.

"I made spaghetti." She trailed behind him.

He walked into the kitchen and lifted the lid

off the large pot sitting on the stove. "Smells good." He covered the dish, and asked, "Where's Jayden?"

"In his room, playing." She smiled.

"I'ma go upstairs and take off this uniform."

"Okay."

He walked upstairs and Aja leaned against the island in the kitchen and opened the bills. Immediately, she could feel the blood rushing to her face. Her cheeks felt hot, and she became angry when she saw several past due notices enclosed. *Is it too much to ask for Hunter to pay the bills on time?* she thought. Barely able to contain her anger, she stormed upstairs. Hunter was in the bedroom taking off his shirt.

"Hunter!" she yelled, waving the bills in the air. "Why are the Visa, telephone, and electric bills past due?"

"You better watch how you talkin' to me," he said in a surprisingly calm manner as he continued to get undressed.

Aja hated it when he tried to man up on her. She wasn't having it. Backing down wasn't something she was accustomed to. *Who does he think he's dealing with?* she thought. Surely, he knew she was not afraid of him. She walked up closer to him, and threw the letters toward the bed, making sure most hit his side.

He grabbed her forcefully by the arm and said, "Woman, don't you ever throw anything at me! I'll break your neck!"

Shocked, Aja blinked quickly. He released Aja's arm, and shoved her backward. Hunter's fingerprints were visible on her arm, and she felt a tingling sensation, so she rubbed it. Aja was so enraged that she saw red. All she could think was this Negro has got to go. No man was going to put his hands on her in her house. *This ain't the Mike Tyson and Robin Givens show.*

Even though Hunter was bigger and stronger, she didn't consider that when she lunged at him, knocking him slightly off balance. He steadied himself on the bed. Then she punched him in the chest, and he pushed her away, causing her to fall to the floor.

"What's wrong with you, Aja? You gone crazy?" he yelled.

The pitter patter of little feet running down the hall snapped Aja out of her rage and back into reality.

"Mommy, Daddy!" Jayden cried. "Why are you fighting?"

He stood in the doorway with tears streaming down his cheeks. *Oh God,* she thought. What was she doing? The last thing she wanted was for her baby to see her acting like a fool.

Aja got up off the ground and walked over to Jayden. She put on a fake smile as her countenance. "Honey, please go back to your room. Mommy and Daddy are fine," she lied.

"No, you're not," Jayden insisted. "Mommy, your arm is red! You were fighting."

Aja saw Jayden's tear stained face, and it broke her heart. She wiped away his tears and gave him a hug. She tried to reassure him that everything was fine, and it was just an accident. The two of them walked back into his

Power Ranger decorated room, and she searched for Diego, Dora the Explorer's cousin, On Demand. While he watched TV, she closed his door and went back into the master bedroom.

"Tell me why you haven't been paying the bills?" she said to Hunter as soon as she walked into the room, closing the door behind her.

"Stop sweatin' me." He sounded frustrated. "I have been paying the bills."

"Not on time." She felt her jaw tightening. "What's up with that?"

"Look, Sunni called me and told me Devin needed braces. I had to pay for that."

"What?" She sounded surprised.

She didn't want to believe what Hunter was saying, but how could she not? *Will Sunni ever stop milking us dry?* Aja was convinced that Sunni wanted Hunter back, and she would stop at nothing to achieve that goal. Sunni had already garnished Hunter's wages. He wasn't obligated to pay anything else, so, Aja wondered, what was the deal with the braces? And Aja resented the way Sunni used their son as a pawn in her grudge match with Hunter.

"I didn't want to tell you, because I knew you would go off," he explained.

"If we could afford it, I wouldn't go off. But we can't. You're taking food out of our son's mouth. We're on the verge of losing electricity, and God only knows what else, because you can't stand up to THAT! Why are you so weak when it comes to her?"

"Don't you ever call me weak!" His eyes narrowed in on her.

"Whatever, Hunter." She dismissed him with the wave of her right hand. "Did you speak with the dentist to find out whether you could make payment arrangements?"

"No. I didn't speak to the dentist, but Sunni faxed me a copy of the bill. I paid half, and she paid the other half."

"Great!" She threw her hands in the air, exasperated.

She opened the door and walked toward the stairs. Suddenly, she felt Hunter forcefully yank her arm from behind and spin her around.

"Don't you walk away from me when I'm talking to you," Hunter hissed.

Aja snatched her arm away and lost her footing. Fear and panic overtook her like a terrorist attack. She was not ready to die, she thought. Who would take care of her son? She reached for the rail, but couldn't grip it. Loud, high-pitched screams emitted from her mouth as she tumbled headlong down the carpeted stairs and landed on the base.

"Bay!" Hunter yelled as he ran down the stairs.

Moaning and groaning, Aja was unable to move. Her ankle throbbed and her head ached. She lay there with tears streaming down her cheeks. *What's really going on?* she wondered. She must've been missing something.

Three
Shania

Every time I converse with my sister, Cheyenne, I end up getting upset or feel like beating her down.

"Cheyenne," I yelled into the receiver, "tell me now."

"Sister," she whined in a nasally tone, "I'll be there in a little while. I'll tell you when I see you. K. Bye."

We hung up. I closed my eyes and prayed that everything was all right. Knowing my sister, it could be anything. It's ten days before Christmas and Cheyenne is driving from Valdosta to Alpharetta, Georgia, to spend the holiday with me. This is the first holiday we're actually spending in the house since our parents died. In previous years, we'd go visit relatives.

Cheyenne's a freshman at Valdosta State University. I'm proud of her for going to college, because it was no easy feat getting her there. In high school, she was notorious for skipping classes. It was favor from God that allowed her to graduate. I'd never seen someone miss as much school as my sister and still graduate with honors. That's favor—it's not fair.

Our parents died when Cheyenne was ten, and I was twenty-two. Fortunately, I had just completed my senior year of college at Auburn University when I became her legal guardian. With my portion of the money we inherited from my parents' life insurance policies, I was able to start my own catering company, *Eat Your Heart Out*.

I tried to raise my sister the way I thought my parents would want. We went to church every Sunday, and were active members. I prayed and taught Cheyenne how to pray, too. I went to PTA meetings, checked my sister's homework, helped her with science projects, and made unexpected visits to her school. I did everything I could to let Cheyenne know that I loved her.

When she went through puberty, I didn't think I was going to survive. She was moody; got on my nerves. I couldn't figure out whether she was thirteen or thirty from one day to the next. It was hard for me to maintain a romantic relationship, because I was too busy raising a child. Most of the men my age weren't interested in taking on that added responsibility. Thinking back, that was probably for the best. At that time, I didn't need the distraction of being in a committed relationship anyway. I was dealing with my parents' death, raising

Cheyenne, and starting a company. When I was emotionally and spiritually ready for a relationship, Greg came into my life.

Greg and I had met at the Corner Café, in Buckhead, during lunchtime. We struck up casual conversation while waiting to be seated separately.

"It's a nice day outside. Do you live around here?" he asked me.

"No. Alpharetta. You?"

"Stone Mountain." He glanced at my mouth. "You have a beautiful smile. Are you meeting your boyfriend for lunch?"

"No, I'm dining alone today." I looked him in the eye and grinned even harder.

"I find that hard to believe." He rubbed his hands together. "A man would have to be crazy to let a gorgeous woman like you dine alone."

"I'm getting my Range Rover serviced across the street at Hennessey," I volunteered. "I'm simply passing the time."

He licked his lips. "I'm here meeting a client. Otherwise, I'd ask you to join me."

"A client, huh? What do you do?"

"I sell insurance."

He reached in his pocket and handed me a business card. I examined the card and noted that his name was Gregory.

"Nice card, Gregory."

He laughed. "I'm sorry. I'm Greg Crinkle," he said, extending his hand. "And you are?"

"Shania Lassiter."

I grabbed his hand, preparing for a handshake. Instead, he gently kissed the back of my hand. His lips were as soft as melted butter. The fine hairs on my arm stood at attention. *What a gentleman*, I thought.

He looked me in the eyes and said, "Nice to meet you, Shania. Beautiful name for a beautiful woman." I smiled as I freed my hand so that I could retrieve a business card from inside of my purse. I handed the card to him. He studied the card for a moment before saying, "I love a woman who can cook. I just might have to marry you."

We both laughed. The hostess notified me that my table was ready.

"Talk to you later, Greg. Enjoy your lunch."

"You, too."

I sat at a table near the window and ate a turkey sandwich. Before Greg left the restaurant, he stopped by my table and spoke, again. He flashed me a top model smile. He seemed nice.

When it was time for me to leave, the waitress advised that Greg had already paid my tab. That made me smile. Not only was he good-looking, but considerate, too. He earned major cool points with me that day. And of course, I had to call the following day, and thank him.

"Hi, Greg," I said. "It's Shania. We met—"

"I was wondering when I was going to hear from you, Shania, from the Corner Café." He chuckled, and seemed genuinely happy to hear from me.

"I just wanted to thank you for treating me to lunch. That was really sweet of you."

"You're welcome. I want to see you, again. Do you have a boyfriend?"

"No. You?"

"No, I certainly don't have a boyfriend." He laughed.

"Hey, this is Atlanta." I giggled.

"And no, I don't have a girlfriend or wife either. So when can I see you?"

"I'm not looking at my calendar; would you call me later?" I deliberately kept the conversation brief, because I didn't want to appear too eager.

"Sure, I can call you back. What time?"

"Seven-thirty should be fine. Talk to you then."

"I look forward to it."

The truth be told, I was looking forward to speaking with him again, too. There was a sincerity about him that made me trust him right off the bat. I thought about his large, white teeth, and yummy smile. Then I prayed.

"Father, thank you for all you have done for me. Keep me on the right path, and protect me from all evil and harms. You know me better than I know myself, and you know exactly what I need. It is not my desire to waste my time, or bring the wrong people into my life. If this man, Greg, has been sent by you, please reveal that to me right away. If he's not for me, have him lose my number. In Jesus' name, I pray. Amen."

Greg called me back at seven-thirty on the dot, and we made plans to get together for dinner that upcoming Saturday. Every day for the rest of the week, I thought about him.

On the night of our date, Greg picked me up at my house, and took me to the Sun Dial restaurant in downtown Atlanta. I absolutely loved the spectacular view of the city from the rotating establishment.

"So, Greg, tell me about yourself," I said, taking a sip of water.

Smiling, Greg said, "I'm the youngest of three children. I have an older sister and brother. My dad's a retired Air Force pilot, and my mom volunteers her time to various charitable organizations. Did I tell you how amazing you look tonight?"

"You just did. Thank you."

Greg looked at me with the most admiring eyes. His gaze bore a hole through my soul and made me feel like the most beautiful woman in the room; no, the world. In an effort to hide my grin, I scanned the bill of fare until the waiter returned to take our orders. When the waiter arrived, I ordered the half rack of lamb, and Greg selected roasted chicken.

"Your food will be out shortly," the waiter said.

"Tell me about your siblings," I said, smoothing out a wrinkle in the tablecloth.

"Sure. My sister, Aleigha, is a pediatrician and my brother, Neil, is a lawyer. Aleigha has been happily married to her college sweetheart for the past ten years. They have beautiful twin daughters, Alexis and Arryana. Those girls are my heart." He chuckled, taking a sip of his water. "And Neil is married, too. He and his wife have been together for five years, and they have a little boy, Nelson. He's two years old and a bundle of energy." Looking at me, Greg said, "I pray that my own family will be as blessed."

"So you want to have children one day?"

"Ah-hem," Greg cleared his throat, "I wouldn't mind having two or three. I love children."

"Do you go to church?"

"I attend every Sunday, and Tuesday night Bible Study, at Saved and Sanctified Baptist Church. I'm one of the youth pastors." I nodded my head and smiled. Then I silently thanked the Lord for sending me a great guy. "Enough about me," he said. "Tell me about your family."

I took a deep breath and exhaled. I didn't like telling this story, but there was something about Greg that made me comfortable enough to open up. "I was away at college. I had just completed finals, and was excited about my up-coming graduation ceremony when I received a phone call from my mom's older sister, Sylvia. She was a rambling mess, crying and screaming. She said, and I quote, 'Your family, your mom and dad. They've been killed in a car accident.' Of course, she was stuttering when she told me."

Greg's jaw dropped. My hand was resting on the table, and he covered my smaller hand with his larger one. "I'm so sorry," he said sincerely.

I gave a faint smile. "It's okay. When I initially heard the news, I had a sinking feeling in the pit of my stomach. I wanted to faint. Surely, Aunt Sylvia hadn't just told me that my mommy and daddy were . . . gone. I could hear the anguish in Aunt Sylvia's voice, and it cut me to the bone. She cried so hard that it sounded like she was hyperventilating. Then she said, 'A drunk driver hit them. Come home right away.'

"I couldn't breathe," I explained as he gently squeezed my hand and looked me in the eyes. "I felt as if the walls were closing in on me. Next thing I know, I dropped the phone and wailed. My heart thumped so loudly that I could hear it. I wanted to die. I couldn't understand why it happened. My parents were both really good people."

"No one should have to go through that. That's one of the reasons why I don't drink. One of my college buddies was killed by a drunk driver. The pain never really goes away."

"That's the truth. I felt as if I was trapped in a photograph—still and lifeless. The pain was so severe; I didn't think I could handle it. My life seemed about as clear as muddy water. The only thing I knew was that I'd never be the same. I didn't think I'd ever smile, laugh, or experience happiness ever again. How was I supposed to live without my parents?" He nodded his understanding. "I can honestly say, that if it weren't for my relationship with the Lord, the support of my family, and pastor, I don't think I would've made it."

"I can only imagine."

The waiter returned with our food, and while

we ate, I told Greg about my younger sister, Cheyenne, and my catering company. After dinner, we took a romantic carriage ride through the streets of downtown Atlanta. He wrapped his arm around me, and I felt safe. That's when I realized I could fall in love with Mr. Gregory Crinkle.

I went into the modern kitchen with stainless steel appliances to put the finishing touches on Cheyenne's welcome home dinner. I must admit that I put my foot all up in it! Baked chicken so tender it'll melt in one's mouth. Pots of collards, sweet potato soufflé, and garlic mashed potatoes covered the eyes of the stove. Freshly baked yeast rolls coated with warm butter, and cornbread dressing occupied the oven. The food smelled so good I wanted to throw down right then, but I knew I had to wait. So, I went upstairs and took a shower. I slipped into a chocolate colored shirt and matching lace skirt; moisturized my face and pulled my hair back in a matching lace bow.

I went back into the kitchen, put dirty dishes in the dishwasher, and started a load. I wiped down the marble counter tops, because I can't stand a dirty kitchen. My mother used to clean up the kitchen as she cooked. She taught me that. She also taught me how to cook. As a child, I would watch my mother as she prepared our meals. Pleasant smells always emanated from our kitchen. My family loved her cooking. Sometimes, when I'm throwing down in the kitchen, I can feel my mother's presence. We were so close. We loved exchanging recipes and trying new things. Even though it's been eight years since my parents died, I still miss them— especially during the holidays.

I felt a tinge of sadness trying to creep up on me like a teenager sneaking into the house after curfew. I quickly thwarted it by focusing on more positive things. I realize that I have a lot to be thankful for. I'm healthy, woke up in my right state of mind, own a successful business, and I have a great guy. I'm fortunate, and truly blessed.

My doorbell rang. I looked through the peephole and saw that it was Greg. He looked good in his crisp white shirt and jeans. His bald-head was freshly shaved and goatee neatly trimmed. He was carrying a bottle of sparkling apple cider in one hand and a Poinsettia in the other.

"Nice to see you," I greeted, and kissed him on the cheek. I took the bottle and he followed me into the kitchen.

"What are you in here burning?" he asked, placing the plant on the island.

"Got jokes, I see." I laughed.

He rubbed his stomach and said, "I'm playing. It smells good. Almost as good as you look." He pulled up a barstool and sat at the island.

"Thanks." I placed the sparkling drink in the refrigerator. "Cheyenne and Jonathan should be here soon," I said, like it was no big deal. In reality, I couldn't believe that I was about to break bread with Jonathan. He's the bane of my existence. I pray that Cheyenne wises up before she lets him ruin her life.

"Jonathan?" Greg crinkled his nose. "I thought you couldn't stand him."

"I can't, but that doesn't stop Cheyenne from dating him."

"Did he ever get his GED?"

"No. He's been popping the same old tired game ever since Cheyenne's known him. And she keeps falling for it. When they were both juniors in high school, and he dropped out, I told her he wasn't going back. She gave me some sob story about his mother abandoning him, and he dropped out of school to support himself."

"Is he still selling drugs?"

"Yes. What can I say? She's got a thing for bad boys."

"She needs to be careful. I don't get a good feeling about this guy. You hear stories all the time about people getting killed because of the company they keep. A bullet doesn't have anybody's name on it. She's got a lot going for herself and could do a whole lot better. I would hate to see her ruin her life because of him, or anybody else for that matter."

"I know. It's like my momma used to say, 'A hard head makes a soft behind.' All I can do is pray."

I started transferring food from copper pots to sterling silver serving dishes. My mom used to use the same expensive silver pieces for holidays, and any other occasion she deemed special. Greg offered to help, so I let him set the

table. By the time we finished, the doorbell
rang. Perfect timing, I thought. I opened the
door. Cheyenne and Jonathan greeted me and I
offered them a warm smile and gave my sister a
hug. I was glad to see her, regardless of how
much she tested my resolve. They came in, I
locked the door behind them, and then we
went into the kitchen with Greg.

Greg acknowledged Cheyenne and Jonathan
and gave Jonathan daps. In the year we had
been dating, Greg had met Cheyenne twice before. During a going away party I threw for
Cheyenne to celebrate her going off to college,
Greg met Jonathan.

"Sister," Cheyenne said. She never called me
by my real name. "I have something to show
you." I sucked air through my teeth and rolled
my eyes. What now? I wondered. She turned
her back toward me, exposing angel wings tat-
tooed on her shoulder blade. I didn't say anything. "Well, do you like it?" Cheyenne asked.

"It's all right," I said. I don't know why she
bothered to ask me. She knew full well that I
wouldn't approve of the tattoo. That's why she
waited until after she had already gotten it to
tell me about it. Then she showed it to Greg.
He simply shook his head.

"And wait." Cheyenne slightly lifted up her
halter style top to reveal a second tattoo—a
cross and rosary on the small of her back. This
just keeps getting better and better, I thought.
The devil is a liar. I'm not about to give in to
this nonsense. I recited The 23rd Psalm in my
mind. I silently said that prayer whenever I felt

an anxiety attack coming on, like right now. "Sister, do you like it?"

"It doesn't matter if I like it. I'm not the one who mutilated her body."

"Why you gotta be so melodramatic all the time?" Cheyenne laughed.

I could tell by the tone of her voice that she was disappointed that I didn't approve of her body art.

I exhaled and said, "Let's eat before the food gets cold."

We went into the formal dining room. We held hands and closed our eyes as Greg blessed the food.

"Lord, thank you for this food we're about to receive. Bless the hands that prepared the meal. And may we enjoy the feast and fellowship. In Jesus' name, we pray. Amen."

Then we took our seats and each fixed a plate.

"So. Shania. How you been?" Jonathan said.

I hoped that my eyes didn't betray me, because secretly I was throwing darts at Jonathan. I couldn't stand the way he talked all slow. Perhaps that's the only way his brain could keep up.

"I've been doing well," I replied.

Until now, I hadn't really paid much attention to Jonathan. He looked as sloppy as he usually did—baggy sweat pants and an oversized white tee. However, he had something on the side of his neck. My eyes narrowed, trying to decipher the scribbling. *Cheyenne*. He had Cheyenne's name engraved on his neck.

"When did you get that?" I nodded my head in Jonathan's direction.

He placed his hand on his neck and said, "Oh, this?" He laughed and looked at Cheyenne. "Not that long ago. Maybe two, three weeks."

I gave Cheyenne a scathing look and said, "Why did you let him do that?"

"Sister, I told him not to, but he said he wanted to do it." She went on to explain that Jonathan said he loved her and would still want her name on him even if they broke up.

I felt disgusted. They were so young and so naïve. They were a perfect example of the blind leading the blind. Not wanting to say the wrong thing, I stuffed a forkful of collards in my mouth.

"Jonathan, what have you been doing with yourself?" Greg asked, biting into a piece of chicken.

"You know. Tryna stay outta trouble."

I wanted to reach across the table and shake him. For the life of me I couldn't figure out what Cheyenne saw in him. He had pimply skin and a chipped tooth in the front of his mouth. He had enough butter on his teeth to spread on every roll at the table. I had to wonder whether she was dating him just to rebel against me.

"You plan on going back to school?" Greg asked Jonathan, sounding like a parent. He reminded me of my dad; the way he used to interrogate my boyfriends.

"Nah. I wanna get my GED."

"So why don't you?"

"I'm workin' on it. I gotta get a copy of my birth certificate from my mom. We ain't speaking right now, so it's hard."

This guy must think that everybody at this table has about as much common sense as God gave to a rock. Who was he trying to fool? I've met his mother, Candace, and spoken with her in-depth. She admitted to leaving her children for a while, but she came back. Candace said that Jonathan was trouble, and warned me to get my sister away from him. She was the one who told me Jonathan was a drug dealer. According to Candace, she found his supply at her house and kicked him out. Having him living with her and her other children posed too much of a threat to the safety of their family. She refused to take him back in until he straightened up his act.

When I confronted my sister about Jonathan being a drug dealer, she tried to down play the whole thing. Insisted Candace was crazy. Not credible because she abandoned her family. I told her I believed Candace's story. Then Cheyenne flipped the script and acted like Jonathan's drug dealing was justified since he had to fend for himself. I looked at her like she had lost her mind. I told her to stop making excuses for Jonathan's bad behavior. He made a choice to sell drugs. She stopped talking. I could tell by the thoughtful look in her eyes that my words were getting to her. At least I gave her something to think about.

For the rest of dinner, we talked about the weather and college life, mostly Greg's recollections. Afterward, Cheyenne and I cleared the dishes from the table. Greg offered his assistance, but I assured him Cheyenne and I could handle it. So he joined Jonathan in the family room, where the Christmas tree was located. This was the first tree I had ever purchased, and Greg helped me put it up. It touched the ceiling. The tree itself was white and the decorations were primarily gold, with red and green accents.

"How do you think you did this semester?" I asked Cheyenne as I scraped leftovers into plastic containers.

"I don't know," she shrugged.

I could tell she was lying by the influx in her voice. "What do you mean 'I don't know'? Have you been going to school?"

She exhaled and closed her eyes, acted like I was getting on her nerves. She opened her eyes and said, "Sister, I don't want to talk about this right now." She unloaded dishes from the dishwasher, making room for the new batch, and put them in the cabinet.

Silently, I fumed. I wanted to go off, but I knew that wouldn't accomplish anything; at least, not anything positive. Besides, we had company and I didn't want to show out in front of them. So I continued to put up the food.

Having finished our domestic chores, Cheyenne went into the family room and I put on a pot of coffee. A few minutes later, I grabbed a deck of Uno cards from the island drawer and joined the rest of them while the coffee brewed. They were as excited as school children at recess when I suggested we play. Greg dealt the first hand and I won. We were having such a good time, laughing and trash talking, that I temporarily forgot about my issues with Cheyenne.

I asked, "Anyone want some coffee?"

Greg and Cheyenne said, "Yes."

We momentarily interrupted the game while Greg and I went into the kitchen. I grabbed three cups and saucers from the cabinet then filled them up. Since the three of us liked our coffee the same way, I spruced up the hot liquid with hazelnut creamer and a couple of cubes of sugar that were housed in a small crystal bowl.

Smiling, Greg said, "I'm really having a good time."

"Me too," I replied.

Greg lifted the corners of two saucers that were balancing cups on top of them and went back into the family room. He set both drinks on the glass table. I followed, carrying my cup.

We played another round of Uno. This time, Cheyenne won. We finished our aromatic brew and Cheyenne announced, "I'm going to drop Jonathan off at his grandmother's house. Be right back."

"Drive safely," I said.

"I will."

Greg stood up, shook Jonathan's hand, and said, "Take it easy."

Jonathan replied, "You too."

As soon as I heard the door close, I exhaled.

"You did good," Greg said, patting my hand. I smiled, feeling as though I had earned a gold star. He slid closer to me on the couch and looked me in the eyes. "Shania, there's something I want to say." He took a deep breath and released it. He seemed serious. "I was trying to wait until Christmas, but I can't."

My heart raced with anticipation, and I gave him an incredulous look. He stood up and reached inside his right pants pocket. He wriggled his fingers around before pulling out his hand. I couldn't see what he was holding. With a balled fist, he knelt down on one knee. I swallowed hard, feeling tears well up in my eyes. He looked into my watery eyes, grabbed my left hand, and said, "I love you. You mean the world to me." I noticed that his eyes were misty, and his lower lip quivered. That totally surprised me. I was usually the one crying to him about my sister. I had never seen him cry. Sweet. I blinked away some loose tears. "Shania," he continued, "would you make me the happiest man in the world and marry me?"

I was so nervous that my palms were sweating. I didn't want to rub my free hand over my skirt, but I did it anyway. With my right thumb, I wiped away his tears. He seemed so sincere, yet vulnerable at the same time. I didn't think it was possible, but I loved him even more. I looked down and noticed a sparkling two-carat, pear shaped diamond ring staring at me. Looking back at Greg, I swallowed hard, and said, "Yes. I'll marry you."

No hesitation; no reservation. Greg was my soul mate. He slipped the ring on my left ring finger and stood up. I stood up, too, and we hugged. This was truly one of the happiest days of my life. I say *one* of the happiest, simply because I expect to have many, many more wonderful days to come.

Four

Rayna

Living with Bryce was not as easy as Rayna thought it would be. She had a romanticized view of marriage, where she imagined married life being about sharing home-cooked meals, spending long mornings in bed, and watching movies every Friday night, like her parents regularly did. Other than her father, she had never lived with a man before, so she used him as the standard. Unlike her dad, Bryce was messy, and she found herself spending a great deal of time cleaning up behind him. No matter how many times she told him to use the clothes hamper, or put the cap back on the toothpaste, Bryce still wouldn't do it. She was frustrated and beginning to feel as if she had inherited a child instead of a husband. This seemed to be a lot more than she bargained for.

Her two-bedroom apartment was starting to feel cramped. When she lived alone, the accom-

modations were fine. She kept the apartment
the way she liked it—neat. Now, as she sat in
the living room, she hardly recognized the
place. The purple colored love seat and sofa in
the living room were barely visible due to Bryce's
clothes scattered all over their surfaces. Writing papers and newspapers covered the glass
dining room table and floor. The place was a
pigsty.

Christmas was a little more than a week
away, and Rayna hadn't done anything to prepare. Decorating wasn't an option, because Bryce
would mess it up. That would infuriate her even
more. With a stressful marriage, Rayna was feeling a bit down, not really in the holiday spirit.

She had been reading the Bible and praying,
yet her spirit was still vexed. Rayna had heard
people say that prayer changes things, and she
believed that. However, she seriously wondered whether prayer could improve her sex
life. Was this a sign that she had married the
wrong man? Were all marriages ordained by
God? They couldn't be, she reasoned. Chris-
tians were divorcing at a rate comparable to
worldly people. Either people were marrying
outside of God's will or giving up before God
could fulfill His promises.

Having recently read a book about marital relationships, Rayna remembered the female author talking about honoring wedding vows no
matter what. The book stated that the Bible
doesn't give a woman any provisions for a divorce, only a man. According to the author, a
man can divorce his wife because of adultery.

She shared personal testimony about how she stood by her husband even after he had an extramarital affair. Commendable, she thought.

According to the Bible, *Marriage is honourable in all, and the bed undefiled: but whoremongers and adulterers God will judge.*

Rayna wished she hadn't slept with Bryce before getting married. That was something she regretted, especially since she knew better. There had only been one other guy that Rayna had slept with prior to her husband. She repented and became a born again virgin. Oftentimes, she wondered whether that was the reason why their love life was so unrewarding. She distinctly remembered what Bryce said to convince her to go all the way.

"We're planning to get married. We have a covenant agreement, and that's what marriage is. Based on that, we're already married. Think about it; when someone dies, he's already dead. Having the funeral is merely a formality," he had explained.

Thinking about it now, Rayna smirked. She couldn't believe she had been so gullible. When she went to church that following Sunday, the preacher addressed the issue of engaged couples and fornication. According to the minister, sex between engaged couples was still a sin. Rayna felt convicted.

Tempted to get some writing done on the manuscript that she had started a few months ago, Rayna walked through the corridor to her bedroom and booted up her computer. While she waited for the machine to warm-up, she thought about that relationship book again. She agreed that people were too quick to divorce. However, she begged to differ when the author advised women to stay with a man regardless. That was a tough pill for Rayna to swallow. She could not get with staying with a murderer, or child molester, or drug addict, or alcoholic, or habitual cheater, or abuser, or even a "down low" brother.

The author did mention that if a woman is being physically abused, she should leave her abuser while he seeks help from a Christian counselor. When the counselor agrees that it's safe for the wife to return, she should reconcile with her husband. What if the husband isn't saved? Rayna wondered. What if he has a history of abusing women? The author did acquiesce that if the abuser refuses to seek treatment, then a divorce may be a viable option.

After having read about physical abuse, Rayna immediately thought about an episode of *Oprah*, where a beautiful young lady whose estranged husband showed up at her job, doused her with gasoline, and set her ablaze. According to the young woman, her ex-husband called her from prison asking for reconciliation. Rayna couldn't even fathom such a thing. The nerve! Having carefully reflected on that, Rayna realized she had the answer to her question—are all marriages ordained by God? She didn't think so, because people had free will.

She remembered Revelation 3:20: *Behold, I*

stand at the door, and knock: if any man hear my voice, and open the door, I will come in to him, and will sup with him, and he with me.

Rayna didn't believe that God would give His children abusive mates, who strip others of self-worth and self-esteem. Since God is omnipotent and omnipresent, He knows what people are going to do before they do it. Thank God He's able to clean up our messes! Rayna rejoiced internally.

Speaking of cleaning, Rayna looked around her bedroom and became disgusted all over again. It looked like a torpedo had hit it. She decided to hold off on writing until after tidying up a bit. She went into the living room and removed all of Bryce's clothes that were randomly strewn on the furniture. As tempted as she was to throw the items in the garbage, she didn't. Instead, she sorted the whites from the colors, and placed them in their appropriate compartments in the hamper. Then she went into the dining room and stuffed all the papers that were scattered all over the table and floor into a large plastic garbage bag. She placed the bag into the bedroom closet.

By the time Rayna finished cleaning, her French manicured nails were chipped. Looking at her hands, she frowned. The scales of an alligator were probably softer than her hands, she thought. An immediate decision was made to go and get a manicure. So she took a quick shower and slipped into a black Baby Phat jogging suit, grabbed her purse from the dresser, and went into the kitchen to grab a sticky note and pen from one of the drawers. While scribbling a note for Bryce letting him know where she'd be, she heard the front door close, and she jumped.

"Bryce!" she yelled, placing a hand on her pounding chest. "I didn't hear you come in. You scared me half to death."

"Where are you going?" he said as he placed his laptop case on the floor, next to the sofa.

He had gone to the library and stopped by his new office to meet some of the people who either didn't have enough seniority or vacation to take off for two or three weeks during the holidays.

"Oh," she extended the fingers on her right hand, "to get a manicure."

He walked over to her and kissed her on the lips. Smiling, he said, "I'll come with you."

What guy volunteers to wait for a woman at a nail salon? she wondered. Having Bryce go and wait for her wasn't what she had in mind, but since he asked . . . "Sure," she replied.

Before Bryce made it into the bedroom, he was already taking off his clothes. He removed his tie and threw it on the arm of the couch. Rayna sighed. Who did he think she was? Florence from *The Jeffersons*? Reluctantly, she picked up the tie and followed Bryce into the bedroom.

"Bryce, I don't want to sound like a nag, but would you please make a conscious decision to clean up after yourself?"

He laughed nervously. "I'll try, baby."

She sat on the corner of the bed, waiting for

him to change into a pair of Phat Farm jeans and hoodie. She fidgeted with her fingers, ran a finger across her arched brows, and felt the area between her upper lip and nose. Both areas were smooth. The little Asian lady at the nail shop had a tendency to say, "You want lip wax today?" Even though Rayna didn't think she needed a wax, she usually fell for it every time.

"I'm ready," Bryce said.

They turned out the lights and Bryce locked the front door. They walked outside to the parking lot and Bryce opened the passenger door of Rayna's Toyota Camry. He waited for her to get inside before closing it. Then he drove them to the shop. As soon as they entered the salon, one of the technicians greeted them.

"May I help you?" the Pinay looked up from behind the station as she applied a coat of polish to a dark skinned lady's finger.

Rayna held up her hands. "I need a manicure and pedicure." Even though she didn't wear open toed shoes in the winter, she still liked to have nice feet year-round. Besides, the pedicures were so relaxing.

"Me, too," Bryce chimed in.

Rayna looked at him from out of the corner of her eye. She had never been with a man who liked manicures and pedicures. It must be that whole metro sexual thing.

"Pick out you color," the Asian lady continued. "Wait ten minute."

Bryce took a seat next to a heavy set woman with a blond weave. She had an infant car seat sitting on the floor with a baby inside, and a toddler climbing on the seat to the left of her. Rayna wondered how the woman was going to get any enjoyment from what should be a pampering session with two small children to tend to. She made eye contact with the woman and smiled. The woman returned the friendly gesture, and Rayna began browsing the wide array of paint colors on the display shelf affixed to the wall. A dark shade caught her attention, so she held on to it. Taking an empty seat next to Bryce, she asked him his opinion of the color she selected. He nodded his approval and they made small talk about what they were going to do for dinner.

Not long afterward, two spa pedicure chairs became available . . . one for Rayna, another for Bryce. She took off her Baby Phat sneakers and socks and sat in the massage chair with her feet soaking in the bubbling tub. The water was a bit hot, but she didn't complain. Like most women, she enjoyed hot baths, so it didn't take long for her body to adjust. The control device for the chair was dangling from the armrest. She alternated between kneading and rolling until she finally decided that she preferred rolling instead. Closing her eyes, she leaned her head against the headrest. This was exactly what she needed, she thought.

Forty-five minutes later, the manicures and pedicures were complete. Bryce paid the tab and tip with a credit card. They were both at stations with small fans emitting air onto their fingernails when one of the Asian ladies walked over and asked Rayna, "Wax for you today?"

Rayna looked at her with questioning eyes before hesitantly replying, "Not today." She smiled, but still wondered whether she really needed a wax. Why else would she keep asking?

The lady returned the smile with a nod before walking away. After their nails dried, they went to dinner at the Orient Express of Vinings. The waiter greeted them.

"And how are you two doing?" the waiter asked.

"Great," they replied in unison.

The staff had always been friendly whenever they visited. The atmosphere was sophisticated and elegant. The Chinese food and sushi were always delicious and fresh. As an appetizer, they ordered spring egg rolls. For dinner, Rayna selected the chicken and Chinese vegetables and Bryce, general tso's chicken. They both chose Jasmine tea to drink. Their waiter retrieved their menus and left. Rayna thought about her friend, Aja.

Looking at Bryce, she said, "I need to stop by and visit Aja. She fell down the stairs and sprained her ankle."

"That's terrible." He furrowed his brows. "Of course, we can go over there."

We? she thought. *Where's all this "we" stuff coming from?* She was feeling as if Bryce was taking the two becoming one too literally for her liking. It seemed as though every time she turned around, Bryce was sticking to her like lint to tape.

"I'm thinking about contacting a realtor to help us look for a house," Rayna announced excitedly.

"A house?" He rubbed his chin.

"Yes. What's the matter?" she asked, perplexed.

He didn't seem as excited as Rayna thought he would be. Quite frankly, he wasn't enthused at all.

"I don't think we're ready for a house," he said seriously.

"Not ready? I don't understand." She scrunched up her face.

"Owning a home is a major responsibility."

"And?"

He leaned in toward her, his lower chest pressed against the table. "Baby, I just started the news anchor job. I don't want to get into debt right now," he whispered.

The waiter returned with their food. There was an awkward silence between them as they abruptly ended the conversation.

"Can I get you anything else?" the waiter inquired.

"No, thanks," Bryce answered as Rayna shook her head.

After the waiter left, Bryce said, "Let's pray." They bowed their heads as Bryce said, "Lord, bless this food and cleanse it of any impurities. We thank you for this meal. In Jesus' name, we pray. Amen."

Although Rayna's stomach had grumbled earlier, after hearing Bryce's comment about not being ready to get a house, her appetite was gone. This was serious, and she wasn't ready to let it go.

"Why?" she inquired.

"Let's not talk about this now," he said as he looked around the establishment to see whether any of the other patrons were looking at them. "This isn't the place."

Rayna swallowed the lump forming in her throat. She was confused and angry. She wasn't used to Bryce talking to her in such a stern manner. And she really didn't appreciate him cutting her off like that. What about her feelings? Does he even care? She picked over her food and tried not to read more into Bryce's reaction to owning a home, but a conversation she had with Aja replayed in her mind.

"Make sure you check his credit report, tax returns and bank statements," Aja had warned.

At the time, Rayna laughed. "You make it sound like a business deal instead of a marriage," she joked.

"If you run your marriage like a business, you'll be all right," Aja had said. "Take it from me. I wish I had followed my own advice. You need to know what you're working with instead of being married strangers. You don't want a man who has more flash than cash. If a man doesn't pay his bills on time, that's saying something. Probably not something you want to hear. Either he's broke or irresponsible. Neither one is good."

Rayna didn't think that was the case. Bryce seemed very responsible. Admittedly, she and Bryce never discussed their credit history, outstanding debts, or financial goals. They conversed about becoming rich in general, but never talked about how they planned on accomplishing that goal.

Rayna looked at Bryce and fought back the small puddle of tears hovering around the borders of her eyes. When his gaze met hers, she looked away. With regret, she felt as if she and her new husband weren't on the same page.

"Sorry I snapped at you," Bryce said. "You know I love you, girl."

She was glad to hear him say that. She hated being at odds with him. "Forget about it." Maybe she was being too hard on him.

Five

Aja

The look on Hunter's face as Aja tumbled down the stairs was etched in Aja's brain. His face was frozen with fright like one of the characters from the movie, *The Ring*. Jayden had bolted out of his room, and she could hear him tramping down the stairs behind her. "Mommy, Mommy," he had cried with a tear stained face.

Hunter had dialed 9-1-1. He and Jayden stayed by Aja's side, holding her hand, until the ambulance arrived and carried her out on a stretcher. Hunter drove himself and Jayden to the hospital. Once there, the doctor examined Aja and gave her an X-ray. That's when they discovered that she had sprained her ankle. Thank God she didn't break her neck! The entire experience was terrifying, and Aja had been in excruciating pain. When the doctor asked her what happened, she thought about Hunter and his shocked expression. His eyes appeared glossy, as if at any moment he would blink away some loose tears. Aja hesitated before telling the doctor that she missed her step. Had she told him that she and Hunter had been arguing, it would've been considered a domestic disturbance. She wasn't in the mood to deal with that. The last thing Aja wanted was for people to think that her husband had been abusing her. There was no doubt in her mind that it was an accident.

Later that same evening, Aja had been released from the hospital, and Hunter had been waiting on her like a manservant. When they arrived back home, he had carried her out of the car and up the stairs to the bedroom where he placed her in bed with her foot propped up on a pillow.

In two days, the daycare would be closed for Christmas break, and Hunter was already taking his scheduled vacation time from work. Aja looked forward to her two weeks away from hyperactive, crying, temper-tantrum throwing, snotty nosed kids. She especially appreciated having Hunter at home to take care of her and help with Jayden.

"Bay, you all right?" Hunter asked as she lay in the queen sized bed with her foot elevated on a pillow. He called her "Bay" as a term of endearment.

"I'm fine." He handed her a glass of cranberry apple juice. "Thanks," she said, taking a sip.

"Iesha is downstairs with the kids," he explained.

When Iesha found out about Aja's injury, she agreed to work full-time hours for the next couple of days while Aja recuperated.

Hunter's cell phone rang. He answered and walked out of the room. What's that about? Aja was determined not to trip, because that's exactly what Hunter would expect her to do. However, she was definitely curious about the call and why he felt the need to leave the room. That was unusual for him. She decided to trust him . . . at least for now. When it came to relationships, her Aunt Bertha gave her this advice, "I'm faithful for as long as he is. Not a minute longer." Aja adopted that philosophy. She figured that in relationships someone was either cheating, just finished cheating, or about to cheat. With that attitude, she figured that as long as she expected the worst, but hoped for the best, she'd never be caught off guard.

At the end of the day, when all of the children had been picked up, Iesha yelled upstairs to Aja.

"Come on up," Aja instructed.

The bedroom door was partially ajar. Iesha stuck her head inside. "Hey lady," she greeted with a smile. She had a medium-brown complexion, wore micro-braids, and was shaped like a pear. The door swung open as she walked toward the bed. "If you needed a couple of days off, all you had to do was say so," Iesha teased.

Laughing, Aja said, "I hope the little people didn't drive you too crazy."

"Never that." She plopped down at the foot of the bed. "They know who's in charge. I don't play that." Iesha pointed to the vast floral arrangement sitting on the nightstand next to the bed. "Are those from Hunter? He sure hooked you up."

"No," she said. Aja couldn't remember the last time she received flowers from Hunter. He justified his actions by telling her that flowers were a waste of money, because they would wither away in a couple of days. Still, Aja thought that getting flowers from a man was romantic. A sweet gesture. And she secretly wished that Hunter would get with the program. "Those are from my girlfriend, Rayna," she clarified. She dropped them off when she and her husband, Bryce, came over for a visit."

"Oh. She must really love you. Those are nice."

"Thanks." She smiled. "Is Jayden with Hunter?"

"That's right." Iesha snapped her fingers. "I almost forgot. Hunter told me to tell you that he was taking Jayden with him to pick up Chinese food for dinner."

Aja nodded her head.

"So," Iesha hesitated, eyes staring at a small ink blotch on the comforter, "how did you fall?"

"Girl, I missed a step," she said, waving her hand like it was no big deal. "Just me being clumsy."

"I'm glad you're all right," she paused and continued. "Aja." She sounded serious.

"Yes?"

"I think you know how I feel about you, and you know I'm not the messy type. I don't mean to get in your business, but I heard something today that concerned me." She bit the corner of her lip.

"What?" Aja's heart raced. She didn't know what Iesha was about to say, but she could tell from the tone that it wasn't good.

"I don't know how to say this." She took a deep breath and held it for a couple of seconds before letting it go.

"Just say it," Aja said impatiently. As far as she was concerned, all of the melodramatics weren't necessary. She could certainly do without it.

"I overheard Hunter on the phone. It sounded like he was talking to a woman."

And? What's the big deal? she thought. "It was probably his ex-wife."

"Sure; you're probably right." She nodded and stood up to leave. "I'm sorry for overstepping my bounds. Forget I said anything."

Curiosity got the best of Aja. "Wait." She halted her hand. "What did he say?" She figured there must have been more to the story; otherwise, why would Iesha bring this to her attention? Up to this point, Iesha had never meddled in Aja's personal business. They had a mutual respect. Even though Iesha seemed to be cool and Aja trusted her, Aja still maintained a certain professional decorum because Iesha was her employee.

"You know what? I shouldn't have said anything. You get some rest." She patted Aja's hand.

"No. You can't leave me hanging. Tell me."

Iesha sat back down and faced Aja. She seemed to search her face as if trying to get re-assurance that she should continue. She pondered for what seemed to be a long minute before saying, "I didn't hear the entire conversation. What grabbed my attention was when Hunter said, 'It was a mistake. I wish you'd let this go. It never should've happened.' "

Aja's heart sank and she licked her lips. "Did you hear anything else?"

"That was it."

That was enough. Aja swallowed hard and rubbed her fingers across her lips in a back and forth motion. She didn't want to believe that Hunter was cheating on her. "You did the right thing by telling me," Aja assured her.

"I hope this doesn't change anything between us," she said sincerely.

"Why would it?"

"I really care about you, and I like working for you. Marriage is serious. I would never try to come in between anybody's marriage. The only reason I told you is because I respect you. You seem like the type of woman who would want to know if something was going on behind her back."

"That's right."

She offered a wan smile. "Do you need anything?"

"No, I'm fine."

"Well, I'm going to leave, unless you want me to wait here with you until your family returns."

"No, you don't have to. Thanks though."

"You sure?"

"I'm sure." Aja smiled to reassure her.

"All right. Take care of yourself."

Iesha stood up and Aja waved good-bye. Once alone, Iesha's words played over and over again in Aja's mind like a scratched vinyl record. She tried to think of a logical explanation, but none came to mind. How could he do this to her? And after she upgraded him from an apartment to a house, bought him a car, and cleaned up his credit? Hunter may be a lot of things, but she didn't think that stupid was one of them. If he were cheating, would he be fool enough to have a conversation so close in Iesha's proximity? The thought of him being intimate with another woman made Aja angry . . . and jealous. She prayed that he wasn't being unfaithful.

"Lord, forgive me for seeing my marriage through worldly eyes instead of spiritual ones. I realize that I've sinned by secretly communicating with other men, and I'm sorry for that. There's no excuse for my immature, selfish behavior. Help me to be a better wife and focus on bettering myself and not the flaws in my marriage. Give me strength, Lord, because if Hunter is being unfaithful, I don't know what I'll do."

Tears streamed down her cheeks as she felt a scream bellowing in the pit of her stomach.

"Bay," Hunter yelled upstairs. "We're back."

She flinched because she hadn't heard him enter the house. Aja quickly wiped away her tears using the sheet as a tissue. She heard footsteps coming up the stairs.

"Mommy," Jayden said, running toward her.

"Hey, baby." Aja sniffled. He climbed on the bed and wrapped his arms around her neck and squeezed. "Careful," she said, nudging him away from her ankle.

"You okay, Mommy?"

"Yes, baby. I'm fine." She kissed him on top of his head.

Seeing her son always gave her the strength to go on. She felt like holding him and never letting go. Hunter came through the door carrying a serving tray.

"I hope you're hungry," Hunter said. "I got us some house fried rice, sesame chicken, and egg rolls."

Aja was hardly able to look at him. She felt like throwing the pillow propped against her back at his head. For the sake of their son, Aja realized that she needed to remain calm. "Sounds good." She forced a smile.

Hunter had three empty plates stacked on the tray. He fixed Jayden's plate and set it on the small table for two next to the window. Aja had watched a talk show that discussed turning one's bedroom into the nicest room in the house. The talk show host suggested putting a dining table in the bedroom for intimate dinners. She liked the idea. Since then, she and

Hunter had shared numerous candlelight dinners in the bedroom.

She and Hunter each fixed their own plates before saying grace.

Jayden actually volunteered to say grace. He sang, "Thank you, Father; thank you, Father, for our food, for our food. Many, many blessings; many, many blessings. Amen. Amen."

Aja thought that Jayden's prayer was adorable. A smile appeared on her face whenever she heard him recite any of his prayers. Additionally, Aja had taught him The Lord's Prayer, The Pledge to the Christian Flag, and The Pledge to the Bible. Hunter joined Jayden at the table, and Aja placed the tray on her lap and ate. Jayden had a difficult time staying in his seat. Every so often, he tended to get up to play.

"Jayden, sit down and eat," Hunter instructed. Jayden reluctantly sat in his seat and stuffed his mouth with food. "That's too much," Hunter said. "Slow down and chew your food."

Jayden laughed. Then he opened his mouth and showed his daddy his food. "See." He pointed to his mouth.

"Stop it," Aja said. "You know better."

"Don't do that." Hunter shook his head. "That's nasty. Keep your mouth closed when your mouth is full."

Jayden giggled, but still did as he was told. After they finished eating, Hunter stacked the plates and took them downstairs. When he returned, he went into Jayden's "under the sea" themed bathroom and halfway filled the tub with water.

"Take your clothes off," he said to Jayden. "It's time to take your bath."

"Okay, Daddy." Jayden bounced around while kicking off his sneakers, wriggling out of his jeans and struggling to get his shirt over his head. They went into the bathroom where Jayden splashed around in the tub and played with some plastic blocks.

"Time to wash up, little man," Hunter said, dropping a washcloth and bar of soap in the water. Jayden fumbled with the soap, causing it to glide off the rag and plop into the water. He slid the soapy rag up and down his leg. After watching Jayden's attempt to bathe himself, Hunter followed up and washed the areas the boy had missed. Then he wrapped him in a towel, escorted him to his room across the hall and laid his underwear and pajamas on the bed. Hunter left the room while Jayden dressed himself.

Hunter went into the master bathroom and took a shower. While Hunter showered, Jayden came into the master bedroom carrying the children's book, *Are You My Mother?* and sat next to Aja on the bed. She put her arm around him and read him the story as he rested his head on her bosom.

Not long afterward, Hunter came out of the bathroom dressed in a T-shirt and boxer shorts. Realizing that it was time for Jayden to go to bed, Aja hugged and kissed him goodnight.

"I love you," she said, blowing him a kiss.

"Love you, too, Mommy."

Hunter tucked Jayden into bed and came back into the bedroom with Aja. He climbed into bed next to her and kissed her on the cheek.

"I don't know how you do it, Bay," he said. "Dealing with kids all day can be stressful. Just watching Iesha tired me out." He smiled adoringly.

"Hunter, we need to talk," she said seriously.

He sighed. "Come on, Bay. Why did you wait until nighttime to talk? I've been home all day, and you wait until it's time for us to go to bed and decide you want to talk."

She ignored his comment and continued. "Do you love me?"

"What kind of question is that? Of course I love you. Why?" He sounded irritated.

"Are you happy?"

"No, I'm not happy," he joked. "Especially not right now with you trying to keep me up. I'm the one who should be asking whether you love me. You won't let a brother get a lick of sleep."

"I'm serious. Are you happy?" she repeated.

"If I weren't happy, I wouldn't stay with your crazy self. Either that or I'm just a glutton for punishment." Hunter put his arm around her and she rested her head against his muscular chest.

"One more question," she said, patting his chest.

"Enough with the questions already."

"Have you ever cheated on me?"

"No." She raised her head off his chest and looked into his eye. "Why are you staring at me? I said, '*No*,'" he reiterated.

"You better not." She rolled her eyes and placed her head back on his chest. The rhythm of his heartbeat soothed her. She adjusted her breathing to match his. She decided not to tell him what Iesha had said because if he were having an affair, she didn't want to tip her hand.

"You ready for Devin's visit?" Hunter asked.

"With everything going on, it slipped my mind. When is he coming?"

"He'll be here this weekend. He's staying for a couple of weeks."

"At least I'll be mobile by then. Wobbling, but mobile," she joked. They laughed. "I'll have the guest room ready for him. Jayden will be so excited. He loves spending time with his big brother."

"Yes. And he can help me put together some of Jayden's Christmas toys."

"You know, Christmas is my favorite time of year," she said. "When I was a little girl, my mom and I would bake chocolate chip cookies. Until I became a teenager, I used to leave a plate full of cookies and a glass of milk for Santa."

The fond memories made her smile. Hunter lightly squeezed her arm and then rubbed it.

"We didn't do that at my house," Hunter admitted. "My dad let me and my two brothers know at an early age that *he* was Santa." He chuckled. "He wasn't about to let someone else get the credit for his hard work. Dad worked two jobs to take care of his family. It wasn't until I was grown that I found out we were considered poor. As a kid, I had no idea. We took family vacations. Granted, we always drove; never flew. Still, my parents made sure we had fun. We didn't get everything we wanted, but we had everything we needed."

Sharing childhood memories with Hunter made Aja feel warm and fuzzy. It helped her remember what she liked about her husband. When he wasn't stressed, he was a joy to be around, easy to talk to. They could relax with each other. She realized that unlike his older brother, Hank, Hunter did not have a bad temper. That's why she was shocked by his behavior the night she had fallen down the stairs. His bark was usually worse than his bite. Whenever Hank drank too much, he physically abused his wife. For that very reason, Hunter refused to drink liquor. He didn't know how it could possibly affect him, and he didn't want to find out.

"I don't think it's good to get children everything they want," Aja said. "Giving children too much can make them materialistic and unappreciative."

"True dat." He kissed the top of her head and said, "I'm going to sleep."

"Okay, boo. Goodnight."

Aja scooted over to the right side of the bed. Just as she pressed her face against the satin covered pillow, Hunter's cell phone rang. Startled, she rolled over. He hopped out of bed and checked the caller ID. When the phone stopped ringing, he turned it off and stuck it in his pants pocket. Then he got back into bed.

"Who was that?" she inquired with a raised brow and a hint of an attitude.

"Sunni."

"Why didn't you answer?"

"I didn't feel like talking to her."

Aja bit her lip. He'd better not be lying, she thought. She rolled back over and silently prayed.

Lord, I pray Hunter's desires are only unto me, and my desires remain only unto him. If he's being unfaithful, forgive him. I pray that you stop him before it destroys our family. If he's not cheating, let me know. Show me how to trust him. Show me how to love him in the way he needs to be loved. Restore this marriage. In Jesus' name, I pray. Amen.

Aja tried to silence the negative thoughts residing in her mind, telling her that Hunter was a liar and a cheat. She wanted and needed to trust Hunter. He draped his arm over her waist, with his hand resting on her stomach, as they lay in the spooning position. The electricity from his touch sent a slight quiver through Aja's body. What's done in the dark will come to light, she silently reminded herself. If Hunter is involved with another woman, it will be revealed, she wanted to convince herself. Tears welled in her eyes. Again, using the cotton bed sheet as a tissue, she dabbed the corners of her eyes and pulled the sheet and comforter up to her neck. Then she sniffled and attempted to clear her mind. Her eyes were closed when Hunter snuggled a little closer to her, and she heard him say, "Love you."

If only that were true.

Six

Shania

"Greg and I are getting married," I said to Cheyenne as I held out my left hand for her to view my engagement ring. After Greg proposed, I had been so excited I felt like jumping up and down. I couldn't wait to share my good news with Cheyenne, so I waited up for her in the family room. The lights from the Christmas tree lit up the room.

Inspecting my ring, she said, "I leave you alone for a couple of hours, and you're getting married?" Her smile was so bright the lights on the tree paled in comparison.

"Yes," I said excitedly. "He asked me right after you left."

"Congratulations, Sister. I'm happy for you." She hugged me.

"Thanks. That means a lot to me."

"Greg's a nice guy. I can tell he loves you. And the ring . . ." she paused, gave me two

thumbs up, and said, "very nice." She smiled
and nodded her approval.

She was about to go upstairs when I said,
"Cheyenne, wait a minute. We need to talk."

"Can we talk in the morning?" She yawned.
"I'm tired."

I could see the sleepy look in her eyes.
"Sure." I shook my head. "I'm kind of tired myself."

Cheyenne waited as I unplugged the Christmas lights. Then we both went upstairs.

"Good night," we both said before going into
our respective bedrooms.

I took a shower before putting on my oversized
white tee that I preferred over a nightgown. It was
comfortable. I wondered whether Greg would approve of my sleepwear after we got married.
Would he prefer lingerie or would it even matter?
I made a mental note to ask him.

Even though I was exhausted, I thumbed
through the Bible until I found Proverbs 21. I
wanted to read about living in the house with a
nagging woman. It reminded me of what not to
do when I got married. Once finished, I kneeled
down next to my bed and prayed.

"Father, thank you for this day. I pray that
you bless Greg abundantly. Make him the head
and not the tail; a leader and not a follower; a
lender and not a borrower; above and not be-
neath. Keep him on the right path, and help
him to be all that you've called him to be. Take
care of Cheyenne and protect her by your
power. I'm thankful that your angels have

charge over us and that no harm will come our way. In Jesus' name, I pray. Amen."

That night, I tossed and turned, excited about my upcoming nuptials. I thought about the type of dress I wanted to wear, flowers, food, and bridesmaids' dresses. There seemed to be a checklist in my mind. Whenever one item got checked off, a new one would pop up and take its place. Eventually, I dozed off and slept soundly.

The next morning, I woke up feeling as good as an NBA player who had scored the winning basket during a championship game. After reading my daily devotional and praying, I went into the bathroom to wash my face and brush my teeth. I was in the mood for a delicious breakfast, so I went into the kitchen and pre- pared strawberry crepes. The smell of eggs, bacon, and percolating coffee must have jolted Cheyenne out of her sleep, because she joined me without me having to yell upstairs for her.

"Good morning, Sister," Cheyenne greeted as she rubbed her sleepy eyes and yawned. She was dressed in a tank top and boy shorts.

"Good morning. Did you sleep well?"

"Like a baby. What are you in here cooking?"

"Strawberry crepes and bacon." I walked over to the baker's rack and picked up a loaf of wheat bread. "Want a piece of toast?"

"Uhm hmm."

I removed two slices of bread and placed

them in the toaster. I pressed the lever. "I made coffee."

She retrieved two cups from the cabinet and poured us each a cup. "The usual?" she asked.

I nodded. "Thanks." The toast popped up. "Would you hand me two plates, please?"

She did, and while Cheyenne spruced up our cups of java, I fixed our plates. I waited for the toast to cool a little before placing a slice on each plate.

"Thank you," Cheyenne said as she carried a plate in her right hand and a cup of joe in her left.

I did the same, and we went to the table. We sat down, bowed our heads, and I said grace.

"Lord, thank you for this nourishing meal. Bless the food, and bless us so that we can carry out your will. In Jesus' name, we pray. Amen."

"So, what's going on in your world?" I asked.

She seemed thoughtful, resting her right index finger on her cheek, and said, "Nothing."

I took a sip of freshly brewed coffee and swallowed. I said, "Okay. How are things with you and Jonathan?"

"Fine."

She cut into the crepe with her fork, and stuffed a piece in her mouth. Obviously, I was asking the wrong types of questions, because she wasn't giving up any information. I decided to take a different approach.

"Tell me what you like about Jonathan," I said.

She became child-like. Shy. "Well, he makes

me laugh." She rolled her eyes upward. Apparently she was thinking. "He loves me for me."

I nodded my head. Why wouldn't he love her for her? She's outgoing, nice, and pretty. What guy wouldn't like that? "What does he plan on doing with himself? His future?"

"He's not sure. He says he wants to be an actor. Then he said he wants to design clothes."

Like we really need another out of work actor. I let out a slight sigh. "How do you feel about that?"

"I'm okay with it. I did tell him that he'd better do something to get his life together. If he doesn't, he won't have me."

"You really told him that?" I looked at her suspiciously with a raised brow.

"Yes, and I told him he needs to get his GED," she laughed. She knew I was skeptical. "I did some research and found out what he needs to do to get it."

"That's good." I ate another forkful of food, dabbed the corners of my mouth with a napkin and said, "Do you plan on marrying him?"

I don't know why I asked that question. She had never mentioned marrying him before. Intuitively, I sensed that she had been thinking about it. In my heart, I hoped she wouldn't.

She seemed stumped by the question, but answered, "Yes. That's part of what I wanted to talk to you about." Her tone sounded serious. "Sister, I'm not going back to school."

"What?" I dropped my fork and probably my jaw, too.

"I don't like school," she admitted. "Never have. The only reason I went to college is because you expected me to. Ever since I was a little girl, I've been told to go to college. I didn't think I had a choice."

I felt a lump forming in my throat, storing all of my words. A few seconds later, all of which seemed like hours, I managed to say, "Why would you drop out of college?"

I looked her in the face, but she averted her eyes and said, "I already told you."

"Okay." I held my hands up in resignation. "I won't lie. I am disappointed."

My mouth felt like cotton, so I drank some more coffee. I wondered why she would quit school when there were so many people who would give up their firstborn child to be in her position. Cheyenne was young, talented, and affluent. She was blessed to have all of her college expenses paid for. She didn't have to work, she drove a cute car, and knowledge came with ease. I couldn't understand why she didn't realize what a gifted position she was in.

"Sister, I'm sorry." She rested her hand on top of mine. "I didn't mean to hurt you."

Ingrate! I thought. "It's your life. You're an adult now. Even though I don't agree with your decision, I have to respect it. I can't force you to go to school."

A broad smile spread across Cheyenne's face. She pushed her chair away from the table, stood up, leaned over, and hugged me. Her left cheek pressed against my right, and she squeezed my shoulders.

I grinned and pushed her away. Regardless of my disappointment, I still saw Cheyenne as my little sister. I couldn't stay angry with her. "Don't get excited," I said. "If you're not going to be in school, you need to get a job."

"Sister," she whined, taking her seat.

"Don't 'Sister' me; I'm serious." I had been so caught off guard by her admission to quitting school that I neglected to mention anything about her plans to marry Jonathan. So I backtracked and asked her what was up with that.

"We're planning on getting married," she answered.

I sighed and said, "Let me share something with you. I don't think you should get married anytime soon. You've heard about two people coming together and making each other whole."

She nodded her understanding.

"That's not right. Two whole and complete people should come together and complement each other. If you don't know who you are or where you're going, you aren't going to make a good wife. When you get married, I want your marriage to have the best possible chance of succeeding. Right now, Jonathan needs to get himself together. He's not ready to be a husband. He's a high school dropout and a drug dealer. If you marry him, you'll be living a dangerous life. If he keeps going the way he's going, he'll end up dead or in jail. I don't want that for you or him."

She smiled and seemed to comprehend my sentiment.

I wrapped up by saying, "Now, if a couple of years down the road, you and Jonathan have your acts together, and you still want to get married, I'll gladly support it. I'll give you one of those celebrity weddings we see in *Ebony* magazine. Just sit tight and enjoy your youth. You're only young once. Don't blow it."

We hugged again before finishing up our breakfast and putting away the dishes. I prayed that she would take heed to what I said and not rush into anything. Even still, I had a nagging feeling that my words fell on deaf ears.

Seven

Rayna

It was Sunday afternoon. After attending mid-morning worship service at Hallelujah Cathedral, Bryce and Rayna went over to her parents' house for dinner. Every year, Mrs. Culpepper went overboard on the decorations. The outside of their five-bedroom stucco house had white icicle lights draped from the roof. A nativity set was prominently displayed in the front yard, and a wreath hung on the front door.

When Bryce and Rayna entered the home, miniature Christmas trees inhabited every room except for the spacious living room, which had a larger than life white tree decorated with gold accessories. The spiral staircase looked like a candy cane with red ribbon wrapped around the banister and a hand tied bow on the end. Every possible surface, including the tile countertop island in the kitchen, the breakfast nook and granite fireplace mantel, had Christmas topiaries, unique garlands, or other decorative elements.

"I love what you did with the place, Mrs. Culpepper," Bryce complimented.

"Thanks, Bryce. But you don't have to call me Mrs. Culpepper," she said, giving him a hug. "Mom or Clara will be fine. Make yourself comfortable."

Bryce smiled. "Okay, Clara."

He joined Mr. Culpepper in the media room where they watched a football game on the widescreen TV. Mrs. Culpepper and Rayna were in the light colored country-style kitchen, decorated with woven baskets and floral motifs, putting finishing touches on the feast. The Cornish hens and cornbread stuffing were baking in the oven. The macaroni and cheese was cooked to perfection. Rayna checked on the Italian green beans in a pot on the stove while her mom stirred the homemade mashed potatoes.

"How's married life treating you?" Mrs. Culpepper asked Rayna.

"It's fine." She placed a lid on the pot and went to wash her hands in the sink.

"Is it everything you thought it would be?"

Rayna really wished that her mother would stop probing. She was making Rayna feel as if she were being interrogated. She had a way of asking the same question over and over while phrasing it differently. What did she expect Rayna to say? For goodness sake, Bryce was in the next room.

"Yes," Rayna lied, tearing a paper towel from the rack and drying her hands.

She immediately noticed the dessert selections—sweet potato pie and a buttery caramel cake. Rayna was beginning to salivate just thinking about all of the scrumptious food.

"Aw, man!" her father shouted from the other room.

Must be a really good game, Rayna thought.

"What happened?" Mrs. Culpepper asked, looking in her husband's direction.

"They're about to show it again," Mr. Culpepper explained, shaking his head.

All eyes were glued to the big screen. Some guy was running along the fifty yard line and got tackled. Rayna wasn't a big football fan, so the replay really didn't faze her.

"Ooh," Bryce said, balling his hand into a fist and pressing it against his mouth.

It was time for a commercial break, so Rayna went into the family room and sat next to Bryce on the plush couch. She asked, "Did you call your mother back? Remember, I told you she called when you were in the shower."

"No," he said nonchalantly.

"Why don't you call her before it gets too late?" She lightly touched him on the shoulder. "I'm sure it would mean a lot to her."

Without saying another word, Bryce pulled out his cell phone and called his mother, Lucille.

"Hey, Mom," Bryce said. He sounded cheerful. Rayna could hear Lucille talking loudly through the earpiece. "Uh-huh," Bryce said. "Okay," he paused. "We're having dinner with Rayna's parents . . . at their house." There was more jabbering from Lucille. "Look, Mom. I got to go." Lucille continued to talk. Bryce got up and walked into the foyer. Rayna followed, wondering whether everything was all right. "Look," Bryce said sternly between clenched teeth, "I said I have to go." Then he hung up the phone abruptly.

"Did you just hang up on your mother?" she inquired, shocked.

She had never personally known anyone who had behaved so disrespectfully to their mother, except when she was in the seventh grade. There was a white girl named Nancy who used to cuss out her mom and run away from home. Besides Nancy, Rayna couldn't think of anyone else.

"You know I can't talk to her very long. She rubs me the wrong way."

"You need to call her back," she chastised. "That was rude. I don't care how much she works your nerves; you should never hang up on your mom."

Mrs. Culpepper walked into the foyer and asked, "Y'all all right?"

Rayna and Bryce exchanged glances.

"We're fine," Bryce said.

"Okay," Mrs. Culpepper said with a concerned look on her face. "Dinner's ready." She walked back into the kitchen.

Bryce gave Rayna a stupid look, similar to

the Robert Townsend character, Duck, while he pretended to be the "shy brother" in the movie *The Five Heartbeats*. Then he held his head down and said, "You're right. I'll call her back."

Rayna watched him as he placed the call to his mother, apologizing to her for his actions. Then he ended the call more civilly. He reached for his wife's hand, and she reluctantly gave it to him. Then she remembered the warning Lucille had given her after she accepted Bryce's marriage proposal. In an effort to get to know her soon-to-be mother-in-law better, Rayna called Lucille the day after Bryce's proposal. Lucille and Rayna had been talking on the phone.

"Are you sure you want to marry him?" Lucille had asked Rayna.

Rayna found her question strange, but she had answered, "Yes, I'm sure."

"He's not the easiest person to live with, you know?" Lucille explained. There was a sinking feeling in the pit of Rayna's stomach. The conversation with Lucille had made her feel uneasy, so she asked her mom to pick up the extension. The three of them were on the phone.

"Lucille, it's nice to finally speak with you," Mrs. Culpepper had greeted.

"You too. Too bad we won't get a chance to meet before the wedding."

Rayna sat quietly on the other end of the phone while their mothers conversed.

"Bryce is a wonderful man," Mrs. Culpepper said. "I'm looking forward to having him as my son-in-law."

"You don't really know him," Lucille warned.

"What do you mean? Has he been to jail?" Mrs. Culpepper questioned.

"No, nothing like that. He hasn't gotten into any trouble."

"I don't understand. Is he on drugs?"

"No. Bryce is just . . . different."

Rayna's ears perked up. She was waiting for her mom to go off after Lucille was being so aloof, but she hadn't. She remained so calm that there wasn't even a noticeable inflection.

"I can only judge him based on what I've seen. He loves my daughter and treats her very well. He's always been kind and polite to me and my husband."

"I guess you'll just have to see."

After they got off the phone with Lucille, Mrs. Culpepper and Rayna both admitted that the conversation was not what either of them had expected. Rayna couldn't believe Bryce's mother had "thrown him under the bus," so to speak. The thought of marrying into such a family didn't set well with Rayna. Feelings of distrust toward Lucille surfaced within her. She really didn't know what to think then anymore than she knew what to think now.

Bryce and Rayna joined Mrs. Culpepper in the kitchen. She was stirring a pot of green beans.

"Clara, the food smells delicious," Bryce said, kissing her on the cheek.

"Thanks. Was that your mom on the phone?" She placed the lid back on the pot and turned off the stove.

"Yes, ma'am." He had a sullen expression.

"How's she doing?"

"She's all right." He chewed on his bottom lip.

"I'm sure she misses you for the holidays." She scraped the mashed potatoes from the copper stock pot and placed them in a serving dish.

"Not really. We didn't have traditional holidays at my house when I was growing up." A solemn expression appeared on Bryce's face. "Being here with you and your family really means a lot to me. I've always dreamt of having holidays like this. I finally feel like I'm a part of a family."

"You are family," Mrs. Culpepper assured him.

Rayna started transferring the food from pots to Cambridge servers with racks.

"Do you need me to help?" Bryce asked.

"No," she said.

He kissed Rayna on the cheek and joined Mr. Culpepper in the family room. Rayna was still feeling uneasy about the conversation between Bryce and Lucille. For the life of her, she couldn't figure out why he treated Lucille with such contempt. How could he have such a resentful attitude toward his mother? He had always behaved toward Rayna's parents with the utmost respect. Rayna wondered whether there was more to the rift between Bryce and Lucille than she realized.

Mrs. Culpepper and Rayna went into the formal dining room to set the table. Rayna's heels clanked against the hardwood floor with every step. The room consisted of vaulted ceilings, ample windows, a natural oak dining set sitting on top of an area rug, upholstered chairs, and a matching buffet and hutch. A huge potted fern occupied a space in the corner. Wooden framed pictures adorned the Burmese gold colored walls. After they finished setting the table, Mrs. Culpepper yelled into the media room for the men to join them.

"Smells good," Bryce commented, rubbing his hands together.

Mr. Culpepper sat at the head of the table and blessed the food.

"Father, we come before you today to thank you for this lovely meal. We ask that you bless the food and the hands that prepared it. In Jesus' name, we pray. Amen." Afterward, they each fixed their plates.

"Son," Mr. Culpepper said to Bryce, looking him in the eye, "how are you adjusting to living in a new city?"

"I'm getting used to it." Bryce smiled and nodded his head simultaneously.

"That's good. What about married life?" Mr. Culpepper said, placing a forkful of macaroni into his mouth.

Bryce looked at Rayna, and said, "It's good."

Mr. Culpepper dabbed the corners of his mouth with a cloth napkin. "Son, let me tell you something. Marriage is a commitment, not a feeling. There are going to be times when you and your wife aren't on the same page. They'll be days when you feel like leaving her, and days when she's going to feel like leaving you. But you have to choose to stay together." He guffawed. "I remember when Clara and I first got married." He shook his head. "Seemed like we used to argue every day."

"You got that right," Mrs. Culpepper said, laughing. "Will and I couldn't agree on anything."

"Love isn't what kept us together all of these years," Mr. Culpepper interrupted.

"No?" Bryce questioned.

"No," Mr. Culpepper replied. "It was our commitment to stay together and honor our vows. Sure, we loved each other; still do. But marriage is more than that. You see, son, love is a feeling and feelings change. You can't base your marriage on your feelings. The problem with folks these days is they're too quick to bail. Marriage isn't like a new car. You can't trade it in once the newness wears off."

"True." Bryce cut into the Cornish hen.

"Son, what I've learned in my twenty-five years of marriage is this: whatever you did to get her, you have to do the same things to keep her. Always date your wife and make her feel special. If you don't remember anything else, remember this: take care of home and home will take care of you. A happy wife means a happy life."

Her dad made sense, Rayna thought. She didn't

have the heart to disappoint her father by telling him that her marriage wasn't working. If she did tell her dad, he'd probably tell her to stick with it. He always encouraged Rayna to finish whatever she started. She looked at her parents adoringly. They seemed so happy and in love. She wished that she had the same type of loving relationship as her parents. Rayna remembered hearing someone say that if you want to know whether a man is a good husband, look into the eyes of his wife. Mrs. Culpepper's eyes were so radiant; they sparkled.

"Rayna," Mrs. Culpepper said, interrupting her thoughts. "Have you registered for school?"

She cleared her throat. "Yes. I plan to start next semester."

"Good for you, honey." She smiled. "Are you still going for film?"

"That's what I intend to do, but I'm looking into journalism as well. I think it would open more doors for me."

"That's a tough field to break in to, but you can do it, honey." She looked at Bryce and continued. "And with you being married to a news anchor . . ."

Bryce smiled back at Mrs. Culpepper, who was noticeably pleased with her son-in-law.

"Thanks, Mom," Rayna said, taking a sip of sweet tea.

"Princess has been writing all of her life," Mr. Culpepper said proudly, referring to Rayna by her childhood nickname. "I remember when she was a little girl. She used to make up words for the dictionary." Everyone laughed. "As she got older," Mr. Culpepper continued, "she loved writing in diaries and notebooks. Anything she could get her hands on," he chortled. "And she's always excelled in English. If my princess wants to be a writer, she's talented enough to do it."

"Thank you, Daddy." Rayna sounded like a sweet little girl.

Mr. Culpepper had always been Rayna's biggest supporter. As a child, she was "Daddy's little girl." He used to read her bedtime stories and tuck her in at night. He'd take her to the park and push her high on the swing. She loved hanging out with her dad, especially when he'd take her to Dairy Queen for their favorite treat . . . strawberry sundaes with rainbow sprinkles.

They finished eating dinner. Afterward, Mrs. Culpepper and Rayna cleared the table. While in the kitchen, Mrs. Culpepper wiped off the countertops. Rayna rinsed the dishes in the sink and loaded up the dishwasher. Mr. Culpepper and Bryce sat in the media room, sipping non-alcoholic eggnog and talking about the game. Not long afterward, Rayna and her mother joined them.

"Princess," Mr. Culpepper said, retrieving a document from the end table. "I have something for you . . . and Bryce." Bryce had a quizzical expression on his face. Rayna wondered what her dad was talking about. She looked at her mom, and Mrs. Culpepper had a smile etched on her face. Mr. Culpepper handed her an envelope. "Go ahead," he instructed. "Read it."

Rayna tore open the envelope, unfolded the document, and skimmed the contents. It looked like a deed, and her name was listed as the owner, and a payment booklet in her dad's name. "What's this?" she inquired excitedly.

"It's a quit claim deed to a house," Mr. Culpepper explained.

"What?" Bryce and Rayna said in unison.

"Yes," her mom interjected. She could no longer contain her merriment. "Dad and I put down half the value of the property as a down payment and bought you a house. We paid the first three months mortgage payments and figured that you guys should be able to handle it from here. Especially since the payments are less than your rent. Merry Christmas!"

Rayna jumped up like a Jack-in-the-Box. "Mom, Dad, thank you." She hugged both of them tightly. "I love you so much. This is the best present ever." Rayna smiled so hard that her face hurt.

Bryce stood and said, "This is way too generous. No one has ever done anything like this for me before. I don't know how to thank you." His eyes filled with tears.

Mr. Culpepper gave Bryce a hug. "Just take care of my daughter. And remember to always keep God first."

"I will," he choked out the words.

"A man can't lead a family without God's help," Mr. Culpepper said. His tone sounded serious.

Tears streamed down Bryce's cheeks as he broke away from Mr. Culpepper and hugged

Mrs. Culpepper. By then, Rayna was also crying. They sat back down, and Rayna bombarded her parents with questions. Why didn't they tell her? Where's the house? What does it look like? When could they see it? Honestly, it didn't matter to Rayna what the house looked like. The fact that her parents invested in it was more than enough for her. This was the answer to a prayer.

"It was so hard for us not to tell you," her mom admitted. "You know that your dad and I have been investing in rental properties for several years now. We were actually going to give you one of the rental properties when you graduated from college. Will decided that we should get you a new house instead, and I agreed. So, we put our realtor to work. After several months of looking, she finally found a lovely home. Since we were planning your wedding, Daddy and I decided that a new home would be the perfect wedding gift. However, things didn't work out that way." She raised a finger as if to say "just a minute." "The contractor that we hired to upgrade the kitchen installed the wrong countertops. That caused a minor delay. The house wasn't ready in time for your wedding day, but it's ready now. We were going to wait until Christmas day, but hey, every day is Christmas, right?" She shrugged her shoulders. "Honey, the house is beautiful. It's a three-bedroom, two-bathroom, ranch-style home. You're going to love it."

"I know we will. How long have you had it?" Rayna asked.

"Six months, but we were having some upgrades done," Mrs. Culpepper said.

"I can't wait to see it." Rayna smiled.

"No time like the present," Mr. Culpepper chimed in.

Bryce and Rayna sat in the backseat of Mr. and Mrs. Culpepper's Lexus. They rode for approximately thirty minutes before pulling into a well-maintained subdivision. They were in Lithonia, a suburb of Atlanta. Rayna noticed that the houses weren't too close together. She never liked subdivisions where the houses seemed to sit on top of one another. No privacy.

The car finally stopped in front of a spacious, yellow stucco house with a two-car garage. Rayna's jaw dropped.

"Is this *our* home?" she asked.

"It sure is," Mr. Culpepper said, handing her the keys.

"It's beautiful," Rayna said.

"Yes, it is," Bryce agreed.

"Let's go inside," Mrs. Culpepper suggested.

Taking a deep breath, Rayna exhaled. She couldn't believe this was her home. They got out of the car and walked around to the back of the house.

"That's a lot of yard," Bryce commented about the half acre of land. "I'm going to have to get a riding lawnmower." He chuckled.

Mr. Culpepper patted him on the back. They circled around to the front door. Rayna's hand trembled as she placed the key in the lock and unlocked the door. She entered cautiously, as if she expected someone else to be there.

Giving Rayna a light nudge, as if reading her mind, Mrs. Culpepper said, "Get in there. This is your house."

"Come on," Bryce said, leading Rayna by the hand. "Let's take a tour."

Rayna soaked up the new house smell. Everything was so clean, she noticed. The living room and adjoining dining room both had plush beige carpet. The walls were painted eggshell white. Next to the dining room was an amazing kitchen.

Rayna screamed, "Thank you, Jesus! Thank you, Jesus! Thank you, Jesus!"

She felt like doing a happy dance when she saw that shiny hardwood floor, maple cabinets, marble countertops, and mustard yellow colored walls. The room was so bright and cheerful that it looked like it had been dipped in gold and kissed by the sun.

"I'm glad you like it," Mr. Culpepper said, grinning.

"I told you it was beautiful," Mrs. Culpepper added.

Rayna ran her hand along each surface, including the stainless steel appliances.

"Clara, Will . . ." Bryce said, looking at both of them with tears welling in his eyes. He shook his head and squeezed the bridge of his nose.

Mr. Culpepper walked over and embraced him. "Son, you don't need to say anything. It's all right," he consoled.

As soon as they finished having their bonding moment, everyone went into the family room. Rayna thought it was very nice.

"This room would be perfect for a black leather wrap-around sofa and big screen TV," Bryce noted. "We could turn this into a media room."

Rayna nodded her head. That wasn't exactly what she had in mind, because the whole black leather couch was such a guy thing. With the beige carpeting, she would prefer to decorate with lighter colors and candles . . . lots of candles. They walked down the hallway, stopping in each of the bedrooms and bathrooms. The walls were painted neutral colors. Rayna visualized painting the bedroom walls with bolder colors like brick red, burnt orange and forest green. She would have to change the wall colors with quickness.

"I'll come over and help you paint," Mrs. Culpepper volunteered, interrupting Rayna's thoughts.

Rayna gave her a warm smile and hugged her around the waist. "Thanks."

The guest bathroom had a garden-style tub, and the master bathroom—a Jacuzzi. Rayna envisioned taking many relaxing baths in there. She felt so full of joy that she silently prayed for her marriage to become blissful so that she could enjoy her new home with her new husband. Bryce held her hand and pulled her away from her parents.

"I can't believe how generous your parents are," Bryce said to Rayna.

Hugging Rayna around her shoulders, Bryce bent over and kissed her. His breath emanated of coffee, and his tongue slithered in her mouth like what she imagined an earthworm would feel like. She nearly gagged and jerked her head away. Rayna wiped her mouth in disgust. She usually brushed her teeth immediately after every meal, but in the midst of all the excitement, it slipped her mind. She preferred kissing Bryce after they both had brushed their teeth, because she had a thing about fresh breath. Bryce knew that, so she was taken aback when he kissed her with breath that was kicking like Tae-Bo. When she caught a glimpse of the disappointed look on Bryce's face, it confirmed that they needed prayer.

God help us.

Eight

Aja

Every Sunday, Aja felt guilty for not going to church. Today was no different. Before meeting Hunter, she used to go to church every Sunday. Even after they started dating, she continued to go regularly. She encouraged Hunter to go to church with her, but he only attended on special occasions. She explained to him that going to church was important to her, and he promised he would once they were married, yet he didn't.

Eventually, Aja got tired of going to church without her husband, so she started going every other Sunday. Pretty soon, her attendance dwindled off to once a month, to every other month, to special occasions when Hunter would go with her. In an effort to stay spiritually connected, Aja would watch church services on TV, listen to praise music, read the Bible, and pray. That still wasn't enough. She missed the fellowship that church provided and promised herself that she would begin going to church as soon as the New Year rolled around. She hadn't shared that information with Hunter, though.

Devin and Jayden were in the family room playing a basketball game on their PlayStation 3. Aja was in the kitchen, and she could see them clearly. She enjoyed watching the two of them together. Their bond was undeniable. The way ten-year-old Devin patted Jayden on the back and gave him kudos whenever he made a basket, was endearing.

"Bay," Hunter said as Aja scraped leftover black-eyed peas into a plastic container. "Go on and relax. I can put up the food."

"You sure?"

Hunter nodded. "Go ahead."

She wrapped her arms around Hunter's neck and kissed him on the cheek. She really appreciated his thoughtfulness. "Thanks."

"Eww, that's nasty!" Devin yelled from the other room. He was looking at them, making faces.

"That's nasty," Jayden mimicked, giggling.

"I thought y'all were playing a game?" Aja said as she removed her arms from around Hunter and walked into the family room.

"I just won," Devin boasted.

"Congratulations. It's about time for you guys to get ready for bed."

"No, Mommy," Jayden whined. "Can we play one more game? Please, please, please."

"Stop whining, Jayden. You know I don't deal with the whining."

"It's cool," Devin said to Jayden. "We can

play tomorrow. Let's go upstairs and put on our pajamas. I'll bet you can't beat me."

He pretended to run with Jayden trailing behind him. Aja limped into the family room and sat on the couch. After putting the leftovers in the refrigerator, Hunter joined her.

"This was great," Hunter admitted. "Having my family around is the best feeling in the world. I can't imagine what I ever could have done to deserve such a wonderful family."

"That was sweet." Aja was touched by his sincerity.

"I love you, Bay." He looked her in the eyes before kissing her on the forehead.

"Devin seems to be having a good time. I'm glad he's here."

"He's a good kid."

"Yeah, in spite of his mother." Aja felt a familiar bitter taste creeping into her mouth. "I still can't believe Sunni sent him here with clothes that didn't fit. Now that was trifling. She knew we'd go out and buy him new clothes and sneakers. She never misses an opportunity to take a jab at us. What kind of a mother does that?" she spat the words out as if they were creating a foul taste in her mouth.

"Don't get me started. I could go on and on about her tactics. I'm just thankful Devin's as well adjusted as he is."

"No thanks to his mother. He's well adjusted because of you."

The mere mention of Sunni tended to elevate Aja's blood pressure. That woman had been a thorn in her side for years. Thankfully, Sunni lived in South Carolina. They had never met face-to-face nor had Aja even so much as seen a picture of her. And she did not want to see her either. She figured she wouldn't have to meet Sunni anyway until Devin graduated from high school. That was years away. Aja imagined that Sunni looked like the gorgon, Medusa, from Greek mythology, and if she ever laid eyes on her, she would turn to stone.

Aja remembered when Sunni found out that Aja was pregnant with Jayden. She had the audacity to call and cuss her out. She called Aja everything except a child of God. Aja thought she was crazy and told her not to ever call her house again. She warned Sunni and told her that the only contact she could have with Hunter was on his cell phone to discuss Devin. At times like these, Aja wondered whether she and Hunter had made a mistake by not seeking full-custody of Devin.

"Bay, how would you feel about Devin staying with us full time?" Hunter said, as if he were reading her mind.

"I don't have a problem with it as long as he's okay with it."

"I'll mention it to him before he goes back home."

"No," she cautioned. "Don't bring it up to him until after you discuss it with Sunni. The last thing we need is anymore of her drama."

Based on the interaction Aja had with Sunni in the past, she knew the woman well enough to know that if they went behind her back on such a serious matter, Sunni would accuse them of trying to brainwash Devin. Although Aja knew they would never do that, she didn't want to give Sunni any ammunition to use against them.

He nodded his head in agreement. "I'm going upstairs to check on the boys."

"I'll go with you."

He stood and helped Aja off the couch. She steadied herself and followed him up the stairs. They found the boys in their pajamas, and Devin reading Jayden a bedtime story. Hunter and Aja stood at the door, watching. She felt full of joy. Seeing their two boys interacting in such a loving manner caused her heart to flutter. Hunter wrapped his arm around her waist and pulled her closer to him. At the end of the story, she and Hunter entered the room.

"You're a good reader, Devin," Hunter said, patting him on the top of his head.

"We came to tuck you guys in," Aja announced. "Go brush your teeth and use the bathroom."

The boys went into the bathroom across the hall and brushed their teeth. When they finished, Devin stepped into the hallway while Jayden used the potty. Then Jayden walked out and waited while Devin went back inside. Not long afterward, they walked into the bedroom together. Aja gave both boys hugs and kisses before tucking them into their beds.

"I love you. Goodnight," Aja said before turning out the light.

"Love you," they replied.

"All right, get some sleep." Hunter followed Aja out of the room.

Hunter went downstairs to turn off the TV and make sure the doors and windows were secured. Aja escaped into the master bathroom and removed the Ace bandage from her ankle before taking a quick shower. She squeezed Black Raspberry Vanilla shower gel from the Bath and Body Works® Signature Collection, onto a mesh sponge and worked it into a rich lather all over her toned body. When she finished, she leaned against the wall to maintain her balance as she dried off with a plush towel and rubbed the accompanying scented body cream onto her soft skin.

With the towel wrapped around her frame, Aja brushed her teeth and gargled with mouthwash. She then hopped into the bedroom where Hunter was sprawled across the bed wearing only the black satin pajama bottoms she had bought him last Christmas. He looked as appealing as her favorite Jamoca Almond Fudge ice cream from Baskin-Robbins. If she had a spoon, she would've scooped him up.

She smiled when she saw the flickering candlelight. Vanilla scented candles were lit throughout the room, and their door was closed. She wondered when he'd had time to create such a magical setting. It didn't really matter; she was pleasantly surprised.

"Come here." His tone was seductive.

She happily obliged and joined him on the bed. He sat up and caressed the back of her neck before covering her mouth with his soft, full lips.

"Bay, let's have another baby," he whispered in her ear before gently nibbling on the lobe.

Her brain was turning to mush. The ear lobe; that was her spot! He caught her off guard. She hadn't thought about having any more children, but Hunter sounded so sincere. She had mixed emotions. On the one hand, she loved her husband. Having his baby, especially a little girl, would be delightful. Then again, children were stressful, even when relationships were solid. She realized that no time was ever the perfect time to have children. Admittedly, there were better times than others. Right now, they needed to focus on getting their finances together, she reasoned. They had so much going on. What if Devin came to live with them? What if they had another boy? So many "what ifs" were going through her mind. Still, she would give his request some serious consideration, because she didn't want to disappoint him.

"I love you so much," he said, turning her face toward his. "You're beautiful."

"I love you too."

They kissed again. Then they explored each other's bodies in loving, intimate ways.

Nine

Shania

"You look nice in that green dress," I said to Cheyenne as she stood in the doorway of my bedroom. "It really complements your complexion."

"Thank you, thank you." She twirled around so that I could get the full effect. Then she stopped turning and batted her eyes. "What about the green eye shadow?"

"I like it." I smiled. "You don't usually wear eye shadow though."

"I know. I wanted to try something different."

I had already taken a shower and was wearing my bathrobe. "Well, it worked. I'll be ready in a minute."

"Okay. I'm going downstairs to wait for Greg and Jonathan."

The mere mention of Jonathan's name tensed my shoulders. It was Cheyenne's idea to invite him to church with us. "Close my door, please."

She closed the door behind her. I untied my robe and spread it across the chaise. Sitting on top of my robe, I rubbed firming moisturizer all over my body. I didn't know why I felt nervous. I had joined Greg's church several months ago, and we usually rode together to Sunday services. That was nothing new. Perhaps I felt jittery because now we were engaged. I know how church folks can be; especially the single sisters. Behind the veneer of congratulatory well wishes, they'd be picking me apart. My hair, makeup, nails, outfit and shoes had to be up to par. Otherwise, they'd think I wasn't suitable to marry him. Besides, I didn't feel like reciting my resumé to prove that I was good enough to be with Greg.

I remember the first time Greg took me to his church. Women were whispering and staring. Some of the women hated on me because Greg had been considered one of the most eligible bachelors at his church. He's six foot four, a muscular 205 pounds and handsome. His sexy light brown eyes, full kissable lips, and even white teeth were definitely assets. Most importantly, he loves the Lord. Being that he was young, pleasant on the eyes, educated, gainfully employed, never married, no children, and straight, he was a hot commodity, and those sisters were ruthless in their tactics.

I'll never forget this one audacious sister, Shannyn, who bumped me out of the way to talk to Greg. She acted like he was a rock star, the way she was throwing herself at him. I had watched her from the corner of my eye as she walked toward us, discreetly unbuttoning the top two buttons of her blouse. Her smile was as fake as her saline implants. I watched her skinnin' and grinnin' all up in Greg's face. He was polite and never once looked down at the midgets in her shirt. I nearly danced a jig when she invited him over for a home-cooked meal, and he grabbed my hand and said, "My lady and I would like that." The look on Shannyn's face was priceless. She couldn't conceal her mad contorted smile. She huffed before getting on her broomstick and flying away.

Continuing to prepare myself for service, I put on my undergarments, dabbed a little bit of Dolce and Gabbana Light Blue on my neck, wrists, and behind my ears before slipping into a chocolate brown colored dress with matching leather pumps. I added some gold accessories, grabbed my clutch purse, and joined my sister downstairs in the family room.

"Ooh, Sister," Cheyenne said, putting down the *Essence* magazine that she was reading. "You look pretty."

"Thanks." I was about to check the time, but the doorbell rang. "I'll get it." I walked to the front door and opened it. Greg, Jonathan, and Greg's mom, Mrs. Crinkle, were standing on the other side. I smiled as I unlocked the screen door. I knew that Greg was picking up Jonathan. Seeing Mrs. Crinkle was a pleasant surprise. She lived in Macon, and I had ridden with Greg a few times to visit. I had met Greg's parents, but not his siblings because they lived out of state. This was Mrs. Crinkle's first time at my house. "Come on in," I said. "Nice to see you."

"You too, sugar," Mrs. Crinkle said with a noticeable southern accent. She hugged me as soon as she walked through the door. "Aren't you as pretty as a Barbie doll?"

"Thank you," I laughed.

"Come here, Barbie, and give Ken a hug," Greg teased as he embraced me and planted a soft kiss on my cheek.

I wriggled free and said, "Hey, Jonathan. Cheyenne's in the family room."

"Okay. 'Cuse me." He made his way into the other room.

Mrs. Crinkle looked around, and said, "Your home is beautiful. I love the decorations."

"Thanks." I was glad that she approved.

"Greg told me about the engagement, and I wanted to come down and congratulate you in person. I couldn't be happier." Her eyes danced with excitement.

She was a sporty older woman. With her short silver haircut and smooth skin, Mrs. Crinkle exuded class and beauty.

"That really means a lot to me," I said as Greg held my hand.

"His daddy would've come down too, but he has a nasty cold." Mrs. Crinkle skewed up her face.

"I understand. You haven't met my sister, Cheyenne. She's home for the holidays."

"No, I haven't, but Greg speaks very highly of her."

"Follow me," I said. We joined Cheyenne and Jonathan in the other room. "Cheyenne, this is Greg's mom, Mrs. Crinkle."

Cheyenne stood up and said, "Nice to meet you."

She was about to shake Mrs. Crinkle's hand when Mrs. Crinkle said, "We're family. No handshakes, only hugs." Cheyenne let out a hearty laugh and hugged her.

Then Cheyenne hugged Greg, and said, "So, Greg, what's up with you wanting to marry my sister?"

"What can I say? I happen to love her." He looked at me, smiling.

Cheyenne pursed her lips and said, "I'm glad you guys are getting married. I've never met a couple as mushy and lovey-dovey as the two of you." She laughed. "What kind of wedding do you want to have?"

"It doesn't matter to me," Greg admitted. "It's not about the ceremony, but the vows and the commitment." He stared into my eyes as he spoke.

"I hear you, but my sister deserves a fairytale wedding. I envision her wearing a beautiful, off-the-shoulder, white gown." She swooped her long, deep walnut brown hair off her shoulder and said, "And an upsweep hairdo with loose curls framing her face."

"You've thought a lot about this," I said, impressed.

"Of course. So you better not even think about eloping." She pointed her finger at us.

Everyone laughed.

"We're only doing this one time, so it's got to be right," Cheyenne continued.

"We?" I asked.

"You know what I mean."

"You know me better than that. I wouldn't shortchange you on being my maid of honor."

"Speaking of which, don't have me wearing no ugly dress." Cheyenne rolled her eyes.

"Remember the bridesmaid's dress Jane Fonda wore in the movie, *Monster-In-Law?*" I joked, trying to keep a straight face.

Everyone laughed again.

"Don't play, Sister," Cheyenne said seriously, pointing her finger at me.

"Who's playing?"

Cheyenne motioned her hand, giving me a dismissive gesture. "Anyway," she sucked air between her teeth, "have you guys set a date?"

"Not yet," we said in unison.

"What are you waiting for, next Christmas?"

"Why are you so worried about it?" I said jokingly.

"Fine. Forget you, meany," she teased.

"I'm just playing."

"No, it's too late." She pretended to pout.

"Drama should be your middle name," I said, laughing.

"Whatever."

Greg checked his watch and said, "All right everybody, it's time to bounce."

I locked the front door after everyone stepped outside, and we all loaded into Greg's Benz. During the ride to the church, we listened to a Mary Mary CD. We talked briefly about whether

Greg and I wanted to get married at the church in which Greg grew up. I didn't have a problem with it, but Greg really wanted to get married on the beach. I noticed that Mrs. Crinkle seemed a little disappointed to hear that. I could understand it, because both of Greg's siblings had already gotten married at the church. She wanted to continue the tradition. In spite of what Greg said, I promised his mother that we'd give it some serious consideration.

Once we reached our destination, Greg parked the car and we went inside. The ushers greeted us with hugs. Several teenagers came up to Greg and they exchanged high fives and an occasional, "Hey, what's up?" We walked down the center aisle and sat in the front row. I wasn't concerned about the many sets of eyes boring holes in the back of my head. I was secure within my relationship with Greg and confident about what I brought to the table. These other women weren't about to intimidate me. It would take a lot more than some eyes rolling and sucking air between teeth. *Why are some women so catty?*

The service began with opening prayer. A robust woman with a pineapple-style haircut and a sparkling gold tooth in the front of her mouth stood in front of the microphone and said, "Praise the Lord, saints."

The congregation stood to its feet and then responded with, "Praise the Lord" and a resounding applause.

We closed our eyes as the woman led us in prayer. "Lord, we invite you into this place.

Enter into our hearts. Heal us where we hurt. Make us whole and meet our needs. Bless the pastor and his family. Give the pastor a word today that will uplift us and edify our souls. Thank you, Father. In Jesus' name, we pray. Amen."

And the church said a collective, "Amen."

She turned it over to the choir who sang "Holy Holy Holy." I continued standing and lifted my hands in the air. I praised God and thanked Him for all He had done for me.

At the end of praise and worship, the pastor came out dressed in all black and greeted everyone. He cracked a couple of jokes, made a few announcements, and then said, "Praise God. I see Brother Greg over there with his lovely mom and beautiful fiancée, Sister Shania." He nodded his head in our direction and motioned for us to rise. "Stand up." Greg and I both looked at each other confused. We stood up, smiling. I was thoroughly embarrassed as I was not expecting that announcement. "Congratulations."

The congregation applauded. Some of the people sitting around us shook our hands, patted us on the back and gave us hugs. Cheyenne and Mrs. Crinkle both smiled. We sat back down, and Greg rested his hand on my lap.

"You were embarrassed; weren't you, Sister?" Cheyenne leaned over and whispered in my ear. I lightly nudged her.

The pastor preached about Peter stepping out of the boat to come to Jesus. He explained that only when Peter took his eyes off of the Lord, he faltered. At the end of the sermon, the pastor prayed a prayer of protection for the congregation.

"Lord, grant us traveling mercies and protect us. Get us to our destinations safe and sound. In Jesus' name, we pray. Amen. Now go out and have the best week of your life," Pastor said in his usual upbeat tone.

My stomach was growling, and I was ready to go eat. We had made our way through the crowd and were standing in the lobby when I heard a familiar voice rapidly approaching from behind.

"Hey, Greg," Shannyn sang. All of us turned around to face her. "Glad I caught you." A grin was plastered on her face. She tapped Greg on the chest. "I guess congratulations are in order."

"Thanks, Shannyn," he said.

"And you, Sister Shania." She turned to face me and shook her head. "It's always the quiet types. You go, girl."

I tilted my head to the side and looked at her like I had caught her eating dog food. You go, girl? What? And who was she calling a quiet type?

"Who might you be?" Mrs. Crinkle asked while noticing the expression on my face.

Cheyenne stifled a laugh and grabbed Jonathan by the arm. She backed him up against a wall.

"Oh, I'm Shannyn," she introduced, extending her hand.

Shaking her hand, Mrs. Crinkle introduced

herself. "How do you know my son?" She looked her in the eye.

Shannyn batted her spider lashed eyes. "He's the youth pastor and my younger sister is, you know, one of his students. That's how we met." Her head bobbed the entire time that she spoke.

"Pleasure meeting you."

"You too, Mrs. Crinkle. I have to go meet my sister. Bye." She waved at us.

Mrs. Crinkle tugged at my arm and said, "You better watch her."

I looked at her, pursed my lips together, and nodded my understanding. I understood what she meant. Nothing against Greg, I trusted him completely. If I had any doubt about his trust-worthiness, I wouldn't be marrying him. There was a determined look in Shannyn's eyes, though, that let anyone know that she's the type of woman who wouldn't stop until she got what she wanted. Right now, it's obvious that Greg was at the top of her list. Too bad, so sad.

We went to eat brunch at the Evergreen Conference Center in Stone Mountain. They had a fabulous Sunday brunch consisting of a salad bar, chilled seafood, breakfast items, a lunch selection, and an amazing array of desserts. Mrs. Crinkle announced that she was going to throw an engagement party for Greg and me. I thought that was great.

Mrs. Crinkle was one of the nicest people I had ever met. The fact that she wanted to throw us an engagement party didn't surprise me in the least. She was a social butterfly.

When her husband, Mr. Crinkle, was on active duty as an Air Force pilot, Mrs. Crinkle made a career out of being an officer's wife. According to the stories Mrs. Crinkle had shared, she used to enjoy throwing social gatherings; everything from tea parties to fund raising events.

After brunch, Greg dropped off his mom at his house; something about her having gastritis. She wanted to take an antacid and lie down. She was spending the night and intended to drive back home to Macon the following afternoon. We made sure that Mrs. Crinkle was resting comfortably before Greg drove the rest of us to my house.

While at my house, we watched *Freedom Writers* on DVD. Halfway through the movie, the phone rang. I checked the caller ID; it was my cousin, Rayna. I picked up the cordless phone and walked upstairs to my bedroom so that I wouldn't disturb Greg, Cheyenne, and Jonathan as they watched the movie.

"Hey," I said as I plopped down on my bed. I was happy to hear her voice. We hadn't spoken since her wedding.

"Hey yourself, cuz. I know it's late, but I was thinking about you."

"I was thinking about you, too. What are you doing for the holiday, old married lady?" I teased.

"Very funny," she laughed. "I'm not hardly old. Anyway, Bryce and I plan to spend Christmas with my parents. It won't be the same without you and Cheyenne. We miss you."

"We miss you guys, too. This will be the first

Christmas that our families won't be together."
We both made an elongated "ah" sound.
"Guess what?"

"What?" Her voice sounded perky.

"Greg and I are getting married," I said en-
thusiastically.

"Cuz, I'm so happy for you," Rayna said. She
sounded sincere.

"Would you be one of my bridesmaids?"

"I'd love to be your bridesmaid. Wait 'til I tell
Momma. She's going to be so excited. You
might as well sit back, because you know Mrs.
Clara is going to take charge." We both
laughed. The way she referred to her mom as
Mrs. Clara cracked me up. I enjoyed talking
with Rayna. She was more like a sister than a
cousin. "Girl, I didn't even tell you this. How
about my parents bought me and Bryce a new
house?" She squealed into the phone.

I was ecstatic too. I couldn't have been happier if someone had given me a house. Wait, the
house I lived in was given to me, too . . . albeit
under different circumstances. Anyway, I
couldn't wait to visit her and get a grand tour of
her home.

"That's wonderful! I can't wait to see it.
How's Bryce?" I asked.

"He's fine. He's right here next to me in bed
typing on his laptop."

"Okay. Tell him I said, 'hi.' "

"Shania said, hi," I heard her repeat.

"Tell her I said, 'hello.' " I heard Bryce's
voice in the background.

"Did you hear him?" she asked.

"Yes, I did."

We finished our conversation and I pressed the OFF button on the phone. Then I set it next to me on the bed. Even though Rayna sounded happy about the new house, and I'm sure she was, she didn't seem elated about her marriage. There was something about the tone of her voice. She didn't sound all giddy like most newlyweds. As soon as I asked her about Bryce, her enthusiasm waned. I wondered what was going on. Was Rayna's marriage in trouble?

Ten

Rayna

An hour had passed since Rayna had spoken with Shania, and she couldn't fall asleep because of all the thoughts occupying her mind. Shania seemed so excited about her upcoming nuptials. Rayna felt that if anyone deserved happiness in this life, it was Shania. She had a heart of gold, always placing the needs of others ahead of her own. Shania and Rayna had always been close, but after Shania's parents died, they became even closer, like sisters. She felt bad about not telling Shania the truth about the state of her marriage. Omission was equally as bad as telling an outright lie, Rayna thought. So many times she had considered calling Shania and confiding in her about her own relationship, but the timing never seemed right. Either Bryce was in her face or Shania was dealing with one of Cheyenne's crises.

"Bryce, we need to talk," she said, poking

her fingers in his chest, doing her best to awaken her sleeping husband.

"What's wrong?" he said with his eyes still closed, half asleep.

"Everything." She sounded annoyed. He sat up in bed, stretched and then yawned. "I'm not happy." Rayna could see disappointment creeping into his sleepy eyes. She felt the need to explain. "It hurts me that you and I don't get along the way I think married couples should. It's like we can't seem to agree on anything. I understand that opposites attract, but this is ridiculous." Even though she knew she shouldn't have, she went down a laundry list of complaints. It went against everything she had ever read in relationship books about communicating and fighting fair.

"When we're in the car," she hissed, "you only want to listen to jazz CD's. I don't have a problem listening to jazz, but sometimes, I like to hear the radio. I like versatility."

He pressed his lips together. Then he said, "I don't like listening to all that bubble gum music. I like to control what I listen to."

"See, that's what I mean." She gritted her teeth. "You're so set in your ways." She could tell by Bryce's solemn expression that his feelings were hurt. She cared, but not enough to stop venting. "And I'm tired of you always wanting to go with me whenever I go to visit my friend, Aja," she continued. "It's like you don't trust me to go out without you."

He lowered his eyes and then looked up at Rayna. "I don't know if I told you this before, but I had a girlfriend, Justine, who cheated on me." Rayna shook her head and listened attentively as he continued the story. "One night, I called her house and asked if I could come over. She sounded strange and was making up a bunch of excuses as to why I couldn't come over. Well, that didn't set right with me. I drove by her house and saw her car and somebody else's, so I called her cell phone from mine. She lied and said that she was not at home. Then I busted her and asked why her car was in her driveway. She told me that she rode with one of her girlfriends. After I got off the phone with her, I kicked in her front door. She was there in the living room with another guy."

Rayna's mouth dropped. That was disturbing, she thought. The fact that he was acting like Rambo was about as convincing as the war in Iraq being about weapons of mass destruction. Regardless of what he may or may not have caught Justine doing was no excuse for violating the woman's home. Bryce was as wrong as OJ Simpson's involvement in an alleged robbery of sports memorabilia. She couldn't help but laugh at the mental image of Bryce acting like a straight up gangsta.

"What did Justine do?" she asked in between laughs.

"She was shocked. She yelled at me and told me to get out."

"What happened with the guy?"

"Nothing." He frowned. "He knew better than to get involved." Bryce actually sounded tough.

Rayna rolled her eyes and gave him a smirk. She tried to conceal her jealousy. The fact that another woman had driven him to such insanity bothered her. "So what happened between you and Justine?"

"We tried to work it out. We stayed together for a little while longer, but I couldn't get past it. I couldn't trust her, so we broke up."

"I see," she said, seriously.

Justine must have really hurt him deeply, she figured. Because of that, she already didn't like Justine. It didn't matter that she had never seen or spoken to the woman.

The following morning, Rayna got up and prepared cheese omelets with red and green peppers for breakfast. She was in a good mood. Last night had given her more insight into Bryce. It helped her to better understand him and his behavior. He had some baggage; but didn't everyone? she thought. Marriage requires hard work and commitment. Rather than holding Bryce's past against him, she decided to show him some love. She even made fresh squeezed orange juice.

Bryce entered the kitchen and asked, "What's all this?"

"I thought we'd enjoy a nice breakfast together." She smiled.

He came up behind Rayna, wrapped his arms around her waist and kissed her on the neck. "You know, I'm in the mood for some eggplant with lots of mayonnaise."

Oh my God! How gross! she thought. "You're nasty, boy." She rolled her eyes playfully as she flipped the omelet in the skillet.

"Smells good," said Bryce. "My wife is fine, and she can cook."

Rayna had to admit that even though she didn't cook every day, when she did, it was off the chain. Between watching her mom and Shania, she had learned her way around the kitchen. Bryce sat at the dining room table reading his subscription to the *Wall Street Journal*, while Rayna fixed their plates. She joined him, and Bryce blessed the food.

"Lord, thank you for the food we are about to receive for the nourishment of our bodies. We pray that you bless the hands that prepared it. In Jesus' name. Amen."

She used her fork to cut a piece of an egg and stuffed it in her mouth. Bryce was smacking his lips and seemed to be enjoying his food.

"How is it?" she asked.

Bryce nodded his head. "Delicious."

"I'm going to the leasing office today to let them know that we won't be renewing the lease."

"When is the actual lease up?" He took another bite.

"I received the renewal notice not that long ago. I think it's sometime next month."

"Okay. I just wanted to make sure we weren't going to be penalized for breaking the lease."

"No, we won't be. But even if we were, I wouldn't care," she enlightened. "We have a house now."

Bryce cleared his throat and wiped the corners of his mouth with a paper napkin. "About that . . . I don't mean to sound ungrateful, because I'm not. What your parents did was extremely generous, and I'm grateful." He looked into her eyes. "I wasn't going to say anything, but I need to get this off my chest." He sighed and placed his fork down on his plate. "Did you ask your parents to get us a house?"

"Absolutely not." She sounded offended.

"Calm down, girl." He started calling her "girl" after watching a few episodes of Martin. He thought it was funny, yet endearing. "It's just that the timing, you know, seemed a bit convenient."

"Believe me; I had nothing to do with that. I was just as surprised as you were."

He searched her face and apparently concluded that she was telling the truth. "The reason why I didn't want us to get a house right away was because I wanted to save some more money first. I didn't want the basic starter house. And I know you. You would want new furniture to go with that new house."

They both laughed, and Rayna nodded her head as if to say, "Yeah."

His laughter ceased and his tone turned serious. "I felt disappointed that your parents didn't put my name on the deed, too. They call me their son, but I guess at the end of the day, I'm

just the guy that's married to their daughter."
He stared at his reflection in the glass tabletop.

Rayna was flabbergasted. She stood and walked
over to Bryce. She hugged him, and he rested
his head against her bosom, arms wrapped
around her waist. In her heart, she had no doubt
that her parents were the biggest supporters of
her marriage to Bryce. Neither one of them
wanted their marriage to fail. In fact, they both
prayed for her and Bryce's success. How could
he question the sincerity of their feelings for
him? she wondered.

"Bryce," she said as calmly as she could,
stroking his soft hair. "You're mistaken. My
parents absolutely adore you. You know that.
You shouldn't feel slighted in any way. We're a
couple. What's mine is yours."

"Yeah, right," he said sarcastically.

"What's that supposed to mean?" She broke
away from him and glared.

"Nothing. Just forget I said anything." He resumed eating.

She sat back down. "Do you really think I'm
going to let you off the hook that easy? No, sir.
Tell me what you meant by 'yeah, right.' " She
waited for a response.

"You really want to know?"

She raised a brow with an "of course, I want
to know" expression on her face.

"I'll tell you," he said. "I feel insecure about
moving into a house that doesn't have my
name on it."

"Then don't move," she wanted to say.

"I don't like feeling like you could get mad

and kick me out," he explained. "Then where would I go?"

Okay, he's a grown man. Bryce had a place to live before they met. If they broke up, he could move into another apartment. She'd just keep the house. Duh?

"Why do you have to be so negative?" Rayna said, more like a statement than a question. "We just got married. Why are you talking as if we won't last? Weren't you the one who said, 'divorce is not an option'?"

Rayna's hand rested on top of the table, and Bryce placed his hand on top of hers. She felt like pulling away, but didn't.

"I shouldn't have said anything," he said.

He still doesn't get it. She felt like screaming. She wasn't upset about what he said, per se. She *wanted* open and honest communication. The problem was how he felt about her parents and their marriage. He tended to have a negative predisposition. His mind seemed to conjure up more negative thoughts than a shrink working with a psychopath.

Rayna picked up her fork and pointed it at him. "Bryce, you need to chill."

"You're right, girl. I'm out of order." He flashed Rayna a sexy smile. "Your parents have been nothing but good to me, to us. I don't know what I was thinking."

Rayna sighed. She truly loved Bryce and wanted to make him happy. She respected his feelings and didn't want him to feel less of a man simply because her parents put them into a house. "If it means that much to you, I'd be happy to add your name to the mortgage before we finalize the paperwork."

"Serious?"

"Yes." She smiled, trying to smooth things over.

"I love you, girl."

They finished eating breakfast and put the dirty dishes in the dishwasher. They went into the bedroom, and Bryce wrapped his arms around Rayna's waist, pulling her closer to him.

"Why don't we stay inside all day and make love? I don't have to go into the station until three o'clock," he said.

"As appealing as that sounds," she lied, "I have a few errands to run. I promised my mom that I would run her around to some stores today."

"Do we have time for a quickie?"

"Sorry, it's that time of the month," she lied again, freeing herself from his embrace.

Being on her cycle was a "get-out-of-jail free" card with Bryce. He wouldn't touch Rayna with a ten-foot pole. He believed that a woman was unclean during that time. Hopefully, Bryce wasn't keeping track, because she intended to use that excuse every other week.

Rayna felt guilty and silently prayed, *Lord, please forgive me. Give me the strength to handle whatever comes my way.*

Rayna knew that the Bible was clear that when a woman marries her body is no longer her own. I Corinthians 7:3-5 states, "Let the husband render unto the wife due benevolence: and likewise also the wife unto the husband.

The wife hath not power of her own body, but the husband: and likewise also the husband hath not power of his own body, but the wife. Defraud ye not one the other, except it be with consent for a time, that ye may give yourselves to fasting and prayer; and come together again, that Satan tempt you not for your incontinency."

Going against God's Holy Word annoyed Rayna. She hated lying. And she especially hated feeling worthless and unfulfilled after having relations with her husband. Things hadn't picked up at all in that area. Seems like the more she complained about Bryce's performance, the more he wanted to do the horizontal polka. What she could do to make things better, she had no idea.

Eleven

Aja

Hunter took Jayden and Devin to the park to play basketball. Aja had been thinking a lot about Hunter's proposition for them to expand their family. The thought of being pregnant again didn't appeal to Aja. When she found out that she was pregnant with Jayden, she was elated. That was the first and only time she had ever been pregnant. Hunter was so loving and supportive. Whenever she had a doctor's appointment, Hunter was right by her side. The problem was that she was worrisome.

Aja could never forget the day she was in the grocery store and ran into Vivian Rose. Vivi and Aja had worked for the same real estate company. She was a statuesque Nigerian woman with a thick accent. Even though Vivi was six weeks further along than Aja, they had both announced their pregnancies within two weeks of one another. They used to talk about baby

names, morning sickness that never seemed to
occur in the morning, healthy eating habits and
their lack of energy. Well, Aja was eight months
pregnant and had taken a leave of absence from
work when she encountered Vivi and asked her
about the baby. Since their ultrasounds revealed that Aja was having a boy and Vivi a girl,
they used to joke around about a pre-arranged
marriage for their children.

When Vivi revealed that her baby had died,
Aja was devastated. Vivi had explained that a
few days before the delivery, she no longer felt
the baby moving. She had asked her doctor
about it, and he told her that the baby was probably just too big for her to feel the movements.
When Vivi went in to have the baby, they discovered that the umbilical cord had wrapped
around the baby's neck and strangled her.

After seeing Vivi, Aja was so worried about
Jayden that she couldn't think clearly. Once,
when she didn't feel Jayden moving, she made
an emergency doctor's appointment for an ul-
trasound. Her doctor authorized the procedure
because she realized that Aja was distraught.
Hunter tried to assure her that everything was
fine, and he attended the appointment with
her. Her fears were somewhat relieved when
she saw Jayden moving on the monitor. Hunter's
chest was sticking out with pride when he had
said, "He's got my nose." Aja smiled and shook
her head. Inside, she felt so in love with her
husband and prayed that their baby would be
fine. Thankfully, Jayden was born healthy and
weighing nearly nine pounds. She certainly didn't

take having a healthy child for granted. To Aja, that meant more than any worldly possession. Occasionally, she still found herself going into Jayden's room just to see if he was breathing.

Aja's cell phone rang to the tune of *Sex and the City*. "Hello," she answered.

"What up?"

"Nothing much, Trevon. How have you been?"

"A'ight," Trevon replied.

"You ready for the holiday?"

"I guess. Everything would be straight if I got to see you."

She smiled. Trevon was an immediate ego booster for Aja. He had caramel brown colored skin with a head full of natural long, wavy, black hair. And he had some kissable looking lips, which Aja hadn't kissed. My, my, my. She shook her head. She needed to stop.

"Do you plan to spend it with your family?" she asked.

"Yeah, but I only have Christmas Day off. I have to work Christmas Eve."

The life of a telemarketer, she thought. "That's too bad."

"It's cool. Anyway, when I'ma get to see you? For real, a brotha is missing you."

"It's hard for me to get away. Especially since my husband is home from work and my stepson is visiting," she explained.

Aja knew that she was playing with fire and like the adage goes, "If you play with fire, you will get burned."

Regardless, Trevon was so sweet and likable.

There was something about him that attracted
Aja like a good girl to a bad boy. Perhaps it was
his idealistic outlook on life. There was a certain innocence that came with youth. Who was
Aja trying to kid? Trevon was good-looking and
fine . . . six foot six and muscular. It wasn't his
conversation that kept her stimulated.

"I wish I could kidnap you for a few days."

Aja laughed. "Oh really? And what would
you do with me?" Why did she say that?

"Whatever you want me to, baby."

Stop it, Aja. The thoughts occupying her
mind were completely inappropriate, as was
the entire conversation. She had to remind herself that she had a husband. Her cheeks felt hot.

"Anyway, I have to go fix dinner."

"Whatchu cookin', baby?"

Trevon sounded so sexy when he called her
"baby." "I'm making fried chicken, collard
greens, macaroni and cheese, and cornbread."

"You rollin' like that, baby? Save me a seat."

"You're crazy," she laughed. "I'll talk to you
later."

"Okay. Be sweet."

Aja smiled as she flipped the cell phone shut.
Her smile waned at the thought of having to
give up her relationship with Trevon. Even
though they hadn't been physically intimate,
there was definitely an emotional connection.
She felt guilty committing adultery. The fact
that she had been lusting after Trevon definitely qualified as adultery, and she wasn't
comfortable with that.

At the same time, it was hard for Aja to give

her all to a man . . . even her spouse. In her previous relationships, her partners always cheated on her. Now, she had come to expect it. Aja understood that life was a self-fulfilling prophecy, that one pretty much gets what she expects. On a conscious level, Aja didn't want any of her former boyfriends to be unfaithful. That was their choice. Was it fair that Hunter was being penalized for the bad behavior of other men? she thought. She shook her head as if to snap herself out of her thoughts.

Aja went into the kitchen and washed her hands. The collard greens and macaroni and cheese were already prepared. She had put the greens on first thing that morning, because she preferred to cook them for hours. Thank goodness for the new cut and cleaned greens in a bag. She never liked the taste of canned collards, but didn't feel as if she had much of a choice since she didn't have any interest in sitting down and cleaning greens. She was glad that now all she had to do was place the greens in water, and add seasoning and turkey meat.

The macaroni and cheese was covered with aluminum foil and sitting on the countertop. The poultry was thawed, so she rinsed and seasoned it. Leaving the chicken on a plate, she filled the black iron skillet with oil and placed it on the stove over high heat. While waiting for the grease to heat up, Aja floured the meat. As soon as she heard the popping noises and saw tiny bubbles forming in the grease, she placed a few pieces of meat into the frying pan. She waited until the skin became brown and crispy before turning it over. After frying the chicken, she placed the pieces on a paper towel covered plate to soak up the excess grease.

Aja preheated the oven to 400 degrees before emptying the contents of two boxes of Jiffy brand cornbread mix into a large glass bowl and blending the ingredients. The boys loved the sweet cornbread taste. Besides, using Jiffy was much faster and more convenient than making cornbread from scratch. She remembered watching her grandmother make crackling. Learning how to make crackling didn't appeal to Aja. When she finished making the batter, she poured the concoction into two non-stick pans and placed the pans inside the oven. Then she went into her room to freshen up.

When Aja came back downstairs, she heard the sound of the garage door opening. She turned the stove off, put on an oven mitt, and removed the golden yellow bread, placing it on the front burner. She retrieved a stick of butter from the refrigerator and rubbed it along the surface of the hot bread.

"Hey, Mom," Jayden said as he walked through the door with Devin and Hunter trailing behind him.

Aja noticed that they were all sweaty.

"Hey, honey," Aja replied. "Did you have fun at the park?"

"Um-hmm."

"You guys go and wash up for dinner," she instructed as she re-wrapped the butter and placed it back in the fridge.

As Devin and Jayden brushed past Aja, she

got a whiff of their musty little bodies. As her grandmother used to say, they smelled "like outside." She crinkled her nose. Hunter rubbed his hands together, licked his lips, and smiled.

"That means you, too," she said to Hunter, smiling.

He kissed Aja on the cheek, and she took a step backward. "You stink," she teased.

He lifted his right arm and sniffed his armpit. His brows knitted together. She laughed as he headed upstairs to take a much needed shower. While the guys were upstairs getting cleaned up, Aja set the table.

During dinner, they talked about how much they enjoyed having Devin spend the holidays with them.

"Devin," Hunter said. "How would you feel about spending more time with us?"

"I would love that, Dad," he said as he hurriedly ate his food.

"Slow down," Aja warned.

Devin gave her a side glance and slowed his roll.

Hunter placed his fork on his plate and folded his hands on top of the table. "Son, Aja and I have been talking, and we want to talk to your mom about possibly letting you live here with us."

"Devin's going to live with us?" Jayden beamed as he got out of his seat and jumped up and down.

"Sit back down, honey," Aja instructed.

He did as he was told. While looking at Jayden, Aja placed her index finger over her lips, indicating that he should be quiet.

"For real, Dad?" Devin looked down at his plate. "Y'all want me here all the time?" His voice was barely above a whisper.

"Of course," Hunter said. "We love you. We thought long and hard about this. Look at me." Searching brown eyes looked deeply into the eyes that peered into his. "At first I was going to wait until I spoke with your mother, but I changed my mind. Before I approached her with this I wanted to make sure you were okay with it."

Nodding, Devin said, "I understand." Then he went back to eating.

Aja felt good about Devin and his wanting to live with them.

"Hey," Aja said to Devin. "Regardless of what happens, I want you to know that your dad and I love you very much. You're an important part of this family whether you physically live here or not. Okay?"

"Okay," he replied.

Hunter and Aja exchanged glances across the table and smiled.

After dinner, Hunter and the boys were downstairs running around chasing each other. Aja went upstairs to sort through laundry. The phone rang. Right when she was about to answer, it stopped ringing. She picked it up anyway, but didn't say anything. Hunter had already answered, and she recognized Sunni's voice on the other end. She nearly cringed at the sound of Sunni's voice. She couldn't stand that woman. What was she doing calling on the house phone? Aja wondered. Maybe since Devin was here she figured it was all right. She started to hang up but decided to be nosey.

"Hold on," Hunter said, sounding frustrated. "Let me get Devin."

"Wait," she yelled. "I want to talk to you first."

"About what?"

"You need to stop being so rude to me and treat me with some respect. I am still the mother of your child. Remember?"

"I don't even feel like going there with you. Say what you have to say or I'm getting off the phone."

"You have a lot of nerve. Why are you being so hateful?"

"I thought you had something real to talk about." He sighed.

"I do. You never explained to me why you left so abruptly after our kiss."

Kiss? Aja almost dropped the phone. Her hand was trembling and her jaw dropped. What kiss?

He whispered, "It never should've happened. I wish you'd quit bringing it up."

"Well it did. That tells me everything I need to know. You still have feelings for me."

"That's a lie. This isn't the time to get into it either."

"If not now, when?"

"Let it go." Hunter sounded frustrated. "Besides, we have some issues to discuss about our son."

"Like what?"

"I'd rather not go into details right now. We'll talk about it when I see you."

"Fine," she said with attitude. "How's Devin?"

"Why don't you ask him yourself?"

Aja heard Hunter call Devin to the phone. That was Aja's opportunity to press the OFF button on the cordless phone and place it back on the charger. Her feelings were hurt. She felt betrayed and angry. How could Hunter kiss Sunni, of all people? He shouldn't have been kissing anybody, but Sunni? What the . . . ?

She paced the floor, wringing her hands, secretly wishing it was Hunter's neck. Her heart felt as though it were going to beat right out of her chest. She wondered whether Hunter had been lying to her all of this time. Was Sunni correct in her assumption that Hunter had feelings for her? Tears pooled in Aja's eyes before escaping and racing each other down her cheeks.

Thinking about Hunter in a lip-lock with Sunni made Aja feel jealous, and oddly enough, competitive. Even though she felt like going off on Hunter, part of her wanted to fight for her man. The thought of Sunni getting him back was more than she could bear. Yet, another part of Aja wanted revenge. She knew it wasn't right, but she wanted to hurt Hunter as badly as he had hurt her. She was tired of being cheated on, lied to, and deceived. History had taught Aja that she couldn't trust any man. And to think, she almost fell for that whole "let's have another baby" spiel. The nerve of him! Enough was enough.

Twelve
Shania

Cheyenne, Greg, Jonathan, and I attended Christmas Eve church services. The church was packed. We sang Christmas carols, had scripture readings, received a unique Christmas message from the pastor, partook of Holy Communion, and closed with a candle lighting ceremony.

The following morning, Cheyenne and I got up early so that we could eat a light breakfast together and get dressed. Greg was coming over at noon to pick us up and drive us to Macon. When Greg informed Mrs. Crinkle that my sister and I planned to spend Christmas alone, she insisted that we come to her house for dinner. Telling her no wasn't even an option.

When we arrived at the Crinkles' house, the garage doors were open with a portable heater generating heat. No cars were parked inside, and people were standing around talking loudly and laughing. I could hear Yolanda Adams' Christmas CD playing in the background.

"What's up, Scooter?" Greg said with a sly grin as he walked up to a guy who was about an inch shorter than he. The man had a smooth, pecan brown complexion.

"Ah, man, no you didn't call me Scooter," the guy said, laughing. He and Greg hugged and he patted Greg on the back. Looking over his shoulder, he looked at me and said, "That must be Shania."

He and Greg broke their embrace. "Yes, that's my girl." Then he motioned his hand toward Cheyenne. "And that's her sister, Cheyenne."

He looked at Greg and nodded his approval. Then he looked back at Cheyenne and me, smiling. "Welcome to the family, you two. In case you hadn't figured it out, I'm Greg's much handsomer big brother, Neil."

We all laughed. Neil hugged Cheyenne and me, and kissed us both on the cheek.

"She looks even prettier than the picture Mom has on the mantel," Neil said as he smiled in my direction. Then he looked back at Greg and said, "You did good."

"Thank you," I said with a slight giggle. Cheyenne nudged me and smirked.

"Hey, why do they call you Scooter?" Cheyenne asked.

He and Greg exchanged glances. Shaking his head, Neil looked back at us and said, "My mom nicknamed me Scooter when I was a baby. She said I used to scoot around all the time. People stopped calling me that," he looked at Greg, "when I was twelve, though."

They both smiled.

"How was the trip from Maryland?" Greg asked Neil.

"Interesting," he sighed. "At least until Nelson fell asleep during the flight. Man, traveling with a kid," he scrunched up his face, "is not a joke. Now I understand why people give kids cold medicine before getting on a plane." He balled up his fists. "Knocks them right on out."

"But you didn't do that, right?" I asked, giving him an incredulous look.

"No, no." He shook his head vehemently.

"I'll bet," Greg said. "Is little man in the house?"

"You know it. He's probably driving the twins crazy." He let out a hearty laugh. "The bad girl's here, too."

"The bad girl?" I asked, confused.

"Oh," he chuckled, "that's what I call my wife."

"I won't even ask how that name came about," I said, smiling.

"It's all good; believe me." He rubbed his hands together.

"Sis already here?" Greg asked.

"They got in from Columbus, Georgia, last night."

"Cool."

"Come on," Neil said.

He introduced us to the rest of the people standing around in the garage before leading us inside the house.

"Momma," Neil yelled as soon as he walked through the door with us following him. "Look who's here."

Mrs. Crinkle walked into the family room and smiled at us. "I'm so glad to see y'all." She hugged us. "How was the drive?"

"It was okay," Greg said. "There wasn't that much traffic. Thank goodness."

"Good," she sighed. "Well, everybody is pretty much spread out. Make yourselves comfortable."

Mrs. Crinkle walked back into the kitchen, and Cheyenne and I exchanged glances.

"I'm going back outside," Neil said as he patted Greg on the back.

Greg took me by the hand as we made our way through the family room where his dad was stationed. Mr. Crinkle was a good-looking man with a whole lot of swagger. The couch, loveseat, and recliner chair were full. There were even three people sitting on the step to the sunken den. People were watching football and yelling at the screen. There were a few delayed head turns, waves, and "Hey, how you doin'?" after Greg announced, "This is my fiancée, Shania, and her sister Cheyenne."

We kept it moving and acknowledged the people sitting at a card table playing dominos.

"Cross my legs!" an elderly gentleman yelled as he slammed a domino on the table.

I laughed.

"That's my Uncle Charles," Greg said.

I nodded. As we made our way over to the group sitting at the dining table playing spades, one of the ladies turned her cards face down and stood up.

"That's my sister, Aleigha, right there," Greg whispered in my ear while he pointed at a petite woman walking toward us.

"What it be like, bro?"

What it be like? That reminded me of something Rerun from the TV show, *What's Happening!* would have said. I wanted to laugh. Whenever I heard bourgeoisie black folks trying to talk slang, I found it humorous. There's just something about it that doesn't sound right.

Greg laughed out loud. "How's my favorite sister?" He released my hand and embraced her.

"I'm your only sister." She thumped his shoulder and pretended to pout. "Hey, Shania. I recognized you from your picture." She kissed me on my cheek. "So nice to finally meet you."

I smiled and chuckled at the same time. Trying to repress my laughter was not easy. "Nice to meet you, too." I motioned my hand in Cheyenne's direction and said, "This is my sister, Cheyenne."

"Hey, you." She smiled. "The two of you look like you should be models or something."

"Heck, naw," Cheyenne said, laughing.

"It's your turn, Aleigha," an attractive light-skinned lady with a black mole above her lip said.

"Just a second." Aleigha held up her index finger and then turned back to us. "The twins are upstairs playing. Go on up and check on them. I know they'll be glad to see their Uncle

Greg and new auntie. I think Nelson is up there, too. "

"Cool," Greg said.

She sat back down, and Greg introduced us to the other three people at the table. The lady with the supermodel Cindy Crawford mole was Neil's wife, Patricia, and the man with lips like actor, Denzel Washington, was Aleigha's husband, Alex. The salt-and-pepper haired gentleman was Greg's Uncle Jr. We exchanged pleasantries before waving good-bye and making our way upstairs.

Once upstairs, I felt as if we had invaded the TV show, *Kid Nation*. Little people were everywhere. It was pure pandemonium. We were nearly knocked back downstairs by a couple of children running down the hall talking about, "Bet you can't catch me."

"Hey, hey, hey," Greg said. "Y'all need to slow your roll. Don't be running in here."

The children looked at us and slowed down but continued to play. We peeped inside the master bedroom and saw two children jumping up and down on the king size bed. I immediately imagined one of them falling and hurried over to them.

"Get down from there," I said, helping them off the bed. "You should not jump on the bed. That's dangerous."

As I was placing the littlest one on the floor, the adorable little boy smiled at me. He had the cutest dimples and longest lashes.

"Yeah, Nelson," Greg said, "you know better than that."

So that's Nelson? Boy, he has grown. He doesn't look like the baby pictures Greg showed me. I felt like giving Nelson a hug, but he broke free.

"Uncle Greg," Nelson sang as he ran into his uncle's arms.

Greg picked him up and swung him in the air like a rag doll. Laughter and giggles filled the room. Not long afterward, two gorgeous little girls with pigtails so thick and long they resembled ropes entered the room. The girls looked like matching bookends—identical.

"They must be Alexis and Arryana," I whispered to Cheyenne.

She nodded her head in agreement and said, "They're cute."

I smiled. Greg placed Nelson back on the floor.

"Twins," Greg called, "come over here and show your most favorite uncle in the whole world some love."

They giggled first before coming over to him and giving him tight hugs. Nelson raised his hands in the air and said, "Pick me up again."

Greg knelt down and complied. While holding Nelson in his arms, Greg introduced us to his nieces then pointed to the different children in the room as he told us who they were in relation to him.

We decided to stay upstairs until dinner. I did not mind, because I enjoyed being around children. Besides, I felt better knowing that the kids had some adult supervision. I did not think they should be running amok.

I enjoyed seeing Greg laughing and playing

with the children. It came natural to him. When he was around them, Greg seemed like the biggest kid of them all. I could not tell whether he or the little people were having more fun.

Cheyenne, on the other hand, was fine because she wanted to watch TV. She flicked through the channels until she found the classic movie, *The Other Side of Midnight*. That was one of her favorite movies of all time, so I did not expect to hear a peep out of her.

An hour passed before Mrs. Crinkle sent Neil upstairs to get us.

"Why are you guys hiding up here?" Neil said when he entered the room. "Momma's been calling you to come and eat."

"For real?" Greg carefully removed his nephew from his back and placed him on the floor. He had been giving him a horsey ride. "I didn't hear her." He looked at me with a questioning look.

"I didn't hear her, either," I said.

"Okay," Neil said, patting his son on the head. "Well, the food is ready."

We instructed the ten children who were upstairs with us to wash and dry their hands. Then we told them to walk, not run, down the stairs. They did as they were told. As I walked down the stairs, I could smell so many delicious foods that I did not even try to figure out all of the menu items.

"What were you all doing up there?" Mrs. Crinkle said jokingly when we entered the kitchen.

Greg kissed her on the cheek. "We were playing with the kids. It was noisy, so we didn't hear you. But dinner smells so good." He licked his lips.

There were two children's tables. After some pushing, shoving, and squabbling over the seating arrangement, the children finally calmed down and took their seats. Mrs. Crinkle had an elegantly decorated buffet table that was draped with a beige tablecloth and a floral arrangement as a centerpiece. The dinner consisted of Cajun turkey, barbecue ribs, dressing, collard and turnip greens, Italian green beans, black-eyed peas, sweet potato soufflé, corn on the cob, and cranberry sauce. And the desserts were equally as inviting. I had to admit that Mrs. Crinkle put her foot all up in it. The homemade pies: apple, sweet potato, and pecan, made me salivate. And I was convinced that Mrs. Crinkle spent days preparing the caramel cake and carrot cake from scratch. As a caterer, I had to give Mrs. Crinkle her props. The woman could burn; figuratively speaking, of course. Seeing the lavish spread reminded me of how the holidays used to be when my parents were alive.

"You all right?" Mrs. Crinkle asked me. She had a concerned look on her face.

"Oh, I'm fine," I said, forcing a smile.

She patted my hand and said, "Everything's going to be all right." She pressed her lips into a smile. "I don't claim to know exactly how you feel," she looked me in the eye, "but I lost both of my parents, too. It can be difficult at times. I want you to know that I love you, and you're a part of this family."

"Thank you." I appreciated her understanding.

Cheyenne wrapped her arm around my waist and leaned her head on my shoulder.

"Everybody," Mrs. Crinkle yelled. "Gather around so we can bless the food."

People started holding hands and Mr. Crinkle led us in prayer. "Heavenly Father, we come humbly before you to give thanks and praise. Thank you for this family and thank you for this food. Bless the food that we are about to receive for the nourishment of our bodies. And bless the hands that prepared it. In Jesus' name, we pray. Amen."

We all said a collective, "Amen" and started fixing our plates. I looked around the room and saw smiling faces. There was such a loving spirit in the Crinkle home. I was happy to be a part of it. I silently thanked God for bringing this wonderful bunch of people into my life. I was glad that Cheyenne and I had not spent the holiday alone.

Thirteen

Rayna

Rayna was so excited about moving into her new home that she had not had a full night's sleep since her parents showed her the house. Like most people, she did not enjoy the packing and cleaning that came along with moving. However, the fact that she was moving from an apartment into her dream home made a big difference. Bryce had gone to work, and she was at home packing. Every room had cardboard boxes lined up against the wall. Dressed in jeans, a T-shirt, and flip-flops, Rayna began packing up the bedroom. She started by removing the hardcover books lining the bookshelves. The books ranged from fictional to inspirational. Rayna's collection meant a great deal to her. Many were signed by the authors. Once the box was full, she sealed it with masking tape. With a black marker she wrote the word "BOOKS" on the outside.

Rayna went into the kitchen and poured herself a glass of chilled apple juice. The glasses were still in the cabinet. Looking around the apartment, she saw an organized mess . . . if there was such a thing. The dining room table was covered with stacks of plates, saucers, and bowls waiting to be wrapped and stored. A roll of bubble wrap was on the floor next to the table. She drained her glass and put it in the sink. The doorbell rang and startled her. She wasn't expecting company. Ordinarily, Rayna would not answer for uninvited guests, so she tiptoed to the door and peeked through the peephole. Surprise, surprise. She unlocked the door and opened it.

"Hey, Fox," she said. "What are you doing here?"

"I was in the neighborhood and decided to stop by. Sorry I didn't call first, but Bryce told me you guys were in the process of moving. Do you need any help?"

"Come on in." Rayna stepped out of the way as he entered the apartment. Thank goodness the living room wasn't in disarray.

"I hope you haven't eaten. I bought us some lunch," he said as he held up a fast food bag in one hand and a drink holder in the other.

"That was nice of you. You were taking a chance though. I could've already eaten or not been at home," she teased.

"True, but I had a feeling you'd be here. You haven't eaten, have you?"

"No. When I'm on a roll, I don't tend to stop for food," she laughed. "This time I'll make an exception."

He looked around. "You've been busy."

"Yes, I have. I get a lot done when Bryce is at work. As you can see," she motioned toward the dining area, "the dining room table is off limits. I do have serving trays that we can use."

"Hey, I'm easy," Fox said, placing the bag on the coffee table.

Interesting choice of words, Rayna thought. According to Bryce, Fox had a reputation for being popular with the ladies. Rayna could see why. Fox was six foot one, had a dark chocolate complexion like Morris Chestnut, straight white teeth, and an athletic build. Even with his loose fitted shirt, his broad shoulders and rippling muscles were quite evident. His trim waist and buns of steel could make a woman lose her mind.

"I'll get the trays," she said, walking into the kitchen where two wooden trays were nestled between the refrigerator and the wall. She and Bryce used the trays whenever they ate in the living room.

When Fox saw Rayna carrying the trays, he walked toward her and said, "Let me get that." He grabbed both trays.

"Thank you."

After unfolding the serving tables, Fox removed a grilled chicken salad with honey mustard dressing from the bag.

"For you," he said, placing the salad bowl in front of her.

"Thanks so much." She smiled. "I love chicken salads from Chick-fil-A. How did you know?"

"Lucky guess."

He removed two chicken sandwiches from the bag for himself. Rayna bowed her head and silently blessed her food before removing the lid from the container. Not knowing whether Fox had prayed over his food, she said a silent prayer for his meal, too. Then she opened the dressing and poured it all over the lettuce and strips.

"So, how's married life treating you?" Fox asked.

"It's cool. Takes some getting used to, you know?" She mixed the salad, trying to evenly distribute the dressing onto each leaf.

"No, I don't know." He sounded serious. "Maybe one day the Lord will bless me with the right woman."

Rayna swallowed the lump forming in her throat. "Do you want to have kids?" She cut the chicken strips into smaller, bite-size pieces.

"Sure. I want to get married and have kids."

Rayna and Fox had never sat down and had a one-on-one conversation. It was refreshing considering that they usually kept their conversations limited to "How are you?" Everything she knew about Fox came courtesy of Bryce.

"Do you attend church?" she asked, stuffing her mouth with salad.

"Yeah. I go to Holy Rollers Church." He took a hearty bite into his sandwich.

Rayna was pleasantly surprised to learn that he attended church. The way Bryce described him, Rayna thought he was too much of a hellion to set foot in church. "I've heard of that church. I go to Called to Conquer. I'm one of the praise dancers." She continued to eat. "How do you like living in Atlanta?"

"The weather is great. Not like all the snow I'm used to, being from Chi-Town and all." He took several more bites of his sandwich before it disappeared.

"Why did you decide to leave Chicago?" She stared at him.

"Oh," Fox said, removing his second sandwich from its pouch. "Before I forget, I got you an ice-dream in a cup. You may want to put it in the freezer until you're ready to eat it."

"I don't know what to say. You're full of surprises. You ordered the exact same lunch that I usually order for myself when I go to Chick-fil-A."

He smiled, obviously pleased. Their connection seemed eerie. She did not see this as some coincidence. It was as if he knew her likes and dislikes. If Fox told her that he ordered a diet lemonade, she may need to run from up out of there.

She removed the Styrofoam cup that was covered with a lid and went into the kitchen to place it in the freezer. When she came back, Fox was inserting a straw into his drink and then took a sip.

Rayna sat back down on the couch and ate some more of her lunch.

Fox set his drink down and said, "I left Chicago because of a business venture."

He went on to explain that he had bought out a company that was going out of business.

According to Fox, he turned the company around and now it was a profitable organization. She was impressed by his business acumen.

He tilted his head in the direction of the drink still in the cup holder. "The drink over there is yours. I wasn't sure what to get you, so I got the diet lemonade. The guy behind the counter assured me it tasted as good as the real thing. I figured it was appropriate with the salad."

What in the world? she wondered. "Uh, uh, thank you," she stammered. This was bananas! Did Bryce put him up to this? If he did, why would he do that? Rayna was on the defense. At this point, she was suspicious of both Bryce and Fox. Either they were in cahoots or Fox really knew women.

Rayna opened a pack of sunflower seeds that came along with the salad, tilted her head back, and sprinkled the seeds directly into her mouth. She felt as if a pair of eyes were searing a hole into the side of her face. With her peripheral vision, she noticed that Fox was staring at her.

"Why are you looking at me?" she inquired.

"You're a beautiful woman."

"Stop it," she laughed. "I'm looking as bummy as all get up and go."

"I don't think you could ever look bad. Bryce is lucky to have you."

Was he coming on to her? she thought. No. He's Bryce's best friend. He wouldn't do that. Would he? The way he was looking at her was almost . . . sensual. She figured that she must have been imagining things. Just in case she wasn't, she decided that Fox had to leave. Even though they were not doing anything wrong, Rayna did not want the appearance of it. Besides, this could have been a trap. What if Bryce was testing her? Better yet, what if this was a spiritual test? Regardless, Rayna refused to fail.

She secured the lid on top of her remaining salad and stood up. "Fox, I really appreciate you bringing me lunch, but I should get back to packing. So much to do and so little time to do it. You know how it is." She nervously smoothed her hair with her hand.

"That's why I'm here, to help you." He crumpled up the empty pouches and stuffed them into the same bag that had been used to carry the food. He stood as he picked up the trash.

"You're sweet. Really, though, I work better by myself. Maybe you can come back when Bryce gets home and help him move the boxes."

"You sure?"

"I'm sure."

"Did I do something wrong?" He raised a brow.

"No, why would you say that?" She rested her hand on her hip.

"It's just that you seem a bit tense."

"Do I?" She giggled. Rayna tended to do that when she got nervous.

"Look, I didn't mean to make you uncomfortable. That's the last thing I want to do." He paused and continued, "A lot of people think that because I have a name like Fox I can't be trusted. I want to tell you it's not true. I'm shrewd in business because I play to win. When it comes to relationships with friends and family, I'm totally different." He searched Rayna's eyes, and she stared into his. "I'm not the type of brotha to disrespect a marriage. Let alone try to push up on my homeboy's wife. Where I'm from, that's grounds for a beat down. Believe that." His laugh was melodious.

Rayna laughed with him. She noticed that he was holding the trash. "Don't worry about that," Rayna said. "I'll throw it out later." She folded her hands in front of her and twiddled her thumbs.

"It's no problem," he assured. "I can take it with me and toss it in the dumpster. Do you have any garbage you need taken out?"

Is he kidding? There was a lot of garbage that needed to be taken out. Seemed like anytime someone moved, every piece of paper needed to be tossed into the recycle bin.

"I don't want to inconvenience you. Bryce can take care of it when he gets home."

"Come on, Rayna. That's what friends are for." He licked his lips.

Friends? So we're friends now? She stopped playing with her fingers and deliberately placed her hands by her sides.

"Fine. If you want to take out the trash, knock yourself out," she said.

He lifted Rayna's hand toward his soft, luscious lips and kissed the back. Her body quivered as she uneasily freed her hand from his.

Her heartbeat sped up. The way Rayna's chest was heaving, she was certain that her breathing was erratic.

"I didn't get a chance to ask you. How was the honeymoon?"

Was he on a fishing expedition or genuinely concerned? she wondered.

"It was great," Rayna lied. She would never say anything negative about Bryce to Fox. To Rayna, that would be disrespectful. "The accommodations were lovely. Bryce and I had a great time. Thanks again for such a generous gift."

"No problem. It was the least I could do," he said sincerely. "Now give me everything you want me to take to the dumpster."

Rayna paused and looked at him for a moment. There was no way he could be in cahoots with Bryce, she convinced herself. She suddenly felt sad. Too bad she had not met him before she met Bryce. The lyrics to Eryka Badu's song, *Next Lifetime*, seemed apropos.

She stopped singing the hook in her mind and said, "Follow me." Rayna forced a smile.

Fox made several trips to the dumpster, discarding full bags of trash bags and a few boxes.

"Thanks for your help," Rayna said to Fox.

"Not a problem. I can stay and help you box up some stuff. Make the time go by faster."

She declined his offer again. He gave her a warm smile.

Rayna stood in front of the door with her hand on the handle. "I appreciate you stopping by. Don't be a stranger."

"Of course not."

"Once we get settled into the new house, we'll invite you over for dinner."

"I look forward to it."

He stood there as if he were waiting for something. There was an awkward pause.

"All right," she said, slightly opening the door. Rayna felt nervous energy moving inside of her as she looked directly into Fox's eyes. She did not know whether to shake his hand or give him a hug. A handshake seemed so impersonal, she reasoned. If she hugged him, he may misconstrue her intentions. She decided to give him a friendly hug like the ones in church. Not too close. She did not want him trying to cop any feels. "See you later," Rayna said.

They broke the embrace, and he left.

The unexpected visit from Fox stayed with Rayna long after his departure. The smell of his citrusy Armani Black Code cologne lingered in the air. She needed to find her journal and make an entry. She often recorded her thoughts, hopes, and dreams in several different notebooks. Sitting on the edge of her bed with her book on her lap, Rayna scribbled her thoughts.

Dear Lord,

I had an interesting encounter today with Fox. He seems much nicer and more considerate than I originally thought. I wonder why Bryce cast him in such a negative light. Bryce made Fox seem untrustworthy and underhanded. After spending a short amount of one-on-one time with him, I could tell that he wasn't anything like that. I'm not sure whether Fox ignited a fire within me. Something inside of me felt alive when he came around. He bought me lunch, offered to help me move, and took out the trash without me having to ask. I realize that Bryce and Fox have a lot of history together. After all, they've been friends since they were children. I'm sure they both have plenty of stories to tell about each other. I respect their friendship, but I respect my marriage more. I made a vow, and I intend to honor it. Heaven forbid if things don't work out between Bryce and me. I'd feel like such a failure. The last thing I want is a divorce, especially one because of something I did. If today was a test, I pray that I passed. If I failed due to lust in my heart, I pray for forgiveness.

In His Service,
Rayna

Writing down her thoughts often felt therapeutic. It helped Rayna systematically think through her issues. She closed her journal and placed it back in the nightstand drawer. Her Bible was resting on top of the stand. She thumbed through the pages until stopping on Proverbs 18:22, which read, "Whoso findeth a wife findeth a good thing, and obtaineth favour from the Lord."

She meditated on that verse for a few minutes. Then Proverbs 12:14 popped into her mind. *A virtuous woman is a crown to her husband: but she that maketh ashamed is as rottenness to his bones.*

Convicted in her spirit, Rayna dropped to her knees and prayed.

"Lord, forgive me. Forgive me for having lustful thoughts about Fox. Remove any impurities from my heart. Show me how to stay focused on you and not get distracted by the physical. Help me, Lord, to have desires only unto my husband. Change my way of thinking about my sex life with my husband. I want to please him, and I want to be pleased. Thank you for all you've done for me. I praise your Holy name. In Jesus' name, I pray. Amen."

Rayna got up and made a checklist of things to do. Keeping lists helped her to stay organized. Rather than taking her living room and dining room suites to the new home, she decided to sell them. There was nothing like buying new furniture for a new abode. She would give the first option to buy the slightly used furniture to her family and friends, but if they did not buy it, she would place an ad in the local newspaper. The next thing on her list was to call her pastor to schedule a day for him to come out and bless the new house. The third and final item on the list was to find a shelter to donate all of the clothing she had not worn in a year or more.

The thought occurred to Rayna that she had forgotten to take some meat out of the freezer for dinner, so she left the list on the bed as she went into the kitchen. As soon as she opened the freezer door and saw the container of ice-dream, her heart raced. She had forgotten it was there. She stood in front of the icebox with the door open, hand still gripping the handle, shaking her head, thinking about the thoughtful gesture. Fox had certainly made an impression on her.

Fourteen

Aja

"Bay, I'm not cheating on you."

"Whatever, Hunter, don't lie to me. I know what I heard," Aja said, referring to his conversation with Sunni.

Avoiding confrontation was not Aja's strong suit. She tried to hold her tongue until after Devin's visit. But not expressing herself was eating her up inside. At least she held out until after Christmas and waited until the boys went to bed.

Hunter took off his shirt and pants. Aja's eyes trailed the length of his toned body as he stood before her in a pair of boxers. Even in the midst of her anger, she still found him to be sexy and enticing.

"Tell me everything," she said as she pulled the blanket back on the bed.

"Whether I tell you or not, it's not going to

make a difference. You've already made up your mind."

"Try me."

"Fine." He plopped down on the left side of the bed where he usually slept.

Aja slid her body between the cotton sheets and sat up, resting her back and head against the headboard.

"We kissed," he continued. "Is that what you wanted to hear?" He looked in her eyes, waiting for a reaction.

Aja could feel the hair prickle on the back of her neck as she nearly shuttered with indignation. How dare he be so arrogant? Is that what she wanted to hear? That's not what she wanted to hear; that's what she heard. He must not know 'bout Aja. He'd better listen to Beyoncé's song, "Irreplaceable."

"You don't care about me," she finally said. "You couldn't possibly care. Not by saying what you said and the way you said it."

"Calm down." He gripped her chin before she could turn away. His grip, although not painful, disabled Aja from turning away as he spoke. "Bay, you're my heart. Don't you ever question my love for you or my commitment to our marriage." He released Aja's chin, his tender lips soothing the place he held so tightly.

"I need to know what happened, and why it happened. You haven't told me that."

Hunter stopped kissing her face. "Promise you won't get mad?"

"I promise," she lied. She was already angry.

"It happened last month. Remember when I decided to drive to South Carolina to pick up Devin instead of buying a plane ticket?"

"I remember." She nodded her head.

"Devin had mentioned that he needed some new sneakers. He told me his mom wouldn't buy him any. I wanted to surprise him, so I bought him two pair and carried the shoes with me. I showed up at the house about an hour earlier than planned. When I got there, Sunni was wearing a robe. I didn't want to go inside, because I don't trust her. Too bad I didn't trust my instincts." He massaged his temple. "Come to find out, Devin wasn't even home. Soon as she told me he wasn't there, I was ready to bounce. That's when she untied her robe and exposed herself to me."

Aja was not a cussing type of woman, but there were quite a few cuss words floating around in her head. She was tempted to call Sunni and give her a piece of her mind. Better yet, she felt like doing a Brenda Richie. Where's the Vaseline?

"She what?" Her jaw quivered with restrained anger.

"She was butt naked, Bay. I tried to get from up outta there, and she pushed me against the door. Next thing I know, she got her big mouth over mine. I was in shock. I couldn't believe she tried to pull a dope fiend move like that. It took me a few seconds to get my bearings and push her off me. She must've mistaken my delayed response for participation. I'm telling you that's not what it was."

"Are you sure you weren't the least bit turned on?" She gave him an incredulous look.

"No," his brows knitted together, "not at all."

"Then what happened?"

"I felt like washing my mouth out with bleach." He wiped his mouth with the back of his hand and frowned. "I told her to call me as soon as Devin got home, and I left."

"That's it?"

"You mean besides Sunni yelling obscenities behind my back?"

A reluctant smile appeared on Aja's face. "I still don't understand why you didn't tell me about this sooner." She wondered whether Sunni was the woman Iesha overheard him talking to.

"I thought I could handle it myself. You and Sunni already get along like Donald Trump and Rosie O'Donnell. I didn't want to add more fuel to the fire."

"I'm your wife, Hunter. You should be able to share anything with me. No matter how painful it may be. You definitely should've told me about Sunni's most recent stunt."

He nodded and wrapped his arm around her shoulder.

Aja figured that she might as well kill two birds with one stone. "By the way, when Iesha was here, she overheard you talking on your cell phone." She looked at him.

He furrowed a brow. "Oh, she must've overheard me going off on Sunni. I'm sorry." His eyes seemed sincere. "I can only imagine what she thought."

"You know what this means, don't you?" she asked.

"What?"

"You can't be alone with Sunni anymore. If you need to take any more trips to Carolina to pick up Devin, I want to go with you."

"Like that's a problem," he joked.

Aja must have been tired, because it did not take long before she fell into a deep sleep. She had a terrible nightmare, or maybe it was a premonition. In the dream, she and Hunter were on the beach having a great time. She was laughing as the wet, grainy sand oozed between her toes. Suddenly, Hunter's expression changed. He became sullen, and his eyes stared off into the distance. She turned her head in the direction of Hunter's gaze and spotted Trevon. When she turned back to Hunter, he was gone. She began to cry uncontrollably. She kept saying, "I'm sorry, Hunter. I'm so sorry."

When Aja woke up, she realized that she was actually crying. She rolled over and was relieved to see Hunter lying next to her. She wiped her tears and got into the spooning position next to him. The thought of losing Hunter deeply saddened her. Aja felt as if this dream were a warning. If she did not change her ways, she could lose the man that she loved.

The next day, Hunter took Devin out to spend some quality time alone with him. They went to the arcade to play games and eat. Jayden and Aja were at home.

"Let's go to the park," she suggested.

Jayden jumped up and down. He was a bundle of energy. "The park? I like the park."

"I know. Go get your sneakers," Aja instructed.

He went upstairs to get his shoes. Aja's cell phone rang and a familiar number popped up on the display. She hesitated. Her initial thought was to let it go to voicemail, but she decided not to delay the inevitable.

"Hello."

"Hey," Trevon said. "What up?"

"Hey. I'm about to take my son to the park."

"Cool. Can I come?" He laughed.

Aja exhaled and looked around the room to make sure Jayden hadn't come back downstairs. She realized that she could not keep doing this. If she wanted her marriage to work, she had to commit. No more straddling the fence. No more playing games. She reminded herself that she was either hot or cold. Being lukewarm would get her spit out.

She chose her words carefully. "Trevon, I really like you. I don't want you to take this the wrong way, but I can't talk to you anymore."

There, she said it. She exhaled. Good for her. Hercules, Hercules. She imagined herself clapping her hands and grinning profusely.

"What you mean you can't talk to me anymore?"

"I'm trying to make my marriage work. The

only way I can do that is to give up my friendship with you. I hate to do it, but I have to. I
can't be a hypocrite and a liar. It's not right. If
Hunter knew about us, he wouldn't approve.
My marriage has enough issues, and I'm not
trying to make it any more complicated."

"So, you just gon' kick me to the curb?"

"Don't say it like that."

"Hey, how else can I say it? It is what it is."
He sounded frustrated.

She heard Jayden trotting down the stairs.
"Look, I have to go. My son's here. You take
care of yourself. Okay?"

"When you get bored again, you know where
to find me."

He hung up, leaving Aja with her jaw dropped.
Bored? Is that what he thought? That she was
some bored suburban wife trying to inject some
excitement into her otherwise dull existence?
Whatever! Forget him. She closed her phone
and stuck it in her purse.

"Look, Mommy," Jayden said. "I tied my
shoes."

"Yes, baby, you sure did. Big boy, I'm so
proud of you."

She cupped his adorable face in her hands.
She could not believe how much he had grown.
It seemed like only yesterday that she was
changing his diapers. She kneeled down and
gave him a big hug before undoing Jayden's
botched attempt, and properly tied his shoe
laces. Aja grabbed their jackets, and they went
to the park.

Once at the park, Jayden took off running down the paved sidewalk.

"Not so fast!" Aja yelled, picking up the pace to keep him in eye shot.

He slowed down a little. There was a ball-game in process on the baseball field. A few people were in the stands cheering the young boy at bat. A fence separated the field from the park. She took a seat on a bench underneath a large tree. It was chilly out, so Aja knew they would not be staying outdoors very long.

Jayden joined several children playing in the play area. He climbed on a few steps before sliding down the winding slide. She gave him a "thumbs up" as he hopped off.

"Is that your son?" A heavyset lady sitting on the opposite bench said.

"Yes," Aja replied with a smile.

"He's adorable."

"Thank you." No matter how many times people complimented Jayden, Aja still felt thankful every time.

Being Jayden's mother was not a job that she took lightly. It meant the world to her. The least she could do was work on her marriage, she felt. Not only did she owe it to Jayden, she needed to open herself up to experiencing a loving, happy marriage. Providing Jayden with a stable home environment was the right thing to do . . . for all parties concerned.

*   *   *

Later that evening, when the boys were in bed, Aja and Hunter were in the family room talking.

"Bay, you'll never guess what happened to me today?"

"What?" She sat up on the couch.

"I ran into Chris Blocker, a dude I went to high school with." He seemed excited.

"Really?"

Aja had no idea who this Chris Blocker was, but she had no doubt that Hunter would fill her in.

"Yes." He shook his head and grinned. "I'll tell you what. When we were in school, Chris was a weed head. You'd never know it by looking at him now. Guess what the brotha's doing now?"

She shrugged.

"You ready for this?" He paused, waiting for Aja's response.

"Yes?"

"He's the pastor of a church." Hunter said that as if he had dropped a major bombshell.

"That's good."

He placed her feet on his lap and gave her a foot massage. "We had a deep conversation about the Lord. He asked me if I was saved. And you know what?"

"What?"

"I didn't know what to say."

"I don't understand."

He stopped rubbing her feet. "I believe in God, and I was baptized as a baby. As an adult, I never really worked on my relationship with the Lord. When I told Chris that, he invited us to go to his church. I told him we would go."

She prayed that one day Hunter would become the man God had ordained him to be. She believed that included covering his family in prayer, taking his family to church, and raising their children according to God's Holy ordinances. She figured this would be the perfect opportunity to tell him about her New Year's resolution.

"I would love that," she said. "This must be divine timing, because I promised myself that I would start going back to church as soon as the New Year rolled in. We need to start going to church as a family anyway. That would be good for us."

Hunter began rubbing her feet, again. "I love you."

"I love you, too."

Maybe this time they would get it right.

Fifteen
Shania

Having spent Christmas with Greg's family, I was in a mellow mood. Even though I had a wonderful time with the Crinkles, there was no place like home. Every room in my house was lit up with Christmas lights. I put on TLC's Christmas CD while I prepared my signature dish, lasagna, for dinner—Greg's favorite, and what I had originally intended to make before being whisked away to Macon. Cheyenne was hanging out with Jonathan.

I was relaxing in the family room, drinking non-alcoholic eggnog, while the lasagna baked in the oven. Then the phone rang. It was Cheyenne. I could tell by the sound of her voice she had been crying.

"What's wrong?" My body became tense. I placed my milky drink on the coffee table.

"Sister," she sobbed.

"Calm down. Tell me; what's the matter?"

"I'm at the hospital."

My heart raced. Lord, not again, I thought.

She told me the name of the hospital and continued, "Come on." She sniffled.

I turned off the stove, put on my shoes and grabbed my purse. I was nervous. I hurried to the hospital. When I arrived, I parked at the emergency entrance and ran inside. I looked around and saw Cheyenne sitting slumped over in a chair in the waiting area. Sitting next to her were an older lady and an ashy black guy who looked like he had eaten a few too many donuts. I thanked God that Cheyenne was all right. I rushed over to her and grabbed her face in the palms of my hands. I noticed that her shirt was soaked with blood.

"What happened?"

Still crying, Cheyenne said, "Jonathan. He's been shot."

I was shocked, and my eyes got wide. "Who shot him? Why did they shoot him?"

"Some guy he'd been arguing with. I didn't know the guy. We were leaving the movie theater, and the guy followed us to Jonathan's grandmother's house. We were walking toward the front door when the guy pulled out a gun." She took a deep breath. "Sister," she bawled, "he shot Jonathan right there in front of me. And Jonathan hit his head on the step."

I hugged her. "How did you get to the hospital?"

"The ambulance." She motioned in the direction of the older lady, who seemed to be praying silently. "His grandmother came rushing to the door. When she saw him lying on the ground bleeding, she became hysterical. One of his cousins, Snicker, was over at the house, and he is the one who called 9-1-1." She wiped her wet face on my shirt. "I couldn't move. I just rested Jonathan's head on my lap. Leaving him alone wasn't an option, so I rode in the ambulance with him."

I continued to hold her and stroke her hair as she cried on my shoulder. I assured Cheyenne that everything would be all right. Seeing her crying moved me emotionally. It made it hard for me not to cry, too. Even though I was not fond of Jonathan, I did not want him to die. In fact, I prayed that he would make a full recovery. Tears began to stream down my face. I used the back of my hand to wipe them away.

"Excuse me." The older lady tapped me on the shoulder.

"Yes." I looked up at her.

"I'm Jonathan's grandmother, Phyllis. Are you Cheyenne's sister?"

"Yes, I am." I wiped my face again. "Sorry we had to meet under such circumstances." I remembered Jonathan's mom telling me that in her absence, Phyllis had cared for Jonathan and his siblings.

Phyllis nodded and gave a faint smile. Smokey Bear walked up behind her and rubbed her back. "This is my grandson, Snicker," she introduced.

"Hey." I waved.

He grimaced.

"What's Jonathan's condition?" I asked Phyllis.

"I don't know," she answered. "They rushed him into surgery. We haven't heard anything else." Phyllis excused herself and asked the nurse behind the counter for an update on her grandson. She came back and informed us that Jonathan was still in surgery.

I patted Cheyenne's hand, and she requested we pray together. My heart rejoiced at the fact that she turned to the Lord. That let me know she knew the power of prayer. We held hands, closed our eyes, and I led us in prayer.

"Lord, we come before you with heavy hearts. We ask that you forgive Jonathan for his sins, oversee the operation, and cover him in the blood of Jesus. In Jesus' name, we pray. Amen."

A couple of hours later, the doctor came out and told us that Jonathan was in a coma. Upon hearing the news, Phyllis squealed like a hit pig. Cheyenne's knees buckled and she collapsed onto the floor. I was shocked. At first I stood there and looked at her. When I realized that she had fainted, I knelt down beside her. The doctor rushed to her side, too, and took her vitals. Fortunately, it only took a few seconds for her to regain consciousness.

"You all right?" I asked.

She still seemed groggy. "I'm fine." She slowly stood to her feet and sat back down in a chair.

Doctor Jordan studied Cheyenne's face for a moment and checked her pupils.

"Have you eaten anything today?" Doctor Jordan asked.

"Yes. I'm fine, really. The news shocked me. That's all."

He nodded and said, "Okay. Maybe your potassium level is low. We can run a few tests."

"No, that won't be necessary."

"Have you ever fainted before?"

"No, never." She shook her head.

"If it happens again, you need to get it checked. Okay?"

"Okay."

"Doctor," Snicker said, "do you have any idea how long Jonathan will remain in the coma?"

"There's no predicting how long he'll stay comatose. He had a single gunshot wound to his abdomen and suffered a concussion from the fall. During surgery, we removed the bullet and didn't see any additional damage. Sometimes after experiencing trauma a person's body goes into a comatose state to help cope. However, I am optimistic that he will recover."

Cheyenne and I hugged and praised the Lord.

Although visiting hours had passed, the doctor made an exception and allowed us to briefly visit with Jonathan in ICU. Phyllis and Snicker went in first. They came out a few minutes later. Cheyenne and I entered Jonathan's room. He looked so peaceful, as if he were sleeping. We stayed long enough to lay hands on him and pray some more. Then we left.

While in the car Cheyenne said, "Sister, I'm scared." Her eyes were puffy and red.

I didn't say anything. There was no need. I took my hand off the steering wheel and patted her hand.

When we arrived home, I called Greg and told him about Jonathan. He wanted to come over, but I told him no. It was late and I was tired. Besides, there was really nothing he could do.

The following day, Cheyenne, Greg, and I went to the hospital to visit Jonathan. He was still in a coma. We stayed and talked to him for about an hour. Cheyenne had bags underneath her eyes and did not have on any makeup. I could tell that Jonathan's condition was taking a toll on her.

When we arrived home, Cheyenne went straight to her room.

"Maybe I should go check on Cheyenne," I said to Greg as we cuddled on the couch in the family room.

"For what? She's all right."

I hesitated. "I can tell she's still upset about Jonathan and—"

"If she needs to talk," he interrupted, "she knows where you are. Leave her alone and let her work this out on her own. You can't keep babying her."

"Is that what you think? That I baby her?" I sat up and looked at him.

"Sometimes you do."

"She's my sister. I love her. When she hurts, I hurt. If you can't understand that . . ." I removed his arm from my shoulder.

"You need to stop."

"Stop what?" I sounded slightly annoyed.

"Trying to create unnecessary stress in our relationship. You know I understand. I understand you better than you do yourself. You need to get a grip. Cheyenne's grown now. Accept it. You've already raised her."

I stared at him for a moment. There was a lump forming in my throat, and I tried to swallow past it. As much as I hated to admit it, Greg had a point. "I know," I said.

He rubbed my shoulders. "It's time to let go. You've prayed about it. Now you've got to leave it in God's hands."

I nodded my head in agreement. I knew he was right.

"Have you decided on a wedding date?" he asked.

He continued to knead my shoulders like cookie dough. I closed my eyes and tried to relax.

"Not yet. With everything going on, I really hadn't had a chance to think much about it," I admitted.

He stopped rubbing my shoulders, and I opened my eyes. As soon as I faced him, he looked me in the eye and said seriously, "I understand, but don't let other people's drama mess up what we have."

"I won't."

He gave me a faint smile and hugged me. "I love you."

"Love you back," I said.

He kissed me, and I heard Cheyenne enter the room, clearing her throat. I was glad that she had gotten out of her room.

"Get a room, why don't you?" she teased.

We stopped kissing and Greg wiped his mouth.

"Whatever," I said as I sat up.

"I'm bored," she pouted, making herself comfortable on the love seat. "I was tired of being cooped up in my room. It's depressing."

"We wouldn't want you to get depressed," Greg said. "At least Jonathan is prayed up. Believe that."

"True," Cheyenne agreed. She looked down at the ground. She seemed to be deep in thought.

"Are you sure you're all right?" I said. "You seem like there's more going on than just Jonathan being shot."

She sighed and her eyes filled with tears. "I'll talk to you later." She stood up. "I'm going back to my room."

It was hard for me not to say anything as Cheyenne sashayed out of the room. I rested my head on Greg's chest as he lightly stroked my arm. I allowed myself to get caught up in the moment instead of worrying about things that I had no control over.

Being with Greg made me feel so safe and secure, as if we were the only two people in the world. We discussed our wedding ceremony and agreed to have an intimate ceremony with an invited guest list of about one hundred. Greg still insisted on a location wedding on the beach. I reminded him about how much it would mean to his mother for us to get married at her church. I suggested having a traditional church wedding and that we spend our honeymoon on the beach. Greg conceded.

Talking about my wedding was bittersweet. It evoked emotions within me that I had been trying so hard to suppress. Not having my parents around to share such a joyous occasion caused me to tear up. I thought about my beautiful mother. Her caramel complexion was soft and smooth to the touch. Sometimes when I closed my eyes, I could smell the scent of her favorite perfume, Passion, lingering in the air.

There are times when I missed my parents so much that my body ached. I allowed myself to grieve, but I refused to become overcome by grief. As a child, my parents taught me to trust God in all things—even when I don't understand. I remember my mom telling me that people don't tend to ask God, "Why me?" when things are going well. She explained that rather than asking, "Why me?" we should adopt the attitude of, "Why not me?" And she was right. Bad things happen in life. It just is what it is.

One of my favorite motivational speakers, Deepak Chopra, explained in one of his lectures that life happens. Basically, people are in one of three stages of life: about to enter a storm, in a storm or out of a storm. Deepak also explained that as humans, if we live long enough, we will all experience similar life situations. Nothing we go through in life is unique or different.

"What's wrong?" Greg asked as I wiped a tear off my cheek.

"Nothing. I was thinking about my parents."

"I figured. I was wondering when it would hit you."

"I miss them so much," I admitted as the tears flowed freely.

"Let it out." He patted me on my back as if he were trying to burp a baby.

I hid my face in his chest and used his cotton shirt like a Kleenex tissue. "I'm fine."

I confided in Greg that I wished he could have met my parents. I'm sure they would have loved him as much as I do. In my heart, I believed that Greg was exactly the type of man my parents would have wanted for me. I loved everything about Greg. He's the yin to my yang. I dried my tears.

He smiled. "Have you thought about who you want to walk you down the aisle?"

"Actually, I have. My Uncle Will, Rayna's dad, and I have always been close. He's been like a second father to me. I can't think of anyone else I'd want more to escort me on my wedding day."

"He's a good guy. I like him. When I met your uncle at Rayna's wedding, I could tell right away that he's a devoted father and husband. I was impressed by the way he doted on both of his girls."

"Yes. When God made Uncle Will, He broke the mold."

Yawning, Greg said, "Sorry. I'm getting tired."

"No need to apologize." I checked my watch. "It's eleven o'clock already. You should get going."

We both stood, and I walked Greg to the door. He kissed me goodnight. I closed and locked the door before going upstairs and knocking on Cheyenne's door. I could hear Eminem's song, "Cleaning Out My Closet" playing in the background. She usually listened to that song over and over again whenever she was going through something.

"Come in," she yelled.

"Hey," I peeked my head through the small opening of the door. "I just wanted to check on you before I went to bed."

"I'm fine. Love you, Sister."

"Love you, too. Goodnight."

I closed her door and went into my room. I could tell that she was dealing with something heavy. Something other than Jonathan being shot. I needed answers, so I knelt down next to my bed to pray.

"Lord, thank you for your multitude of blessings. Please keep your hand on Cheyenne and bless her abundantly. Give her clarity of thought, wisdom and knowledge. Order her steps and help her to make the right decision every time. God bless Greg. Help him to live according to your will and to be all that you've called for him to be. Bless my aunts, Sylvia and Clara. Take care of them and their families. Provide for their every need. Continue to heal Jonathan. Allow him to seek your face and not your hand. I pray your will for my life. In Jesus' name, I pray. Amen."

I stood up and picked up a framed picture of my father sitting on top of my armoire. I held the picture close to my chest.

"Oh, Daddy," I said aloud. "I miss you so much."

I swallowed the lump in my throat and continued holding the photo as I sat on the edge of my bed.

"Dad, there's so much I have to tell you," I said to the photo. "Greg and I are getting married. He's a great guy, and I think you would approve of him. He makes me very happy and I love him so much."

A tear escaped from my left eye.

"I pray that you and Mom are proud of Cheyenne and me. I raised her the best way I could. She's a typical teenager, you know?" I laughed. "My catering company is doing great—thanks to Mom's recipes and God's favor."

I paused as I felt an onset of tears. "I love you so much, Daddy. I wish you could be here not just in spirit but in flesh."

I felt a calming presence and remembered John 14:16, *And I will pray the Father, and He shall give you another Comforter, that he may abide with you forever.*

I laid Dad's picture on my bed as I went into the bathroom to take a shower. The pulsating water felt so good. I allowed the water to wash away my tears. When I finished, I applied baby oil gel all over my body before drying off with a towel. Then I slipped into a pair of Joe Boxers and a matching tee.

As I placed my weary body into bed, I could not help but wonder what Cheyenne was keeping from me. Whatever it was, I hoped she was not in any trouble.

Sixteen

Rayna

"You," Bryce said as he turned Rayna's palm upward and kissed it, "are everything I want in a woman."

"You're sweet." She smiled, looking him in the eyes and running her fingers through his hair. "Want some more honey vanilla chamomile tea?"

"No, thanks." He placed his empty cup and saucer on the coffee table next to hers.

"Can you believe this was our first and last holiday together in this apartment?" she sighed.

Rayna looked around at all of the boxes. The entire apartment was packed, with the exception of the living room furniture, bed, and a few dishes that they washed and reused daily. The movers would be there after the first of the year, and Rayna and Bryce were both excited about the upcoming move.

"Have you decided whether you want us to go to Watch Night services tonight?"

He rested his hand on her lap. "You know, I've never attended Watch Night services before."

"I'm not surprised. It's really more of an African American tradition that dates back to slavery."

"Really?"

"Yes." She repositioned herself on the couch so that she could look him in the face. "I took an African American history course in high school and learned that many of the Watch Night services can be traced back to gatherings on December 31, 1862, also known as 'Freedom's Eve.' On that night, African Americans came together in churches, meeting places, and private homes throughout the nation, eagerly awaiting news regarding the Emancipation Proclamation being passed as law. At the stroke of midnight, it was January 1, 1863. According to Lincoln's promise of emancipation, all slaves in the Confederate States were legally free. When word spread, there were prayers, shouts, and songs of praise as people fell to their knees and thanked God."

"I see." He lightly squeezed her knee. "If you really want to go, I don't have a problem with it."

"Thanks, but I'm not necessarily set on going." She licked her lips. "The truth be told, I was straddling the fence. I mean, there was a time when I used to go to church before attending some New Year's celebration. Then that got

old, and I started just going to the church services. But on two separate occasions, I was
nearly hit by drunk drivers while driving home
after hanging out on New Year's Eve. After
that, I pretty much started staying at home. It's
too dangerous."

"I can appreciate that." Bryce laughed. "Besides," he leaned toward her and kissed her
lips, "I'd rather be at home with you anyway.
We can bring the New Year in the right way."
He gave her a lingering kiss on the lips.

Rayna and Bryce had been getting along a lot
better lately. It had been at least two days and
counting since their last disagreement. Rayna
actually appreciated his company, started asking about his day, and was genuinely interested
in his responses.

"I would like that," she said sincerely.

He kissed her on the forehead. "Come with
me." He took her by the hands and pulled her
off the couch.

"What?" She giggled as she followed him.

"You'll see."

They went into the bedroom where Bryce
stripped down to his birthday suit. "Your
turn."

Rayna ran her tongue across her smooth top
teeth and smiled seductively. She took off her
clothes and stood full monty in front of Bryce.

"Beautiful," he said as he eyed her curva-
ceous body. "Simply beautiful."

He stroked the side of her face with the back
of his hand and eased his way down to her neck.
She closed her eyes and enjoyed the sensuality

of his touch. With the tip of his finger, Bryce traced the fullness of her lips. The corners of her mouth curled upward, and Rayna looked at him. He smiled and led her into the bathroom where they showered together.

After they finished taking a shower, Bryce stepped out first and got towels for both of them. He wrapped a towel around his waist before enveloping his wife's body into the absorbent cloth. In a swooping motion, he reached down and picked up Rayna.

Laughing, Rayna said, "What are you doing?" She wrapped her arms around his neck.

He carried her into the bedroom and placed her on the bed. With a single tug to the towel, it fell on the floor. Bryce swiveled his hips and did his best male stripper impersonation.

"You're so crazy!" She clapped her hands, enjoying the show. She had never seen Bryce act so fun and carefree before. And she liked it.

When Bryce finished "dancing," he turned on the portable boom box and pressed PLAY. A slow jams CD was already inside. As the song, *Forever My Lady* by Jodeci, played in the background, Bryce explored the intimate parts of his wife's body. For the next couple of hours, they pleasured one another.

"Big head boy," Rayna said, slightly panting. She called him that whenever he did something that she really liked. She giggled, because she could not believe how much her husband had satisfied her. "What's up with you?" She rested her head on his chest and closed her eyes.

"What do you mean, pig?" He smiled. He affectionately called her "pig" because she snored.

"I mean, you've never been like *that* before. My body is still tingling." She rubbed his chest and exhaled. "Make a sister want a cigarette, and I don't smoke." She laughed.

With the back of his hand, he dabbed sweat from his brow. "I'm glad you enjoyed it."

"I did." She snuggled closer to him. "Are you going to tell me what was going on with you? It was like you were in complete control." She placed the tip of her fingernail in her mouth. "I can't explain it."

He repositioned the covers so that part of his thigh was exposed. "I have a confession."

She propped her elbow on the pillow and positioned the side of her face on her fist so that she could get a good look at him. "I'm all ears."

"Don't get upset."

"Uh, boy, here we go," she sighed. "What is it?" She sat up in the bed, still facing him.

He ran his fingers through his hair. "I'm going to tell you, but I want you to promise not to say anything until I'm finished."

"Promise." She pretended to zip her lips.

"Okay." He nodded his head. "Don't get angry." He paused and continued. "I had a talk with your father."

Rayna's jaw dropped.

"Close your mouth and just listen." He held up a finger. "I was concerned about not being able to satisfy you."

"Oh, my God!" she yelled. She leaned back

and pulled the sheet over her head, embarrassed. "You talked to my *dad*? How could you? That's so . . . disgusting." She frowned.

Bryce yanked the sheet from her head. "Let me explain."

"Ewww," she shivered.

"You're making me wish I hadn't told you." He held his head down.

She pursed her lips and sucked air between her teeth. "Sorry. You can tell me." She sat back up.

"I want you to understand how much this marriage means to me. I was willing to put my pride aside because I thought Will could help us. There's nothing," he looked her in the eye, "nothing, I wouldn't do for you."

She sensed his sincerity and figured that what he was about to tell her was not easy. She encouraged him to continue with a smile.

"As a man, my ego was deflated when you told me during our honeymoon that I didn't satisfy you sexually. It made me feel insecure. Every time I saw you looking at another man, even the ones on TV, I felt threatened. It was eating me up inside." He clenched his teeth.

"I didn't know." She grabbed his hand.

"Anyway, I didn't want to lose you, so I went to talk to someone who knows you better than anyone—Will. I knew he would tell me the truth, especially since he has kept his own marriage together for so many years."

"What did he say?" Her tone softened.

"A lot of what we talked about was man-to-man. But one thing he did say was that I needed to take you off the imaginary pedestal when it came to our intimate dealings."

"He did?" she sounded surprised. She felt uncomfortable knowing that her dad had learned explicit details about her sex life. In her mind, the fact that her father even knew she was having sex was not even measureable on the creepy scale. As unrealistic as it was, a small part of her wanted to shelter her daddy from knowing that she was doing "the nasty" as she called it. She was not ready to stop being daddy's little girl.

"Yep," he chuckled. "I'm not saying Will wasn't uneasy with the topic for discussion. He was. But he let me know that even though you'll always be his little girl, he respects you as my wife."

"Really? What else did he say?"

He rubbed his chin. "He told me to release and let go. That's what I did."

"May I ask you something?"

"Sure."

"What's the deal with you and Lucille?"

"I'm about to go take another shower," he said seriously. Bryce sat up like he was about to get out of bed, feet dangling over the side.

"Wait." She placed her hand on his shoulder. "Tell me, please."

He inhaled a lung full of air and released it. With his back still facing her, he said, "I love my mother."

She kissed him on his shoulder and hugged

him from behind. Her head rested on the same spot that she had kissed.

"When I was around six or seven years old, I caught my mom having sex with a stranger." He cleared his throat, and his eyes became misty. "She begged me not to tell my stepfather, but I did. She never really forgave me for that. Our relationship has been strained ever since."

"Why didn't you tell me this before?"

A tear escaped and landed on his lap. "I was ashamed. It was bad enough that I was the product of an extramarital affair, but I didn't want people thinking that she was a . . . you know, garden tool."

Rayna could tell that Bryce was hurt. She squeezed him tighter. "You don't think of Lucille that way, do you?"

"I honestly don't know." He sniffed. "There are times when I think that I've forgiven her, and other times when I don't respect her."

"Have you ever talked to her about it?"

"Not really. Every time I bring it up, she shuts me down."

That explains a lot. "Do you think that all women cheat?"

"I'd be lying if I said the thought hadn't crossed my mind. Trust is hard for me. I know where it stems from, and I've been trying to work on it."

Rayna released him and gave him a pat on the back. "I feel like taking a bath instead of a shower. When I get out, I'll give you a back massage. Okay, big head boy?"

"You got it."

She sat next to Bryce on the edge of the bed. Not really knowing what else to say, she bit into her bottom lip. She felt compelled to pray. "Wait."

Bryce turned his head in her direction and stared. He did not say anything.

Grabbing both of his hands, she said, "Let's pray."

Overcome with emotion, Bryce became all choked up. He smiled as his wife led them in prayer.

"Father, thank you for the breakthrough today. We pray for your continued favor and blessings in our household. We're coming to you praying that whatever resentments, judgments, and anger that Bryce may be holding on to regarding his mother, that you will release him from them. We are praying for his deliverance, and we bring those issues to the cross. Help him to leave his past hurts with you and not take them back. Restore his relationship with his mother. Forgive Lucille for her past transgressions and help her to be the woman that you've ordained her to be. In the mighty name of Jesus, we pray, Amen."

She reached over and wrapped her arms around Bryce as he sobbed uncontrollably. "Let it out, sweetie. Just let it out."

After a couple of minutes, Bryce wiped away his tears with the back of his hand. Grabbing a tissue from the nightstand, he blew his nose. "I'm sorry for breaking down like that."

"You don't have to apologize to me for that. I'm happy that you got it out."

"I owe you an apology for something else."

She looked at him questioning. "What is it?"

He swallowed hard and rubbed his mouth. Then he said, "I never told you this before, but the reason I seemed so distracted whenever we made love was because these images," he squeezed his eyes shut and shook his head, "of my mom would pop into my head. I tried to block it out, but they just kept coming back."

"Oh, my God." She hugged him. "I'm sorry, too, for being so hard on you. I never could've imagined."

He pulled away and said, "You don't think I'm crazy, do you?"

"No, no. I certainly don't think that. I love you." She planted kisses all over his face. When she finished, she bit the inside of her lower lip. "Hey, I think we should go to Watch Night service."

"What made you change your mind?"

She exhaled. "We might as well start the New Year off on the right foot. We've made so much progress in such a short amount of time. I feel as if our marriage has been restored, and I'm thankful for that." She paused and leaned back onto her elbows. "The fact that you opened up to me means a lot. I feel closer to you now than I ever have."

With his pointer finger, Bryce drew an imaginary line on Rayna's stomach and stuck his finger in her concave belly button. She giggled. Rayna felt that his touch was oh, so sensual.

"My marriage means everything to me," Bryce said as he rubbed her stomach. "I want to be the man you need me to be. Someone you can count on."

Tears welled in Rayna's eyes. "You already are."

Seventeen

Aja

As Devin and Jayden lay in their bunk beds sleeping, Aja stood in the doorway and reflected on her past. She thought about her father who had abandoned her family. She wondered whether his lack of involvement in her life had affected her choice of men. Although she had been surrounded by strong women all of her life, she couldn't help but wonder how different her life would have been had her father stuck around. Regardless of what her mother taught her about self-esteem and confidence, a small part of Aja felt inadequate, as if she wasn't good enough.

As Devin let out a snore and gritted his teeth, Aja smiled. She felt fortunate to have her husband and two amazing sons. She pressed her hands together. There was so much to be thankful for, she mused. Having her kids tucked safely in their beds made her heart feel full of joy. Her smile faded when she thought about meeting Sunni for the first time when they took Devin back home. She wasn't looking forward to the trip. Devin belonged with her and Hunter, she reasoned. The boy seemed happiest when he was with them. Not that Sunni was a misfit. It's just that at some point, a boy needs his dad to teach him how to be a man, she felt. Hunter was ready, willing, and able to do the job. Besides, Sunni seemed to be having a tough time as a single parent. If she were smart, she'd take the help being offered to her and not fight it, Aja thought. Then she smirked. They would find out soon enough.

She walked downstairs and into the family room.

"The boys are knocked out 'sleep," Aja said to Hunter as she entered the room. She grabbed a mug of hot apple cider off the coffee table and took a sip. She set the cup back down and adjusted her plush, fuschia-colored bathrobe before taking a seat next to Hunter on the couch. "Is it time for the ball to drop?" she asked, looking for the remote control.

Hunter set down his plate of quiche. He placed his hand in the space between the cushion and the sofa and pulled out the remote. He handed the device to Aja. "We have fifteen minutes left."

"Cool." She looked at TV and saw some show counting down celebrity highlights of the year. She flipped through the channels until she found a station televising the Times Square New Year's Eve celebration. "There we go." She set the remote next to her and tucked her feet underneath her behind.

"Bay," he sucked a piece of food out of his tooth and swallowed it, "what's your New Year's resolution?"

She hugged the back of her neck with the palm of her hand and said, "I don't like to make New Year's resolutions, because I never stick with them."

"I feel you. My resolution is to not make any resolutions."

They laughed.

Touching the side of his face, Aja said, "Does Sunni know that I'm coming with you when it's time to take Devin back home?"

As his smile faded, his shoulders slumped. "Yeah, she knows."

"Why did you say it like that?" She tried to mentally prepare for the backlash. She could only imagine all of the mess Sunni must've been talking. Suddenly, her throat felt parched, and she took another swallow of cider.

"Let's just say she wasn't too thrilled."

"I'll bet." She smirked, setting the drink back down. "Tell me what happened."

Head down and hands in praying position with a few of his fingers touching his lips and the tip of his nose, Hunter said, "She went off at first. But she calmed down after I explained to her that we needed to discuss our custody arrangement." Hunter turned his attention to the television and said, "They're getting ready for the countdown."

Aja used the remote to increase the volume.

Hunter grabbed two party hats. He handed one to Aja and placed the other on top of his head. There were also two noisemakers on the table. After Aja put on her hat, Hunter handed her one of the whistles. They watched with excitement, eagerly awaiting the lighted ball to descend seventy-seven feet in sixty seconds. At the stroke of midnight, they blew the noisemakers, and wished each other "Happy New Year."

"We need to make a toast," Hunter said as he hurried into the kitchen and removed two flute glasses from the cabinet. He retrieved a bottle of champagne from the refrigerator and filled the glasses. He walked back into the family room with Aja and said, "Here," as he handed her a glass.

"Thanks." She smiled as she placed the glass near her mouth.

"Wait," he held up his pointer finger, "I want to make a toast."

"Sure." She lowered her hand.

"Here's to excellent health, lasting relationships, and prosperity in the New Year."

"Here, here," Aja said as they clanked their glasses together. She took a sip and set the sparkling drink down. She rubbed her nose. "The bubbles tickle."

Hunter drained his glass and set it next to hers on the table. "Come here, Bay."

She smiled and stepped toward him. "What do you want with me?"

He wrapped his arm around her shoulders and planted a wet kiss on her lips. "Love you."

"Love you, too."

Her purse was sitting on the end table, and she heard her cell phone vibrating inside of it. She had forgotten to turn off her phone. She wriggled out of Hunter's embrace and retrieved her phone. She looked at the display and noticed that she had a few text messages. The first message was from Rayna, wishing her a Happy New Year. She smiled. The next message was from Trevon, also sending her well wishes. There was a tightening in her stomach. She was taken aback when she saw Trevon's message. They hadn't spoken since she ended their friendship. She looked over her shoulder to make sure that Hunter wasn't near enough to read her messages. When he looked at her, she smiled and turned away. She decided not to respond to Trevon's message. Instead, she replied to Rayna with a generic, Happy New Year!

After she finished texting, she turned off her phone and said, "My friends were wishing me a Happy New Year."

Hunter nodded. "You want to go upstairs and bring the New Year in the right way?"

She yawned. "Boy, it's too late for all that. I'm about to go to bed and get some sleep. I suggest you do the same. You know the boys get up early." She ran a finger along his chest. "If you're a good boy," she teased, "maybe we can sneak one in later today."

They held eye contact and Hunter said, "Cool."

Aja thought about Trevon. She hoped that by her not responding to his text, he'd get the message to leave her alone. This was a new year, and for her, that meant a fresh start. She wanted to leave the past in the past. There was no point in telling Hunter about Trevon because that would only hurt him and cause unnecessary strife in their marriage. Besides, she wasn't even speaking to Trevon anymore. "Let it go," she said in a tone barely above a whisper.

"What?" He had a confused look on his face.

"Oh." She rolled her eyes. "I was talking to myself." Just let it go.

Eighteen

Shania

I waited until New Year's Day to take down all of the Christmas decorations.

"This ornament is nifty," Cheyenne teased as she held a gold bulb in her hand.

"Nifty?" Cheyenne has such a way with words, I thought. "Be careful not to break anything. I may want to use these decorations again next year."

"Okay."

She removed the small metal hook and placed the ornament in the box. After clearing all the frou-frou from the artificial Christmas tree, we disassembled it. Cheyenne stopped and stared at me.

"What's wrong with you?" I asked. "Why are you looking at me?"

She smiled. "It's just that watching you reminds me so much of Mom."

I stopped packing the box. Hearing Cheyenne's

comment brought a reluctant smile to my face. Being sentimental was not one of Cheyenne's strong suits, so I was a bit suspicious. I wondered whether she was trying to "butter me up." Admittedly, people often told me that I looked a lot like my mother. I took it as a compliment. We have the same smooth, warm caramel complexion and brownish sable-colored eyes. Cheyenne has the same cinnamon colored skin as our dad, but her high cheekbones, deep set eyes and full lips made her look exotic like Naomi Campbell.

"That's sweet," I said. "Thank you."

Cheyenne sat Indian-style on the floor. I took a seat on the chaise lounge. Even though I'm relatively young, my knees cracked and ached from all the years of running track. I was not about to get down on the floor and give Cheyenne the satisfaction of helping me get back up. She already teased me enough about getting old. Being stuck on the floor would only add to her argument.

"Sister," Cheyenne said. "Do you think Mom and Dad know what's going on with us?"

I bit my lower lip. "I don't see why not."

"I'll bet Dad is probably like, 'It's about time you got married, Shania. I was beginning to think I was never going to get any grandchildren from you.' " She did her best male impersonation and gnawed on her fingernails.

Cheyenne had been a nail-biter for as long as I could remember. Her habit was so bad that when she couldn't snag a fingernail, she bit her toenails. Occasionally, she got sculptured nails.

Even then, if she got nervous enough, she'd cut them off just so she could chew up her natural nails.

Grandchildren? I thought. Where did that come from? After raising Cheyenne, I had not even considered having any biological children.

"You're silly," I laughed. I stopped giggling and said, "You all right?"

"I miss them." Her tone sounded serious.

I nodded my head in agreement and lowered my eyes.

"But you know what?" she said, spitting a nail in the air.

"What?"

She patted her chest. "I keep them right here . . . in my heart."

I smiled. "I know you do." I sensed that something was up with her. "What's going on with you?"

Cheyenne's eyes took on a far-off look as she spoke. "Sister, I wish I could talk to you about more things."

"What do you mean?"

"It's like you're my mom more than my sister. My friends have sisters that they can kick it with. They hang out together, wear each other's clothes, stuff like that."

I leaned back. "I understand what you're saying, and I feel the same way. I wish we could be closer." My gaze met hers and I said, "I love you, and sometimes I can be overprotective of you. Our relationship is unique in that our age gap is greater than a lot of siblings. The fact that I had to raise you makes it hard for me not to act like a mother to you, because in a way, I was." I felt myself becoming emotional. Moisture began to well up in my eyes. If I'd have blinked hard, tears would have flowed. "Cheyenne," I continued. "You're my little sister, but you're not a little girl anymore. Unless you invite me into your world, I have no way of getting close to you. I wish you'd trust me."

Cheyenne nodded and continued to bite her nails. I knew that something was wrong. I could feel it. Her eyes seemed sad, as if she were deliberately keeping something from me.

"Whatever is going on with you," I continued, "won't make me stop loving you. It won't change my feelings for you. Nothing could ever make me stop loving you. You know that, don't you?"

"Yes."

"You can talk to me about anything. I've got your back like a sweater."

We both laughed.

"Okay," she said.

I waited, hoping that Cheyenne would confide in me about whatever was weighing heavily on her heart. To my disappointment, she did not. She checked the watch on her left wrist and stood up. "I hate to leave you, but I'm about to bounce."

"Going to see Jonathan?"

She nodded. "He's still the same, but I like being around him."

"I understand. If it were my man, I'd be there just like you." I gave her a faint smile. "Give him my love."

She placed her hand across my forehead as if she were checking to see if I had a fever. "Who are you, and what did you do with my sister?"

I brushed her hand away. "Very funny. Get out of here."

We both laughed. To my surprise, Cheyenne bent over and kissed me on the cheek. "I love you, Sister."

"Love you more."

Cheyenne walked out of the room and I continued putting away the holiday frills. When the last box had been stored in the closet, I called Greg. I missed him and looked forward to seeing his handsome face. A surge of excitement passed through my body as I looked at my diamond engagement ring prominently displayed on my left ring finger. I could not wait to become his wife. Mrs. Gregory Crinkle. That has a nice ring to it. Shania Crinkle. I like it.

"What time are you coming over?" I asked after Greg answered on the third ring. I took a seat on the couch and crossed my legs at the ankle.

"Hello to you, too," he teased.

I laughed.

"I'll be over there in a couple of hours. What's up?"

"Nothing. I miss you. That's all."

"I miss you too, baby. What are we going to do about dinner?"

"I'll cook, if that's all right with you."

I could hear him laughing on the other end. "I'm about to marry a gourmet cook and you're asking me if it's all right for you to make dinner. If it were up to me, you'd make dinner every night."

"Thank you . . . I think."

We discontinued the call, and Cheyenne entered the room.

I looked at her and said, "You're looking mighty cute."

"Thank you, thank you." She turned around to give me the full view of her form fitting jeans, cashmere sweater, and fur trimmed boots. She flung her designer purse over her shoulder and said, "See you later."

"Will you be back in time for dinner?"

Shrugging her shoulders, she said, "I don't know, depends. What are you cooking?"

"Does it matter?" I joked.

"Not really. Save me some of whatever it is." She waved as she turned on the balls of her feet and opened the door. "Love, peace, and hair grease."

"Later," I said, waving as she closed the door.

Greg arrived looking dapper in a dark shirt and slacks. He greeted me with a kiss on the cheek. We went into the dining room where a romantic candlelight dinner was waiting for us. A smile spread across his face.

"Nice," Greg said, giving me a hug.

Then he pulled out my chair, and I sat down. He sat across the table from me as a small, floral centerpiece with two candles separated us.

We bowed our heads as Greg blessed the food.

"Lord, thank you for this food we're about to receive for the nourishment of our bodies. Bless the hands that prepared it. In Jesus' name. Amen."

"Amen," I concurred.

"Shrimp fettuccini," Greg said, licking his lips. "One of my favorites."

"I know." I smiled slyly as I fixed myself a hearty helping and passed the serving dish to him.

"Where's Cheyenne?"

"She's at the hospital with Jonathan."

"Any change in his condition?"

"Not really . . ." My voice trailed off as I stared at the rose pattern design on my plate.

"What?" He placed the tray back on the table.

"I have an unsettling feeling in my spirit."

He looked at me intently as if to say, "What do you mean?"

I exhaled and said, "Earlier today, Cheyenne was acting strange. She was helping me take down the decorations, and next thing I know, she's telling me I remind her of our mom."

"What's so strange about that? I've seen pictures of your mom and you do look like her. Cheyenne was probably feeling sentimental."

"Not just that. She admitted that she wishes we were closer." I didn't feel like recapping the entire conversation, so I gave the abbreviated version.

"What's wrong with that?"

"Forget it." I was becoming frustrated. "It's hard to explain."

"Try." He stared at me.

"She also hugged me and told me she loves me. Cheyenne doesn't usually do that unless she's going through something or is trying to soften me up. Either way, something is going on with her."

"Maybe she's just growing up."

Growing up? Yeah right! Cheyenne is sneaky. Drama is her middle name. She's up to something. I could see the deception in her eyes. "You're probably right," I acquiesced.

Without proof, I didn't feel like trying to sway Greg to my way of thinking. For now, I decided to keep the peace. At least until I found out what was happening with Cheyenne.

After dinner, Greg suggested we take a drive to downtown Atlanta. I loved taking drives with Greg. And I enjoyed the scenery—cars and trees. He dropped the top on his convertible Mercedes. Even though the top was down, our windows were up. The night air felt so good. Not too chilly or muggy.

"It's a beautiful night," I said.

He nodded in agreement. As we drove along the interstate, Byron Cage's song, "I Will Bless the Lord," played softly in the background. I felt so peaceful . . . and in love. Looking out the window, I silently prayed that Greg and I would always enjoy simple moments like these.

Greg caught me staring at him and reciprocated with a smile. He reached across the console and grabbed my hand. "What were you thinking?" he asked.

I hesitated before answering. I was not expecting him to intrude upon my thoughts. Especially since I was reflecting upon how much I loved him. Besides my parents and Cheyenne, I have never loved anyone as much as Greg. "How much I love you," I admitted.

He lightly squeezed my hand before returning his own hand to the wheel. "I love you, too."

I resumed looking out the window, basking in the ambiance that could only be Atlanta. Riding along Peachtree Street, there seemed to be a restaurant every few feet: Houston's, Justin's, and Mick's, to name a few. There was no other place I would rather have been, and no one else I would have preferred to be with.

Nineteen

Rayna

The apartment was completely devoid of furniture and pictures. Rayna stood in the empty living room and looked around at the bare walls. She was happy to be leaving her first apartment and moving into her starter home. Feelings of sadness and excitement surged through her body. She had done the final walk-through inspection and was preparing to turn in her keys. The thought of walking out and never returning caused her to become teary eyed. Change was good, she reasoned.

Rayna inhaled and exhaled deeply before closing the door and locking it. She went to the leasing office and handed over her keys. Then she drove to the new home where the movers had already delivered all of her personal belongings.

When she arrived at her house, marked boxes

were in every room. Rayna decided to unpack the kitchen first. She figured that if the dishes were put up, she could cook in that fancy kitchen. Besides, the kitchen was the heart of the house, she believed.

After a couple hours of lining the kitchen cabinets with contact paper, wiping off the countertops, placing all of the dishes in the cabinets, silverware in the drawer, and pots in the bottom of the island, the kitchen was complete. She hauled the empty boxes into the garage and stacked them neatly on top of one another. Rayna felt a sense of accomplishment.

She was about to take a break when the phone rang. She answered the kitchen phone.

"Hello."

"Hey, it's Fox. How are you?"

She leaned against the countertop. "Fine. You?"

"Can't complain. Congrats on moving into the new house."

"Thank you."

"I'm not far from your new house. Wanted to know if I could come over and help you unpack?"

She paused for a moment to think about it. Since Bryce was at work and wouldn't be home for a few hours, she could use the extra set of hands. With Fox's help, she could probably finish most of downstairs. "Sure. I'd appreciate that."

"Great. See you shortly."

"Bye." She hung up.

Not long afterward, the doorbell rang.

"Welcome to our new home," Rayna said after opening the door.

"This is a nice neighborhood," Fox said as he entered. He handed her a nicely wrapped present.

She noticed that the jeans he wore showed off his bowlegs.

"Thank you. That was very thoughtful." She accepted the gift and kissed him on the cheek.

"I bought us some caramel apple spice too." He held up his other hand, which contained a two-drink holder from Seattle's Best Coffee.

"You're full of surprises. Follow me." She led them into the kitchen.

"I love the layout of this place. It's so spacious." He set the drinks on the island.

"Thanks."

"I see you've been busy." He chuckled. "Already got the kitchen appliances laid out. Check you out."

"Yeah." She scratched her head. "It took a little while, but I put all of the kitchen stuff in its place." She held up the package. "Can I open this?"

"Of course. It's just a little sumthin'-sumthin' I thought you'd like."

She ripped through the paper and opened the box. "This is beautiful," she said as she held the decorative candle. "I've never seen one like this before."

"I'm glad you like it. I thought about you when I saw it."

Rayna smiled. She couldn't help but admire the colorful flowers displayed inside of the wax. Pure genius, she thought. "I know the perfect place for it." She walked over to the fireplace mantel and set the candle on top.

"Looks good." He nodded his approval and gave her a sincere smile.

When she walked back into the kitchen, she removed one of the cups from the container and took a sip. "Ready to get started?"

He looked her in the eyes and said, "I'm ready whenever you are."

"Okay." She smacked her lips together. "The movers did a good job putting the boxes in the right rooms. What I need help with is setting up the bed in the master-bedroom. If you could put that together, that would be a big help."

"No problem." He sipped his drink.

"Follow me."

They both grabbed their drinks. She led him upstairs and into the master suite. The metal bed frame was on the floor next to two mattresses. The headboard rested against the wall. An armoire and dresser with mirror were already in the room.

"This is a big bedroom," Fox commented.

"You aren't kidding," she laughed. "We had to order a living room suite and upgrade to a king sized bed just to fill up the place." She pointed to the sitting area with a window. "I want that to be my reading area. We're going to put a bookcase and daybed over there."

"That's a good idea. What kinds of books do you like to read?"

"Some of everything. I like fiction, mystery, inspirational, memoirs, and biographies."

"Gorgeous and smart."

Her cheeks felt hot. "Anyway, while you put the bed together, I'll go downstairs and work on the family room. The living room furniture and formal dining room will be delivered some time tomorrow."

"Sounds good."

They both raised their cups to their mouths at the same time.

"Oww!" he yelled as the lid slipped off the top of the cup and hot liquid spilled on his cotton shirt and his hand.

"Oh no! I'll get a towel." She set her cup on the dresser and ran into the bathroom. The towels were still boxed up, so she grabbed a handful of toilet paper instead. "Here."

He started laughing. "Toilet paper, huh?"

"Sorry. It was all I could find. I haven't unpacked the towels, yet."

"I understand. I'm just kidding." He wiped off his hand and dabbed his shirt.

"Look, I feel really bad about your shirt. The washer and dryer are already connected. I'll wash your shirt and throw it in the dryer."

He halted his hand. "No, that's all right."

"Really, it's no problem," she insisted.

"As long as you're sure." He took off his shirt and handed it to her.

She felt herself staring at his muscular chest.

He didn't have that tightly curled, beaded looking chest hair like some black men. Instead, his hair was soft. It was a mixture between straight and curly. And it wasn't too much. She grabbed his shirt and cleared her throat. "I think that Bryce put some T-shirts in his drawer. Let me check."

"I appreciate it."

She checked the dresser drawer and found an undershirt. "Here, put this on." She handed the shirt to him.

The tips of their fingers touched as he grabbed the shirt. His touch felt almost like an electric impulse. She shuddered.

"Thanks." He slid the shirt over his head.

"I'll leave you now. Let me know if you need anything."

"I do need something." He held up a finger. "Got a wrench?"

"As a matter of fact, I do. Be right back."

She went into the garage and retrieved a wrench from the tool box. Before going back upstairs, she sniffed his shirt. It smelled good, like Herrera cologne. She left the shirt on the counter while she gave Fox the tool. When she came back downstairs, she placed the shirt in the washing machine and started the cycle. She couldn't get the image of a shirtless Fox out of her head. She couldn't believe how fine he was. The way his muscles flexed when he handed her his shirt. "Um, um, um," she said to herself, shaking her head. It doesn't make any sense for a man to be that fine. A broad smile appeared on her face. She closed her eyes and exhaled.

"Lord, help me. Don't let me have inappropriate thoughts about this man. Bryce and I are getting along, and I love him. I'm committed to my marriage. Give me strength. The spirit is willing, but the flesh is weak."

She closed the lid on the washer. Temptation had been staring her right in the face. She was convinced that this was only a test. If and when she passed, her relationship with Bryce would move to the next level. The phone rang and interrupted her thoughts. The phone was resting on the island, where she had left it from her conversation with Fox.

"Hello."

"I was thinking about you. How's everything coming along?"

"Hey, honey." She perked up upon hearing Bryce's voice. "I finished the kitchen."

"That's good."

"And Fox came over to help out. He's in the bedroom putting the bed together."

He cleared his throat. "Is that right?"

"Yes. That's one less thing you have to do." She laughed.

"Since you've been working around the house, I'll stop off and bring dinner home. Okay?"

"You know that's fine with me." She ran her fingers through her hair. "I miss you."

"Miss you, too. Love you."

"Love you back."

They disconnected the call. Rayna placed the phone back on the charger. Her eyes scanned the family room. She grabbed the scissors off of the counter and cut open one of the boxes marked

FRAGILE. Removing the bubble wrap from the delicate trinkets, she placed them each on a shelf in the entertainment center. Then she unloaded the remaining boxes and placed every piece of crystal, picture frame and statue in its proper place. When she finished, she stacked all of the boxes and rubbish in the garage. She looked around the room to make sure nothing was out of place. Perfect, she thought.

"I forgot about the shirt," she recalled.

Rayna threw the shirt in the dryer on a low heat setting. She didn't want to take any chances on shrinking it. Then she went into the half-bath and added a few decorative touches. She placed a couple of hand towels on the towel bar, set a small floral arrangement on the back of the toilet tank, and displayed bottles of scented hand soap and lotion on the sink. In the corner, she placed a hand blown glass angel fish statue. After putting on the toilet seat cover and laying down an area rug, the bathroom was finished. She felt a true sense of accomplishment. Her house was becoming a home, and she was happy about that.

"Hey, Rayna," Fox yelled down the stairs. "I'm finished with the bed. Come and take a look."

"I'm on my way." She practically sprinted up the stairs. As soon as she rounded the doorway, she noticed the bed. "It looks great." She smiled before covering her mouth with both hands. Then she released her hands to her side. "Thank you so much." She walked over to the bed and sat down. Bouncing a little on the edge, she said, "Good job." The bed seemed sturdy to her.

"I try," he said with a smile. "What else you need me to do?"

"The cable guy came out and connected the cable, but he didn't connect the DVD player or surround sound to the big screen TV downstairs. Would you please do that for me?"

"No sweat."

She got off the bed. "Your shirt's in the dryer. It should be done any minute."

"Thanks."

"I really appreciate your help today."

"Any time." He turned away.

"Bryce mentioned that he was stopping off and picking up dinner. The dinette is setup in the kitchen. Would you like to join us?"

He turned back around. "You really want me to stay?" His tone sounded serious.

Swallowing the lump in her throat, she said, "You're always so helpful. That's the least I can do."

"That's a nice offer; maybe some other time. You know, after you and Bryce get good and settled."

She held her head down and stared at a speck on the carpet. "I understand." There was a pregnant pause. She shifted her eyes in his direction. "I guess I'll make up the bed."

"Good idea. I'll be downstairs."

After Fox left the room, she chastised herself for feeling disappointed that he wasn't staying for dinner. She tried to convince herself that it was no big deal. What was this effect that he had on her? she wondered. Whether it was his good looks, bedroom eyes, sultry voice, or enticing smell, the mojo was working, she mused.

Rayna went into the linen closet that was already filled with sheets and comforters, and pulled out a dust ruffle, fitted sheet, and top sheet. Once she placed those on the bed, she went back and got a plush comforter. She fluffed some pillows, covered them with matching pillowcases, and set them on the bed.

For the most part, the furniture in the bedroom was already in its right place. Some of Bryce's clothes were still on hangers, draped across the arm of the couch. She decided to hang those up. Her clothes and shoes were arranged in her walk-in closet. That was one of the first things she had done—unpack her clothes.

The master bathroom was next on her radar. She had gone shopping and purchased new items for the bathroom. The bags were sitting on the bathroom floor. Rayna emptied the bags and hung up a shower curtain, placed throw rugs on the floor, and hung pictures on the wall. There was a double vanity, so she placed Bryce's toiletries underneath his sink. Then she stored her personal items underneath the other sink. On the counter, she displayed their toothbrushes in a holder, soap dispenser, lotion, and a vase containing floating candles.

Although she was pleased with the result, something was missing. She stood in the middle of the floor and searched the room. Towels, she remembered. There was a large box sitting on her bedroom floor filled with towels. Rayna folded them and neatly stacked them on the freestanding towel rack in the bathroom. Then she draped a few decorative towels over the towel bar. She smiled as she admired the indigo blue and gold colored bathroom. She really liked it!

Rayna washed her hands before going downstairs to check on Fox. As she rounded the corner, she saw him sitting on the leather couch with a remote control in hand. He was flipping through the TV channels.

"Seems to be working," Rayna said as she patted Fox on the back.

He smiled. "Check this out." He picked up another remote and pressed some buttons. All of a sudden the volume boomed from the speakers loud and clear.

"Is that the surround sound?" she wanted to know.

"Yes. It's like a theater up in here." He laughed.

"You're the man," Rayna teased. "I'll get your shirt."

Removing his shirt from the dryer, she handed it to him. Just as Fox was pulling the shirt over his head, she looked away. Suddenly, she heard the family room door open. She saw Bryce standing in the doorway with a strange look on his face, holding a bag filled with Chinese food.

"Bryce!" She sounded surprised.

"What's going on?" he asked in a serious tone as he closed the door behind him.

Rayna stood there in disbelief. She couldn't believe this was happening!

Twenty

Aja

It was Friday and the daycare would be re-opening on Monday. Aja missed "her" children. She cared about them so much. Her ankle was feeling fine, and she was ready to run around with them. Right now, though, she had a more pressing issue to handle.

"We've got to go," Hunter said. He had finished loading the luggage in the car.

"I'm ready," Aja said. "I'll get the boys." She went upstairs where Devin and Jayden were rough-housing. "All right, fellas. It's time to bounce. We have to get to the airport."

They stopped playing.

"Yes, ma'am," Devin said, unenthusiastically.

"Hey," she patted him on the head, "everything's going to be all right. I promise." She loved that little boy so much. It broke her heart to see him so sad.

He gave her a weak smile, and they all went downstairs. Aja knew that Devin wanted to stay with them full time. That was the purpose of the trip to South Carolina. She and Hunter were going to sit down with Sunni and talk about the custody issue. The two of them had rehearsed their lines so much that she knew what Hunter was supposed to say before he said it. They basically covered every possible objection from "I'm his mother" to "So, you think I'm an unfit parent?" They were prepared to handle whatever guilt or blame Sunni might try to throw their way.

"Get in the car," Hunter said.

The boys ran into the garage and got in the backseat of the car.

Aja lightly grabbed Hunter's arm. "Baby, Devin seems upset about going home."

"We expected that." He kissed her on the forehead. "Everything locked up and turned off?"

"Yes."

They locked the door behind them and joined the boys in the car. On the way to the airport, the boys watched an episode of *Sponge Bob Square Pants* on their portable DVD player. Aja and Hunter didn't talk much, except for a couple of comments about the nice weather. Aja rested her head against the headrest and stared blankly out the window. She lost herself in her thoughts, wondering whether she should look for a job in corporate America or get back into real estate. It wasn't that she didn't enjoy being an entrepreneur; she did. This was strictly about the money. With her college degree, project management certification, and real estate license, she had high income earning potential. If she put her skills to use, she and Hunter could easily afford the boys and a new baby.

She was tired of the financial struggle. Living in prosperity and abundance was something she wanted. If there was a way she could relieve Hunter of some of the financial strain, she would. Being able to pay the bills on time and still have disposable income made Aja think that her marriage would be even happier than it currently was. She knew that the number one reason for divorce was money.

She turned her head and glanced at Hunter as he stared straight ahead. Then she looked away as soon as he darted his eyes in her direction. Her hand was resting on her lap, and he grabbed it. She smiled as she continued to stare out the window.

When they arrived at the airport, they utilized the airport park-ride shuttle. The shuttle dropped them off at the terminal. There was a long line, but it seemed to move at a decent speed. In addition to Devin's luggage, the rest of the family had a carry-on bag and a small suitcase. They were only staying for one night, so they packed light.

After getting checked in, they went through the security screening and caught the train to their gate. Even after being on the crowded train, the walk to the gate seemed like a country mile. Once there, they found four seats and relaxed.

So many people were hurrying through the airport. Some were dressed ultra casual, others were more casual chic and quite a few wore uniforms—military and airline. Aja realized that she didn't bring a book to read on the flight. She looked around and spotted a nearby bookstore.

"I forgot my book," she said. "I'm going to go over there," she pointed in the direction of the store, "and get me something to read."

"Hurry back," Hunter told her.

She told the boys to stay with their dad and that she would be right back. While perusing the magazine rack, she heard a familiar voice whisper in her ear.

"What up, shawty?"

She blinked hard and whisked around. "Trevon, what are you doing here? Are you stalking me?"

"Whoa, watch out there nah." He backed up with his hands up in surrender. "You give yourself too much credit. Why would I stalk you? I might be a lot of things, but I'm not the nut in anybody's equation."

"I'm just saying. What are you doing here?" she repeated. She attempted to hide behind one of the displays so that Hunter couldn't see her.

"I'm 'bout to catch a flight to Miami to hang with my cousin. He works security for a well-known rap star and invited me to a party."

"For real?" She skewed up her face as if she smelled a foul stench.

"Fo' sho'."

She relaxed a little and smiled at him. "Good

for you. I'm going out of town, too. Mine is for business."

"Cool." He eyed her up and down. "You're looking good. On the real, I miss kickin' it with you. The way we used to go to the movies, chill out at the bookstore and hang out at the mall. You were like my homegirl. I sent you a text message to wish you a Happy New Year, but you didn't hit me back. Guess you were busy, huh?"

She didn't say anything.

"I know you probably thought I wanted to get at you. But the truth, after I found out you were married, I just wanted to be your friend. I wasn't trying to push up on you."

She looked him in the eyes, and he seemed sincere.

"Anyway, it was nice seeing you again." He licked his luscious lips. "I don't want to hold you up, lil' mama. Take it easy."

"I will. Good-bye." He walked away, and she loved his swagger. Trevon was so cool, like the rapper LL Cool J. Aja felt stupid for thinking that Trevon would stalk her. The man that she had seen was good looking, sexy, and confident. The brother definitely had game. He did not have to stalk her, or any other woman, for that matter. He was certainly the type of guy any woman would be fortunate to have on her team. "Oh, well," she sighed. That was a done deal. At least she had closure, she mused.

She grabbed a hardcover novel by James Patterson, an *Essence* magazine, and a pack of gum and paid the cashier. Then she re-joined her family.

"They should be calling our row soon," Hunter said as she took her seat next to him. "Some of the other rows are being seated now."

"Okay."

Devin and Jayden were talking and laughing with each other.

"Hey," he lightly nudged her, "who was that guy you were talking to?"

"What?" She sounded surprised.

"I saw some guy talking to you in the bookstore. What was up with that?"

"Oh." Her heartbeat sped up. She tried to think of something clever to say without telling a lie. She giggled, as she often tended to do when she was nervous. "He's an old friend. I hadn't seen him in a while." She pretended to verify the contents of her bag. She could feel Hunter's eyes searing a hole in the side of her face.

The flight attendant called their rows, and Aja was relieved. "That's us," she said as she gathered her belongings. She stood up and extended her hand to Jayden. "Hold Mommy's hand, please." Jayden grabbed her hand and swung her arm. "Stop that."

He stopped, and they entered the long line.

"You sure there's nothing you want to tell me?" Hunter asked, halfway serious.

She gave him a sideways glance and said, "Baby, you know it's all about you. You have nothing to worry about."

Not long afterward, they were handing the flight attendant their boarding passes. Aja and

Jayden sat next to each other, while Hunter and Devin were seated in the row directly behind them. After buckling Jayden's seatbelt, she handed him a stick of gum.

"Chew this so that your ears won't pop when the plane is taking off." She pinched his cheek. "I love you." She smiled as she handed him a coloring book and a pack of crayons. That should hold him over until they got there.

She cracked open the novel that she had just purchased and began reading. By the time the plane taxied down the runway, she was already on the third chapter. She reached over to grab Jayden's hand, but he was asleep. He looked so sweet and innocent, almost angelic. She almost hated to admit that her favorite times of the day were his naptime and bedtime. That boy sure was busy. He kept her on her toes. She grimaced and put her nose back in the book.

Aja's reading was interrupted when the pilot announced that they would be arriving in ten minutes. She closed her book and yawned. Her ears had that popping, numbing thing going on that usually happened whenever she flew. Yawning helped unclog her ears.

She looked over at Jayden, whose mouth was open with drool oozing out of the corner. She hated to awaken him. There were just some things she dreaded doing: waking Jayden up and dealing with him when he hadn't had a nap. That was asking for trouble.

When they were getting ready to land, she woke up Jayden. She could tell that he was in a disoriented state. The way he rubbed his eyes and looked around let her know that he was trying to get his bearings.

"We're about to land, baby," she said. "Look." She pointed out the window.

He looked outside and placed his hand on the window. He seemed to get excited. "We were flying, Mommy."

"That's right, baby. We were flying in the sky. Be still because we're about to land."

She reached inside of her purse and removed a tissue. She wiped Jayden's face and mouth. They held hands as the plane prepared for landing. Once safely on the ground, they picked up their luggage and rental car.

"First, we're going to check into the motel," Hunter said as he drove the compact car. "Then, we can get something to eat."

"Sounds good to me," Aja said. She peeked over the seat and saw the boys playing, "rock, paper, scissors." Jayden had lost. He was the rock and Devin was the paper. At that moment, the paper was covering the rock. She turned back around and stared out the window. She enjoyed watching the different cars pass by.

When they arrived at the motel, Hunter went inside to check in while Aja stayed in the car with the kids. She saw Hunter strutting along, looking side-to-side as he held the room card in his hand. As he approached the car, Aja unlocked the door.

"All right," he said as he entered. "We're ready to rock and roll."

He drove them to the side of the motel,

where their room was located. Hunter carried the suitcase and Aja placed the strap for the overnight bag on her left shoulder. They walked up the stairs to the second floor and searched for their room. When they found it, Hunter swiped the card and let them in.

"This is nice," Jayden said as he ran inside and plopped down on one of the two queen size beds.

"Yeah, I really like it," Devin said.

Aja walked around, flicking on light switches. She checked the bathroom. It appeared to be clean and had a lovely garden-style bathtub. Although she enjoyed relaxing baths, she never felt comfortable taking baths in hotel tubs. She preferred to shower instead. "I like it, too," she said. Then she set the bag on the floor and opened the curtains, revealing a hint of sunlight.

"Don't get too comfortable," Hunter said. "We're about to go eat. Then we have to take Devin home."

"No!" Jayden said. "I don't want you to take Devin home." He stopped bouncing on the bed and got up to hug his brother.

Kneeling down to look Jayden in the eye, Aja said, "Hey. You know Devin has to go see his mom. We explained that to you. Remember?"

He searched her face and released his brother. "I remember."

"Good." She peck kissed him on the cheek. "Now give Mommy a hug." She smiled. He wrapped his arms around her neck and squeezed. "Thank you." His grip tightened, so she pried his arms from her neck and stood up. Her eyes darted from Hunter to Devin to Jayden when she asked, "Where are we going to eat?" As expected, the children wanted McDonald's. She shook her head. "Not today."

"I got you," Hunter said, looking her in the eye. "I'll take us to a spot that all of us will enjoy. Let's go."

They followed him. He drove them to a steakhouse.

"Daddy, what is this?" Jayden said as they entered the restaurant.

"It's a steakhouse, son."

The hostess immediately greeted them, grabbed a paper placemat and some crayons, and sat them in a booth. She placed the paper and coloring utensils in front of Jayden. "May I start you out with drinks?" she asked.

"Yes," Hunter said. "Two lemonades for them," he pointed at the kids, "and put his in a kiddie cup with a lid, please. And I'll have a sweet tea. What about you, Bay?" He looked at his wife.

"Give me a Sprite, please," Aja ordered.

"Coming right up," the waitress said as she whisked away.

Resting his hand on top of Aja's thigh, Hunter asked, "So, what do you think?"

Grinning, she looked around at some of the other patrons and said, "I like it."

They perused the menu for a while, and by the time the waitress returned with their drinks, they knew what they wanted.

Hunter ordered for the family. "They will

have hamburgers, onion rings, and a side of coleslaw." He gave the boys two thumbs up. He nodded his head in his wife's direction. "She'll have the grilled chicken Caesar salad. And I'll have the steak, medium-well, with a loaded baked potato and vegetable medley." He closed his menu and handed all of the menus to the waitress.

"Thank you," she said. "I'll place this order for you right away.

Hunter rubbed his hands together. "Told you I had something for everybody," he said proudly. Aja rested her head on his shoulder. "Tired?"

"Not really." She rubbed his arm. "Just felt like being close to you."

They didn't talk much. Between connecting dots, trying to figure out a maze, and coloring, Jayden was in his own world. Devin mostly observed other people. Aja simply sat back, relaxed, and took it all in stride.

The waitress returned with their food. "The plates are hot," she warned as she set them down.

"I can't wait to dig in," Hunter said, licking his lips.

"Would you lead us?" Aja asked.

He smiled. "Let's pray." They closed their eyes and bowed their heads. "Heavenly Father, thank you for getting us here safe and sound. Thank you for this food we're about to receive. Lord, bless the hands that prepared this meal. In the mighty name of Jesus, we pray. Amen."

"Amen," they said in unison.

"This burger is big," Jayden said as he opened his mouth wide and took a bite.

Everyone laughed. Devin stuffed his mouth full of onion rings. With her fork, Aja mixed the salad with the dressing. Hunter poured A-1 on top of his steak and cut a sizable chunk before placing it into his mouth.

"This steak is delicious," he said. He cut another piece and lifted his fork. "Want a bite?"

"No, I'm good," Aja said. "But thanks."

They finished eating dinner, and Hunter paid the tab. He waited until they were in the car before using his cell phone to call Sunni.

"Hello, Sunni. I just wanted to let you know that we're on our way over. Devin has already eaten dinner. We should be there shortly." He paused for a brief moment. "Okay, bye." He hung up and placed his phone in the center console.

Aja twiddled her thumbs. She prayed silently that the Lord would give her strength. She felt as if they were about to step into a minefield.

Twenty-One
Shania

Jonathan was still in a coma, and Cheyenne was an emotional wreck. At night, I could hear her crying in her room. Some days, she would complain of feeling nauseated. On a couple of occasions, I passed by the bathroom and saw her praying to the porcelain god. I told her that she needed to pull herself together. She was making herself sick. Seeing her in such agony made me feel helpless. I hated watching her suffer and not being able to do anything about it.

"Cheyenne, you've got to eat something," I said. "If you stop eating, your immune system will weaken and you won't be able to fight off anything. You know you have a history of upper respiratory infections."

"I know." She started to cry again. "I'm really not hungry. Every time I do eat, I can't keep it down."

"Maybe you've already caught something. Want me to make you a doctor's appointment?"

"No." She wiped her tears with the back of her hand. "Sister, sit down. You're making me nervous with all that pacing."

"Sorry." I sat down next to her on the couch. "How are you feeling?"

She squeezed her eyes tight. "I can't take this anymore." She sobbed even harder.

I wrapped my arm around her and tried to console her. "Calm your spirit. You'll be all right." I rubbed her back.

She buried her face in my shoulder and cried a while longer. She stopped crying and used the sleeve of her shirt to wipe her eyes and her nose. "I'm sorry, Sister."

"Sorry for what?"

"I wanted to tell you before now, but I didn't want to disappoint you." She exhaled.

I had no idea what she was talking about, and I could tell it wasn't going to be pretty. I braced myself for the worst.

"Jonathan and I got married."

An invisible vacuum sucked the air out of the room. I couldn't breathe. I had to get out of there. I got up without saying a word and sprinted to my bedroom faster than Jackie Joyner-Kersee. Without notice, I bellowed a gut-wrenching scream. My soul ached, and I felt a migraine coming on. Next thing I knew, I was sprawled out in the middle of the floor crying. I must've looked like a two-year-old throwing a temper tantrum, but I didn't care. I felt as if someone had sucker punched me in the gut and stabbed me in the heart.

"Sister, please! Calm down; pull yourself together," Cheyenne pleaded.

"Leave me alone, Cheyenne! How could you do this?" I cried. "Just get out!" For a moment, she stood there. She looked dazed and confused. I stopped rolling around on the floor and said, "Didn't I tell you to leave me alone?"

She opened her mouth as if she wanted to say something, but nothing came out. She turned and walked away, leaving me to wallow in my misery. I was so disappointed in Cheyenne that I couldn't stand to be around her. There's no telling what I might have said. For all parties concerned, it was best that I was alone.

I went into the bathroom and splashed cold water on my face. When I looked into the mirror, I didn't recognize the person staring back at me. My eyes looked like they had been doused with hot sauce. I had an intense headache; I could see the veins pulsating at my temples.

All I wanted to do was sleep and get rid of this headache. I patted my face with a hand towel until it was dry, then I searched my medicine cabinet until I found a bottle of Tylenol® PM. I popped a couple of geltabs and washed them down with some bottled water sitting on my counter.

I crawled into my bed without even bothering to take off my clothes. I pulled the covers over my head and closed my eyes. Just as quickly as the tears fell, I wiped them away. I continued to do that until I fell asleep.

"Shania, wake up!" Greg said as he shook me like a rag doll. "What did you do? What did you do?" he repeated.

"Greg?" I said groggily as I tried to awaken from my deep sleep. I thought I was dreaming.

He hugged me tightly. "Thank God you're all right. I was so worried about you."

I rubbed the sleep from my eyes and covered my mouth as I yawned. "What are you doing here? What time is it?" I looked at the clock: 6:30 P.M. I did a quick mental calculation and figured that I must've been asleep for two hours. What was the big deal?

He released me and said, "What are you trying to do, kill yourself?"

I was shocked. "Are you crazy? I would never do that."

"What did you take, Shania?"

"Why?"

"Why?" he repeated. His eyes were bulging and there was a vein popping out right in the middle of his forehead. I couldn't figure out why he was so upset. "You slept through the entire day."

My jaw dropped. I smacked my forehead with the palm of my head. "Oh, my God." I started to cry. "I remember now."

"Yeah?" He wagged his index finger. "I called you last night, and Cheyenne told me you were sleeping. When you didn't call me back, I got worried. I came over to check on you, but you were still sleeping. We decided to let you get some rest. Your sister told me you were upset, but she didn't tell me why. So, I left and called you first thing this morning. You were still sleeping. It wasn't until Cheyenne called me this afternoon and told me that she wanted me to come over. She had tried repeatedly to wake you up, but you wouldn't get up. The only thing that stopped her from calling an ambulance was the fact that you were snoring, flip flopping and had a normal pulse. Then she heard you get up a couple of times to use the bathroom, and go back to sleep.

"I left work early to come over here. Then I called an advice nurse to determine whether to take you to the hospital anyway. She didn't think that was necessary. I've been sitting here, watching you, and waiting for you to wake up. I couldn't take it anymore, so I put some smelling salt under your nose. That's what woke you up. What's going on with you?"

I sniffed and wiped my nose. "Where's Cheyenne?"

"She went to the hospital to visit Jonathan. She hasn't been gone that long. I promised to call her to let her know how you're doing. Are you going to tell me what's going on?"

I extended my arms. "Come here; I need a hug."

He sat back down and held me. "Talk to me." He softened his tone.

"I don't even know where to begin."

"Try the beginning."

"I'm emotionally tired, Greg. I hate to admit this, but a part of me is tired of loving Cheyenne."

"Don't say that. She's your sister, and you love her."

"That's the problem. I love her, but I'm not sure she loves me." I raised my head off his chest and looked at him. "You know how disappointed I was when she dropped out of college? And now," I shook my head, "she ran off and married Jonathan."

"What? She married Jonathan?" He massaged his temples.

"That's why I was so upset. I feel so betrayed by her. She's been making bad decisions for a long time now." I scooted back on the bed until I felt my back press against the headboard. Then I folded my legs and wrapped my arms around them. "I'm hurt that Cheyenne acts without any regard for anybody else. She's so self-absorbed."

"I understand. I think she's too young for marriage, but it doesn't have to be the end of the world. You could look at this from a different perspective."

"How so?" I listened attentively.

"You raised her with morals and values." He wrapped his arm around my shoulder. "Through the years, you've been a great role model for her. Maybe seeing you so happy and in love has made her want it for herself. Be thankful that she's not acting like a lot of girls her age. Your sister actually holds the institution of marriage in high esteem. Marriage is honorable in the eyes of God. At least she's not being promiscuous."

I rubbed my fingers across my lips. "You're right. It's just that I thought she would've finished college, fallen in love with someone who had something going for himself, and then gotten married."

"That was what you wanted for her. There's nothing wrong with that as long as she wants it for herself. Don't beat yourself up over this. You didn't do anything wrong. This is her life. Let her live it."

"I don't have a problem with letting her live." I didn't mean to sound defensive, but I did. "My problem with both of them is that they don't have anything going on. He dropped out of high school, and she dropped out of college. That tells me that neither one of them has the commitment to finish what they start. Neither one of them has a job, so how are they going to live? They've got another thing coming if they think they're going to live here with me."

"If they both get jobs, you could help them get an apartment."

"I could do that. But I still think Cheyenne has made things more difficult than they need to be. Her husband has a criminal record and no education. What kind of job is he going to be able to get?"

Greg stood up. "You know what? It's not for us to worry about. The best thing we can do is pray for them. Pray that he becomes the best husband he can be and that she becomes a wonderful wife. Instead of discouraging them, we need to support them."

Support them? I couldn't force my mind to comprehend the concept.

"Don't turn your nose up at me," he said. "I'm serious. I know you don't want to hear this, but lots of people get married young. Not all of those marriages end in divorce, either."

"Okay." I uncurled my legs. "We can do things your way. But what happens when she pops up pregnant?"

"We'll cross that bridge when we get to it," he sighed.

I got out of bed and gave him a hug. "I'm about to freshen up. Would you wait for me downstairs?"

"Sure. You want to order a pizza?"

I smiled. "That sounds good. I'm famished."

"You should be, Sleeping Beauty."

I laughed. "Would you order it, please?"

"Yes." He left and closed the door behind him.

I realized that I needed to get a grip. Worrying about Cheyenne wasn't helping anybody, especially since she didn't seem to be worried about herself. Not to mention the fact that she was a grown woman. I had already raised her. My job was done. It still hurt, but Greg was right. I had to let it go.

I went into the bathroom and washed my face and brushed my teeth. Then I took a hot shower. I was beginning to feel like my old self again. After I finished, I put on a fitted sweater, a pair of jeans and some comfy socks. When I walked downstairs, Greg was browsing through the DVD collection.

"Find anything good?" I asked as I entered the room.

He looked over his shoulder and held up a video. "Let's watch your favorite movie, *Sparkle.*"

I squinted my eyes and sucked my lower lip. As I opened my eyes, I said, "I know that's not what you really want to watch, but thanks for indulging me."

"Anything to make you feel better."

I plopped down on the couch and waited for him to put on the movie. The film started, and Greg sat next to me. We were holding hands, and I was singing along with the actors.

"Sister! Thank God you're awake," Cheyenne said excitedly as she walked through the door. She leaned over and hugged me.

"I'm fine," I said dryly. I didn't hug her back. Greg nudged me.

She let go of my neck and sat on the loveseat. "I was so worried about you."

"How's your husband?" I asked with an attitude. I smirked.

"He's the same."

"Look," I pushed the pause button on the remote, "I don't want to argue with you. I have one question, though. Why did you elope?"

"It seemed like the right thing to do."

"The right thing to do?" What was so right about it? I wondered.

"Yes. We were in love." She sounded giddy. "I

couldn't imagine being with anybody else." She paused and leaned back on the couch. "You're the one who always told me to save myself until marriage. Well, I did that." She had a smug look on her face.

I heard Greg chuckle, so I cut my eyes at him. I hated when Cheyenne used my words against me. She had a point, though. I had always told her to wait until marriage before having sex. Although I never imagined that things would turn out like this, I couldn't help but smile. At least she had listened. The glacier was melting.

"Congratulations on the nuptials," I managed to say.

"Thank you." I imagined her saying, "Checkmate," but I didn't let that bother me. "I was thinking that maybe Jonathan and I would renew our vows on our one year anniversary."

"Whatever makes you happy. This is your world, I just live in it," I said sarcastically.

Greg cleared his throat. "Have you thought about what you want to do after Jonathan gets released from the hospital?"

She scratched her scalp. "I've been thinking about transferring to a school in the city. I would probably start in the spring. I also have some apartment guides that I've been looking through."

"That's good," I said. I was glad that she had given this some thought. At least her plans didn't include moving her and her husband in with me. I didn't have a problem living with Cheyenne, and she knew that, but Jonathan was a different story. Perhaps she was more mature than I had given her credit. I had a feeling that it was time for me to cut the apron strings, and as Greg had said so many times, let her live her life. I had to let go and let God.

For the first time, I realized that it wasn't my responsibility to stop Cheyenne from making mistakes, especially after giving her the fundamentals to help her make it in the world. My obligation was to support her when she fell and help her get back on her feet. Was I ready to stop being her mother and start being her sister?

Twenty-Two
Rayna

Rayna was relieved that Bryce hadn't reacted negatively to finding a shirtless Fox standing in the living room. The incident had made Rayna feel self-conscious and embarrassed. She was certain that Bryce would have suspected something. Fortunately for her, that day Bryce hadn't displayed any signs of jealousy or insecurity. In fact, she was amazed, and thankful, at how calm and trusting he was. Fools and babies, she thought. Not that he was a fool, rather that her behavior had been foolish. She was determined not to put herself in anymore compromising situations.

While Bryce was in his home office reviewing the latest news stories, Rayna went into her bedroom and read Psalm 119. When she finished, she knelt down next to her bed and prayed silently, after which, she went down the hall and into her husband's office.

Bryce was sitting in front of the computer

monitor. He appeared to be checking his emails.

"How much longer are you going to be?" she asked.

"Not much longer. Why?"

"I miss you. That's all." He swiveled his chair around in her direction and smiled. "It's Saturday. I was thinking that maybe we could catch a movie today." She sat on his lap and delivered a peck to his lips.

"You check the movie times and let me know. And no chick flicks, either."

She laughed and ran her fingers through his hair. "Hey," she sounded serious, "we never really discussed it, but did it bother you at all when Fox came over?"

"Why would it? He's my best friend, and I trust you."

"I was just checking."

"Believe me, if I thought anything inappropriate was going on, you would've known. Besides, I know Fox, and he wouldn't even try it."

She gave him an incredulous look. "What do you mean by that?" She got up and sat on the floor in an Indian-style position.

"I don't even want to bring this up." He rubbed his chin.

"Bring what up?"

He sighed. "I probably shouldn't even say anything, because I don't want to change your opinion of him."

She swallowed the lump forming in her throat and her heartbeat sped up.

He leaned forward. "A couple of years ago, Fox told me that he was bi-sexual."

Rayna's jaw dropped. The heavy beating of her heart prompted her to glance at her chest to make sure the pounding wasn't noticeable. "Are you kidding me?"

"No, I'm not." He leaned back in the chair.

"You and Fox never . . ."

"Of course not." He skewed up his face. "How could you even ask me that? You know me better than that."

"It's not that I think you would. It's just that I didn't sense that about Fox. Since he's your best friend, I needed to be sure."

"Rest assured, you don't have to worry about that." He turned his chair back around to face the computer screen.

Rayna wasn't ready to let this go. None of this made any sense to her. Fox was drop dead gorgeous and accomplished. Maybe that was the problem. He was so fine he could have any woman *or* man he wanted.

She couldn't think of anything about him that wasn't alpha male. How could she have been so blind? she wondered. On second thought, she remembered that God always made a way of escape. This was definitely her way out; a prayer had been answered. Whether Fox was a switch-hitter or not really wasn't her business. She decided not to give Fox, or his sexual preferences, any more of her energy.

"Fine." She struggled to stand to her feet. "I'll go online and order the tickets." Her laptop was already booted up and waiting for her in the master bedroom. So, she went online to check show times for the latest fantasy/adventure movie. When she found something that she thought both she and Bryce would enjoy, she purchased tickets. "We have an hour before we have to leave," she yelled into the other room.

One of the things Rayna liked about being married was having someone to hang out with. She enjoyed having a permanent date. She felt like looking extra cute for her hubby, so she started getting ready. While in the bathroom, she took off her nightgown and raised her arms over her head. She could see some new growth, so she got some hair remover and slathered it on her pits. Then she ran her hand along her leg and felt stubble. She sat on the side of the tub and lathered her legs with shaving gel and shaved. She grabbed a washcloth and ran it underneath the hot water before wiping off the gook stuck on her armpits. Using the same rag, she ran it under the water and wrung it out. She wiped the residue from her legs.

Rayna wrapped a towel around her body and rubbed her finger across her eyebrows. There was stubble on both. She grabbed a pair of tweezers off the counter and plucked the extraneous hairs. When she finished, she closed the bathroom door and stepped into the shower.

She thought about her relationship with Bryce. Their intimacy level was where she felt it should be. They were talking more and laughing more, too. And when Bryce wasn't working, they were spending more quality time together.

Although her marriage still required work, she was more optimistic than she had ever been. One thing was for certain, she was in love with her husband. She figured that her attraction to Fox was merely a test. Now that she knew her weakness, she would spend more time in prayer. She made a mental note to order the book, *Battlefield of the Mind: Winning the Battle in Your Mind* by Joyce Meyer.

She believed that the spirit of adultery was attacking her to destroy her marriage. The thing she couldn't figure out was why. Everything she had ever read about adultery usually involved some sort of generational curse. She wasn't aware of anyone in her family who had committed adultery. She shrugged it off and turned off the water.

"Is there any hot water left?" Bryce asked as he wiped off the steamed mirror.

He startled Rayna because she hadn't heard him come in. She smiled as she stepped out of the shower. "I think I saved some for you."

She retrieved her robe, which was hanging on the hook behind the door, and wrapped it around her body. Entering her walk-in closet, Rayna browsed through her jeans. She found a fitted pair with pockets on the rear and removed them from the hanger. She matched them up with a ribbed, plum-colored sweater.

By the time she stepped back into the bathroom, Bryce was taking a shower. Rayna got dressed and put on some eyeliner and lip gloss. She could see Bryce's reflection in the mirror. He had a towel wrapped around his waist and his chest glistened. Rayna looked at him approvingly.

"You better stop teasing me before we end up missing the movie," he joked. He removed his towel and popped her with it.

Laughing, she said, "All right, all right; I'll leave you alone." She picked up her plum colored suede heels and left the room. She got back on her computer and went to Amazon.com to order Joyce Meyer's book. Suddenly, Rayna remembered a sermon that she had heard a while ago, before getting married, from a TV evangelist about choosing a mate. When the minister talked about things to look for when choosing a mate, she had wanted to order the message then but never did. She typed in the ministry web site in her browser and clicked on the bookstore tab. There she found a DVD titled *Life Skills: Choosing a Mate*. She decided to order two copies— one for herself and the other for Shania.

While still waiting for Bryce to get dressed, she called her mother.

"Hey, Mom. What are you doing?"

"Nothing. Just sitting here watching *Lifetime*."

"You're always watching something on *Lifetime*. That's your weekend ritual."

She laughed. "Be quiet. They have the best movies."

"Anyway, Bryce and I are getting ready to go to the movies. I wanted to know if I could stop by and see you later."

"You know you don't have to ask me that. You can come over anytime you want."

"Will Daddy be there?"

"Probably not. You know he likes to play golf on Saturdays."

"Okay. I think Bryce is ready now, so I have to go. I'll see you later."

"See you later."

She hung up the phone and then turned to her husband. "You finally ready?"

He nodded. "Let's go."

During the drive to the theater, Bryce mentioned that he'd had a serious conversation with his mother.

"What exactly did you and Lucille talk about?"

His eyes shifted from the road to Rayna and back to the road, again. "I had been thinking a lot about how my feelings toward my mother were having a negative impact on my relationships. I prayed about it and decided it was time for me to address the situation. Long story short, I told my mom that I forgave her for everything and that I loved her. I want to work on a relationship with her."

"What did she say?"

"At first she was defensive, like she hadn't done anything wrong and didn't need my forgiveness. I expected that, though. I told her that I no longer blamed her for the mistakes of her past. If she would've known better, I believe she would've done better. Then I extended an olive branch."

She raised a brow. "What?"

"I offered to buy her a plane ticket so that

she could come visit us and see our new house."

Rayna let out a long, full-throated laugh.

"What's so funny?" He scrunched up his face.

"I'm surprised, is all; but in a good way. I never thought I'd see the day that you would want your mother to come and visit with us. I think it's great." She reached for his hand. "I'm so proud of you."

"Yeah. I told her I'd discuss some dates with you and call her back."

"Sounds good to me. I can hardly wait."

They arrived at the theater and went to the automated ticket dispenser to print out the tickets Rayna had ordered online. Being around Bryce taught her that it was better to buy tickets in advance and avoid waiting in long lines. She was glad she had, because the line was long. They gave their tickets to the attendant.

"Want some popcorn?" Bryce asked.

"Yes."

"You go and save our seats, and I'll get the refreshments."

"Okay." She kissed him on the cheek.

Rayna went into the theater and climbed up the stairs until she reached the top row. She sat smack dab in the middle of the row and propped her feet up against the back of the chair in front of her. Four teenagers came up beside her and sat a few seats over to her left. Sitting by a group of teenagers was usually problematic. They either talked too loudly, laughed too much, or walked around at inopportune times. Depending on the group, it could be any combination thereof. As soon as she heard the roaring laughter coming from the bunch on her row, Rayna looked in their direction. She hoped they would get the message and kill that noise. One of the girls saw her looking at them and tried to shush the group.

There were advertisements being displayed on the big screen. She felt around the bottom of her purse until she found a stick of gum and stuck it in her mouth. Soon, Rayna spotted Bryce walking toward her carrying a large bag of popcorn and a large soda. He looked so sexy. She snickered when a blond-haired woman nearly got whiplash turning her head so fast when Bryce walked by. The woman eyed him all the way until he took his seat and kissed his wife on the lips.

"I think you have a fan," Rayna joked as she casually turned her head in the blonde's direction.

With his fingers, he made the "rock star" sign, and they both let out slight chuckles. Bryce grabbed a handful of popcorn and stuffed it in his mouth. The previews started playing and Rayna snuggled up against Bryce's arm.

At the end of the movie, Bryce drove them back home.

"I told my mom that I'd come over after the movie," Rayna said. She got out of the car and went to the driver's side.

"Everything all right?"

"Yes, all is well. I wanted to spend some time with her. I should be back in a couple of hours."

He kissed her. "Have fun. I'll use the time to get some work done."

She could see the change in Bryce, and she found it attractive. He seemed more confident and secure. Not that long ago, he would've wanted to go with her. Now, she could come and go as she pleased. She appreciated being treated like an adult. It made her less resentful of him.

When Rayna arrived at her parents' house, her mom greeted her with a hug and kiss.

"Come on in," Mrs. Culpepper said. The smell of a sugar cookie candle scented the air. The house was immaculate, as usual. "How was the movie?"

"It was good."

"What did you go see?"

"*Harry Potter 6.*"

Mrs. Culpepper scrunched up her nose. "Not my type of movie. Anyway, what brings you by, Miss Lady?" She held her hand.

"I needed to talk," she sighed.

"Let's go in the family room. Tell me what's going on."

They sat next to each other on the couch. Rayna rested her arm on top of a pillow.

"I didn't mean to sound like I was in some sort of crisis; I'm not. So, before you ask, no, I'm not pregnant." She smiled. "And my marriage is not in trouble."

Mrs. Culpepper breathed a sigh of relief and placed her hand against her heart. "Okay."

"Mom, I'd appreciate it if you would keep this conversation between just the two of us."

"So you don't want me to tell your dad?"

"No," she said seriously.

"All right. What is it? I'm listening."

She told her mom about her encounters with Fox and the chemistry between the two. She followed up with, "Mom, I'm upset with myself. I always wondered how people could commit adultery and now I see how it could happen. That's not what I want. That's not who I am."

Mrs. Culpepper removed a strand of hair from Rayna's brow. "Be glad that you didn't act on your feelings. Given the right set of circumstances, anyone could be tempted. As for you, are you happy in your marriage?"

"I am now," Rayna admitted. "It was rough in the beginning. We're getting more settled and used to each other, though. We've also talked about our issues. We're both making concerted efforts to make our marriage work. I know he loves me, and I love him, too."

"I'm glad to hear that." She squeezed her daughter's hand. "Your dad and I have been very open in letting you know about our rough beginning." She looked her in the eyes. "When we first got married, we argued all the time. Your dad spent a lot of time at work, and I felt lonely and neglected. I really wasn't happy. I wanted out of the marriage. There were times when I felt as if I deserved better. One night, I got all dressed up and went to a nightclub with some of my friends. I thought that if another man showed me some attention, it would validate that I still had it going on." She chuckled. "I ended up meeting a nice-looking guy who turned my head. He was a personal trainer, but outside of that, he didn't have anything else going on. He didn't make a whole lot of money," she held up her fingers to accentuate each point. "He lived in a raggedy apartment, drove a used car, lacked ambition, and he wasn't saved." She paused. "I realized that what I was doing was wrong. I felt so guilty that I confessed my affair to your father."

Rayna was speechless. She exhaled. Her insides quivered.

"I'm telling you this because I want you to understand that the grass is not always greener on the other side. If you water your own lawn, you could have green grass, too. Let me make one thing perfectly clear; I was not in love with the other guy, nor did I intend to leave my husband to be with him. It was a mistake to get involved with him. The only reason I did it was because he gave me something that Will didn't. Attention. As I matured, I came to the realization that marriage was not based on how you feel. Feelings change but the commitment remains the same."

Rayna swallowed the lump forming in her throat and said, "Dad actually forgave you for cheating on him?" She sounded shocked.

"I was just as surprised as you. I expected the worst, but yes," she nodded her head, "he forgave me. He's the most amazing man I've ever known. Of course, we both had to make some changes. I had to give up my so-called friends. I was fine with that, because they were all having affairs, anyway. I stopped going to clubs unless Will was with me. And I found more productive ways to spend my time. Your dad started spending more quality time with me. We even went to marriage counseling. The counselor administered personality tests, and we gained so much insight into each other's thought processes. For example, we learned that my personality type needed compliments and daily reassurances as a way of showing love. Will started doing that. And when we spent time together, we were more loving toward each other."

"Wow! I wasn't expecting to hear anything like that." Rayna shook her head. "Weren't you afraid that Dad would cheat on you out of revenge?"

"The thought crossed my mind on more than a few occasions." She smiled. "But you know what?"

"What?" Rayna listened intently.

"I repented for my sins and changed my ways. Not only did God restore my marriage, He turned my husband into the man I had always dreamed of. To this day, I haven't had any reason to doubt Will's loyalty to me. Aside from my one indiscretion, he hasn't had to question my commitment, either."

"What happened with the other guy?"

"Well, I ended the relationship. I never saw or spoke with him again."

Mrs. Culpepper stroked the side of Rayna's face. Rayna leaned forward and hugged her mom. "I love you, Mom."

"I love you, too. You've got a good husband who truly adores you. Don't let anyone come in between that."

"I won't."

Rayna was thankful that her mom had been open and honest. At least now, she knew where the spirit of adultery that was attacking her had come from. Although she had been stunned by her mom's revelation, it didn't change Rayna's opinion of her. She was still the same wonderful mother and devoted wife that Rayna always thought she was.

Rayna continued resting in the security of Mrs. Culpepper's arms. She closed her eyes and thought, Thank God for the benefits of other people's experiences. She was more determined than ever not to let history repeat itself. To heck with generational curses!

Twenty-Three

Aja

When they pulled up in front of Sunni's house, Aja didn't know what to expect. Nervous jitters consumed her. Her palms were sweaty and her heartbeat sped up. In a matter of moments, she would be standing face-to-face with her arch nemesis.

"Ready?" Hunter asked as he patted her hand.

"As ready as I'll ever be."

She silently recited the 23rd Psalm. When she finished, she quietly counted backward from ten to one. She drew a deep breath and exhaled.

They got out of the car and went to the front door. Devin rang the doorbell a couple of times before a younger looking version of the former Miss America, Vanessa Williams, answered. Aja was floored to see such a striking beauty standing before her. Sunni was dressed casually in jeans and a sweater, and her naturally long hair hung midway down her back.

"Come on in," Sunni said. She greeted them with a warm smile.

"Hey, Mom," Devin said. He gave her a hug and she kneeled down to kiss him.

"Hi, Jayden," Sunni said. "Nice to meet you."

"Hi," Jayden replied.

"Devin, why don't you take Jayden to your room so that the grown-ups can talk?"

"Okay. Come on." Devin waved his hand.

The boys went upstairs while the adults sat in the living room.

"Can I get either of you something to drink?" Sunni offered.

"No, thanks," they both replied as they took their seats on the faux suede sofa with colorful pillows.

Aja couldn't believe how normal Sunni appeared. Not only was she very attractive, which caught her by surprise, Sunni had manners. The condo was also nicely decorated and clean. So clean, in fact, that it smelled like Fabuloso.

"So what's on your mind?" Sunni asked as she took a seat on the matching faux suede chair.

Hunter rubbed his hands together. "Let me just start by saying that we think you're a good mother. Very loving. Your parenting skills aren't in question."

Sunni stared at both of them. "Go on," she said calmly.

"It's just that Devin is getting older, and we think that he needs his dad to have more of a presence in his life. I want to teach our son how to be a man. As a woman, you can try, but you shouldn't have to. And you don't have to, because you've got me. That's what I'm here for." He patted his chest.

Sunni took a deep breath and exhaled. She crossed her right leg over her left. "Before we go into that, would you mind if I had a woman-to-woman talk with Aja?"

Aja and Hunter exchanged confused glances. Sunni had thrown a monkey wrench in the equation. Aja touched her ear lobe and looked at Sunni.

"Sure, we can talk," Aja said seriously. She had a few things that she wanted to get off her chest, too.

"Are you sure?" Hunter asked, searching Aja's face for the slightest indication that she didn't really want to be left alone with Sunni. There was none. If she was bluffing, he couldn't tell.

"I'm sure. You can go check on the boys or something," Aja told him.

He leaned over and kissed her on the forehead. "I'll be upstairs." As he got up, he looked at Aja. She didn't say anything, so he walked upstairs.

Sunni waited until she heard Hunter enter Devin's room before she spoke. "Aja, I wanted to talk to you alone, because I didn't want there to be any misunderstandings."

"Misunderstandings?" Aja felt her stomach tighten.

"Yes. For all these years, you and I have gotten along like oil and water. You probably don't even know why. Do you?"

"I assumed it was because I was involved with your ex-husband."

She laughed. "Not even close. The reason I was so confrontational with you was for several reasons. When you and Hunter got engaged, I thought you would've wanted to talk to me to find out why we got divorced. There are two sides to every story, and if you're going to marry someone, you should find out as much as possible about their previous marriage, or in some cases, marriages. But you didn't. I felt like a nonentity. And then when I found out that you were pregnant, you made me feel like an outsider. Our children are siblings. I didn't expect us to be best friends, but I at least thought we could've been cordial."

"Sunni, I—"

"Wait," she halted her hand, "please let me finish."

"Go ahead."

"The fact that Hunter and I share a son means that we'll be in each other's lives until one of us dies. My son is too young to fight for himself, so as his mother, I have to battle for him. Just because his daddy remarried and has a new family, I didn't want my son to feel insecure, as if he could lose his daddy. So many men forget about the old children when they get new ones. I wasn't about to let that happen to my child. It's hard being a single mother." She lowered her eyes. "You just don't know. Hopefully, you'll never have to find out."

"Sunni, I understand your plight. I apologize if I offended you. That was never my intention."

A single tear streamed down Sunni's cheek, and she wiped it away.

"Please forgive me," Aja said.

She nodded.

"And just so you know, I love Devin very much. He's as much a part of our family as Jayden. You can believe that."

"Thanks."

"Since we're talking," Aja said, "I need to know what was up with the kiss between you and Hunter."

"Oh, God." She covered her face with her hand. "I'm so embarrassed. I had just broken up with my boyfriend, and I was really going through some emotional turmoil." She rested her hand on her head. "Hunter happened to be at the wrong place at the wrong time and caught the brunt of my confusion. I regretted it as soon as I did it. You should have seen him hurry out of here. That was the one and only time anything like that ever happened between us." She removed her hand and caught a full view of Aja's face. "Sorry. I didn't mean to disrespect you."

Aja sensed her sincerity. "Apology accepted."

"Just for the record, Hunter and I got divorced because we couldn't handle the financial and emotional strain. You know how it goes; no romance without finance. I resented him because he couldn't support us financially on his own. I never cheated on him, though, and to the best of my knowledge, he didn't cheat on me either. We were young when we got married, and we thought that our love would sustain us. When those bills started hitting," she laughed, "love went out the window."

Aja understood better than she cared to admit. She, too, had felt the emotional and financial strain of having to make ends meet, having more month than money. "I understand."

"You sure I can't get you something to drink? I have plenty of juice and bottled water."

"Actually," Aja said, "bottled water would be nice."

Sunni flashed a bright smile, exposing even white teeth. "Coming right up." She went into the kitchen and brought back a chilled bottle. She handed the drink to Aja.

"Thank you." Aja twisted the cap off the bottle and took a sip.

"I guess I'll get Hunter so that we can discuss this custody issue."

Standing at the foot of the stairs, she yelled, "Hunter, we're ready."

Sunni waited until she saw Hunter before going back to her seat.

"Everything all right in here?" he asked, rubbing his hands together and eyeing both Aja and Sunni.

"We're fine," Sunni said, smiling.

Aja smiled, and Hunter sat next to her. "In that case," Hunter said, "where were we?"

"I believe you were about to tell me why you should have more of a presence in Devin's life." With her fingers, Sunni placed her hair behind her ears.

"Right," Hunter nodded. "Devin is my first-born son, and he has a special place in my heart. I love that boy. He's a good kid, and this is an important time in his life. He needs his dad to help school him on life." He paused and placed his hand on top of Aja's. "That's why I want full-custody of Devin."

Sunni exhaled. "I see." She rubbed the side of her face.

"Of course, you can see him whenever you want."

She seemed thoughtful. "I'm not going to fight you on this."

"You're not?" Aja and Hunter said in unison. They both sounded surprised.

"No, I'm not," she said seriously. "As a matter of fact, I've been doing some serious soul searching. I want to go back to school. The only reason I hadn't was because I've been working two jobs to support Devin and me." She played with the crucifix hanging from her neck. "I refuse to get on any government assistance. I feel guilty spending so much time working, but I really don't have a choice. Not if we want to live in any type of decent neighborhood.

"In all honesty, I've been thinking about letting Devin come and stay with you while I finish school and get a better job. I want a better life for both us, but not at my son's expense. I worry about losing him to the streets. It's tough on these young boys. It breaks my heart seeing them wearing pants so baggy that they trip; all for the sake of trying to be cool. I don't play that. Clothes aren't cheap. With the little bit of extra money that I do have, I have to make it stretch. I can't afford to waste money on oversized clothes or $300 sneakers."

"You got that right," Aja said.

Sunni smiled. "So, as much as I will miss Devin, I think it would be best if he stayed with you all for a while. Give me a chance to get on my feet."

"Thank you, Sunni," Hunter said. "You won't regret it."

"I better not," she teased.

"I know that was hard for you," Aja said. "As a mother, I can completely understand your decision." She felt her eyes stinging from fighting back tears, so she fanned her eyes with her hand. "Girl, I have to tell you, though . . . before we met, I had a totally different impression of you. I'm so glad you don't have snakes for hair."

They all laughed.

"Yeah, and I'm glad you don't have a bone stuck through your nose, either," Sunni laughed.

Still laughing, Aja said, "Oh, no, you didn't say a bone."

Devin and Jayden came running down the stairs.

"What's so funny?" Devin asked.

"Come here, sweetie," Sunni said, patting her lap, indicating for him to take a seat.

He sat on his mother's lap.

"We have something to tell you," Sunni said.

"What is it?" Devin asked.

"Your dad and I love you very much, and so does Aja. We've been talking about your living arrangements. We all love having you live with us." She squeezed him. "Since Mommy wants to go back to school and get a better paying job, we think it would be better for you to live with your dad, Aja, and Jayden for a while. That way, after I finish school, I can work only one job and have more time to spend with you. Would you like that?"

"You're going to let me live with Dad?" Devin was surprised.

"Yes, sweetie, I am." Without saying a word, Devin hugged his mother's neck. She patted him on the back as tears streamed down her cheeks. "Your mommy loves you very much. I'm doing this for us."

Hunter cleared his throat and Aja released her tears. She grabbed Jayden and hugged him tight.

"What's wrong, Mommy?" Jayden asked. "Why are you crying?"

"I'm crying because I'm happy."

"So, does that mean you want to stay with your daddy?" Sunni asked Devin as she held his face in her hands.

He nodded his head.

"All right then. It's settled." She smiled.

The boys went back upstairs to play. For the remainder of the visit, the adults talked about leaving their joint custody order intact. They would simply work on Devin's new living arrangement amongst themselves. They decided to wait until the end of the school year before making the change. When it was time to leave, Jayden didn't want to leave his big brother. Sunni suggested letting Devin stay with them at the hotel, and everyone agreed.

Back at the hotel, the boys took their baths and put on their pajamas. Then Aja and Hunter took separate showers and got ready for bed. After watching TV, Devin and Jayden fell asleep. Aja rested her head on Hunter's chest.

"Sunni turned out to be a lot nicer than I ever imagined," Aja whispered. She looked over on the other bed to make sure the boys were good and sleep. When she saw that they were, she put her head back down.

"She surprised me, too."

She thumped him on the chest. "Why didn't you tell me that she was so doggone pretty?"

"What?" He laughed.

"Don't even try it," she joked.

"Come on, Bay. It's not that serious."

She sucked her teeth.

"What did y'all talk about anyway?"

"None-ya," she teased.

He smirked.

"I don't really feel like going into every detail of our conversation. I will tell you that we understand each other a whole lot better. Truth be told, we wasted too much time disliking each other."

"Well, I'm glad y'all ironed things out. That's less stress for me. Being caught in the middle was messing with my pressure." He chuckled.

"You're so silly." She tapped his chest.

Yawning, he said, "I'm tired."

"Me too." She kissed him on the cheek. "Goodnight."

Aja turned onto her side and stared at the wall. She thought about all of the things she wanted to do and be. She wanted to be a good mother, travel, and pursue her passion, which was baking. For so long, she thought that money would make her happy. Of course, she wanted to be financially secure. However, she now understood that peace and joy weren't based on money. The only reason she never pursued baking professionally was because she didn't think she could earn enough income doing it.

In the past, she had taken cake decorating classes for fun. As a child, her grandmother taught her how to bake. By the time she was twelve, she could bake cakes, pies, and cookies from scratch. Her mother was so impressed that she relied on Aja for all of the holiday desserts. Since then, Aja mostly baked for church functions, family gatherings and friends. Everyone would rave about her treats. Baking was the one thing that she enjoyed, did well, and would do for free. It occurred to her that she had found her calling a long time ago, but now it was time for her to answer it.

After listening to Sunni, Aja realized that the best thing she could do for herself and her family was to be happy. That was one of the best gifts she could give to her children, she felt.

She might not have everything she wanted, but thank God she had everything she needed. Aja remembered Psalm 128:2: *You will eat the fruit of your labor; blessings and prosperity will be yours.* She closed her eyes. That's exactly what she intended to do.

Twenty-Four

Shania

Greg and I were sitting in chairs next to Jonathan's bed while Cheyenne sat on the bed and held his hand. It had been a week since I found out that Jonathan was my brother-in-law, and I was still getting used to the idea.

"He looks so peaceful, like he's in the middle of a pleasant dream." Cheyenne kissed his eyelids.

I agreed. If I hadn't known he was in a coma, I would've thought he was sleeping.

"Let's pray for him," Greg suggested.

"That's a good idea," I said.

We walked over to Cheyenne and held hands. She stood up, and we formed a circle. Greg led us in prayer.

"Heavenly Father, you said where two or more believers are gathered, you are there in the midst. We come before you today to plead the blood of Jesus over Jonathan. Father, your

Word says that by Jesus' stripes we are healed. We ask that you give Jonathan complete healing right now. Heal his body and get him out of that bed. Restore him, Father. In Jesus' name, we pray. Amen."

"Hallelujah! Amen," I said, clapping my hands. I touched Jonathan's leg and declared, "You are healed! In the name of Jesus, you are healed!"

Cheyenne bounced up and down like a pogo stick. "Glory be to God!" Tears streamed down her cheeks.

I could feel the presence of the Lord. Tears welled in my eyes, too. I couldn't stop praising God, nor did I want to.

After about ten minutes of continuous praise, we wiped away our tears and hugged each other. In my heart, I believed that the Lord had heard our sincere prayers. I had faith that Jonathan would be restored.

"You ladies hungry?" Greg asked. His arms were wrapped around both of our shoulders.

I looked at Cheyenne.

"That's fine with me," she said. We grabbed our purses. Cheyenne leaned over and kissed Jonathan on the cheek. "I'll be back in a little while. Love you." Then she whispered something in his ear that I couldn't hear. Before we left, we went to the nurses' station. Cheyenne requested that they call her cell phone immediately if there was any change in her husband's condition.

Greg took us to Gladys Knight and Ron Winans' Chicken and Waffles ™ on Peachtree

Street. We were seated and the waitress took
our orders. For drinks, we ordered three Up-
towns. Cheyenne and I both selected the brown
sugar salmon as entrees, and Greg chose the
midnight train, which consisted of four chicken
wings and an original waffle.

"I'm glad we came here," I said. I looked
around at some of the memorabilia hanging on
the walls.

"I was hungry and needed some food that
was going to stick to my bones," Greg admitted.

I smiled and shook my head. "Anyway," I retrieved my calendar from my purse and flipped
through a few pages, "I want to get married on
this date." I pointed at the date that I had previ-
ously circled.

"That's only three months away," Cheyenne
said. "You better get busy."

"Three months?" Greg said. "Why so long?"
He sipped his drink.

I nudged him with my elbow. "Before I had
my meltdown," I joked, "I hired a wedding
planner. Since then, I've already booked the
church, and scheduled meetings with the florist
and caterer." I looked at Cheyenne. "I found a
beautiful gold-toned dress that I think will look
fantastic on you." Her hands were resting on
the table, so I reached over and grabbed them.

"You've been busy. I can't wait to see it." She
squeezed my hand. "And what about *your* wedding dress?"

"I thought we'd shop for that together." I
smiled.

"I'd like that."

"I figured that I needed to get the ball rolling on this whole wedding thing." I glanced at Greg. "By the way, I contacted my travel agent and she's putting together some honeymoon packages for us."

"I can't wait." He laughed.

The waitress returned with our food. I released Cheyenne's hand. Everything looked and smelled so good. Greg blessed the food, and we delved right in. There wasn't much talking going on, only jaws chomping and lips smacking. Halfway through the meal, Cheyenne's cell phone rang. She retrieved the phone from her purse and checked the caller ID.

"It's the hospital," she said before taking a deep breath. "Hello."

Greg and I put our forks down and looked at Cheyenne.

"Really?" she paused. She raised a brow. "Thank God," she gasped. "I'm on my way." She hung up the phone and looked toward the heavens. "Jonathan is out of his coma."

"Praise God," Greg and I said in unison.

"The nurse told me that she was in the room with him when he started wiggling his fingers. The doctor came in, saw that he was trying to take his ET-tube out, and removed it. She said that Jonathan was responding to verbal stimuli."

Greg summoned the waitress and asked for to-go boxes. He paid the tab with a generous tip, and drove us back to the hospital. We were shouting and rejoicing all the way there. When we entered the room, Jonathan was propped up on a pillow.

"Hey," Jonathan said in a raspy tone.

The doctor had warned us to remain calm and not to over stimulate the patient. Cheyenne walked over to him and placed two fingers over his lips. "Shush, don't try to talk. Thank God you're all right." She covered his face in kisses. "I'm so happy to see that you're awake."

"Welcome back, man," Greg said from across the room.

I gave him a smile and waved. We stuck around and kept our conversations upbeat and positive. We told Jonathan that we had been praying for him and how thankful we were that our prayers had been answered.

The doctor came back and kicked us out. He was professional and tactful, though. He explained that Jonathan needed some rest. We understood. Greg and I left the room so that Cheyenne and Jonathan could say their goodbyes in private. When Cheyenne came out, she requested to speak with Doctor Samson. We all stood there while the doctor talked to us about Jonathan's condition.

"I know you have a lot of questions," Dr. Samson said. "I'm afraid I can't give you any comprehensive answers just yet. I'm going to have to do some exams over the next week or so."

"When will he be better?" Cheyenne asked. "Will he get back to normal?"

"That's hard to say," he said. "As far as I can see, he doesn't exhibit any signs of long-term damage. The slurring and the word loss are usually temporary. That's quickly regained. There's some processing difficulty. He stumbled while he was trying to count backward. And there's some muscle regression and a little bit of coordination loss."

"When will he get his strength back?" I asked.

"I can't really say." He turned his head in my direction. "It's so different from patient to patient."

"Any cognitive impairment?" Greg asked.

"None that I can see." The doctor clasped his hands together. "Now, emotional difficulties may be another issue."

"What can we do to help?" Cheyenne asked.

"You're off to a good start. Go easy and don't upset him. I'll give you a recommendation for a psychological coordinator. Remember to keep the stress to a minimum."

"Thank you, Dr. Samson." Cheyenne shook his hand.

"Yes, you've been a big help." I shook his hand, and Greg did the same.

Dr. Samson left, and Greg drove us home. Once we got to the house, we sat around in the family room and talked. I said something that seemed to nearly floor Cheyenne.

"If you want Jonathan to stay here while he's recuperating, I don't have a problem with it."

"Serious?" Cheyenne pressed her head so far back into her neck that she looked like a turtle.

"He's your husband, right?" I shrugged my shoulders.

"Yeah, but, Sister, that's so not like you. You're actually being nice to Jonathan. Are you feeling okay?"

I smirked. "I didn't say I wanted to *live* with him. Get it right," I said as I wagged my finger at her. I figured that if God can bring Jonathan out of a coma, the least I can do is show him some compassion. After all, God commanded us to love one another. I was still not thrilled about having him as a brother-in-law, but that's what he was and I couldn't change it. Therefore, I had to get used to it. He was a member of the family now.

"Before I forget," Greg said, "I have a lunch-time appointment with Shannyn at the church tomorrow."

"For what?" I eyed him.

"She's having problems with her kid sister. Since I'm the youth pastor, she wanted to talk to me about it."

"I'm sure she did," I said sarcastically. I gave him an incredulous look.

The following morning, I woke up with extra vigor. I even noticed a little pep in my step. I dolled myself up and put on a cashmere crew-neck tunic with a pair of nicely fitted pants. After checking myself out in the mirror, I applied some mascara to plump up my lashes and smeared a couple of coats of shimmering lip gloss across my lips. I pressed my lips together, puckered, and blew myself a kiss. To top it off, I sprayed on some Calvin Klein Euphoria perfume. By the time I finished getting dressed, it was almost lunchtime. I slipped on my leather boots, grabbed my purse and headed to church. Along the way, I stopped off at Zaxby's and picked up lunch for Greg and me. I ordered a grilled chicken salad for me, and chicken tenders with fries for Greg. I had no intention of eating lunch with him; I just wanted a reason to run into Shannyn.

When I pulled up at the church, Greg's car was parked outside. I checked my watch and figured he should've been wrapping up the meeting so that he could get back to his office. I left my salad on the passenger seat and carried the bag containing Greg's food inside.

"Hi, Darla," I said to the receptionist. "Greg told me he had a meeting here today, and I wanted to bring him some lunch." I held up the bag and smiled.

She was such a nice older lady that I didn't have the heart to tell her that her wig was crooked. But I had to, especially since she took the time to spruce herself up with that gold metallic shirt.

"Go on back, baby," she said with a southern drawl. "He's in the first office on the left." She pressed the buzzer to unlock the door.

"Thanks, Darla." I hesitated before saying, "Do you have a mirror?"

"Yes." She handed me one from on top of her desk.

I looked around to make sure no one was around and whispered, "Adjust your hair."

She laughed out loud and said, "Ah, thank you, baby," then adjusted her wig.

I waved and walked through the double doors. I pulled down my sweater before knocking on the door where Greg and Shannyn were conversing. The door was partly ajar.

"Come in," Greg said.

I walked in, swaying my hips and smiling. I brushed past Shannyn who was sitting on a leather chair with her back facing the door. "Hi, honey. I was in the area and thought I'd bring you lunch. You haven't eaten, have you?" He stood up to greet me, and I kissed him on the cheek. I sounded so sappy sweet that I could've given myself diabetes.

"No, I haven't."

"I didn't think so." I set the food down on the desk. "I didn't mean to interrupt your meeting; I'll talk to you later." I looked at Shannyn. "How are you today?"

"Fine, thanks." The expression on her face was as sour as if she had eaten lemons dipped in vinegar.

Greg reached for my hand. "We were actually finished talking. Right, Shannyn?"

"Oh, yeah, right." She picked up her purse, which was sitting on the floor next to the chair.

He grabbed a folder off his desk and said, "Let me drop this off at the office. Be right back."

Shannyn stood up as if she were about to leave.

"Hey, did Greg tell you we set a date?" I said, looking her in the eye.

"No, he didn't mention it." She scratched her scalp.

"Yeah, we did." I smiled. "We're getting married in three months."

"Lucky you." She placed the strap of her purse over her shoulder.

"I remembered that you told me a while ago that you were a cosmetologist."

"That's right." She nodded her head.

"Whenever I've seen you, your hair and makeup always look nice. How would you like to do the hair and makeup for my bridal party?"

Her face lit up. She seemed surprised. "I would like that. And thanks for the compliment." She reached inside of her purse and handed me a business card.

"Thank you," I said as I studied the card. Her picture was on it. "This is a nice card."

She smiled at me. "Please be sure to use it. Since we go to the same church, I'll give you the hookup. I'll do your hair and makeup for free, and give your bridesmaids a fifty percent discount."

"That's very sweet of you. I really appreciate that."

Greg came back and I walked over and hugged Shannyn. She hesitated for a brief moment but hugged me back. "I'll call you soon," I said.

She left, and Greg and I walked to our cars together.

"I appreciate you bringing me lunch, but that's not the real reason you came over here, is it?" He leaned against my driver side door.

"I don't know what you're talking about." I played coy.

"You didn't have to do that. I can handle Shannyn."

"Of course you can." I patted him on the chest. He moved out of the way and opened my car door.

"I love you. I'll call you later."

"Do that. Love you, too."

He waited until I was inside before closing the door. As I drove away, I couldn't help but laugh to myself. My momma always said, "Keep your friends close, and your enemies closer." Shannyn had been caught off-guard, especially when I hugged her. I'll bet she expected me to cuss her out for hitting on my man. Not saying I didn't feel like going there with her at first, but that's not me. My momma raised me better than that. I had prayed about that situation, and the Lord revealed to me that the best way to handle the situation was with love. Love covers a multitude of sins. Reacting in the flesh wouldn't have accomplished a thing. She and I would've been bitter enemies, and I'm convinced she would've gone after Greg even harder. I still thought it was funny, though. The expression on her face was priceless. She didn't know what hit her. *Sit at my right hand until I make your enemies a footstool for your feet.*

*   *   *

A week had gone by, and Jonathan was scheduled to come home. Cheyenne and I went to the hospital to pick him up.

"Man, being shot ain't no joke," Jonathan admitted. "I thought I was gon' die."

"There's a reason why you've been given another chance," Cheyenne said.

"Yeah, God obviously has a plan for you," I told him.

"Uh, Shania," he looked at me, "do you think I can go to church with you when I get from up outta here?"

"Of course you can." I smiled. "Can I ask you something?"

"Sure."

"Are you saved?" I said seriously.

He scratched his chin. "I don't think so."

Before we left the hospital, I pulled out my pocket size Bible that I carry in my purse and showed Jonathan Romans 10:8-10, which explains that as long as you confess Jesus Christ as your Lord and Savior, and believe in your heart that God raised Him from the dead, you shall be saved. I asked Jonathan whether he was ready to receive the gift of salvation, and he replied, "Yes." I told him to repeat after me as we said the sinner's prayer.

"God, I know that I am a sinner," he said. "I know that I deserve the consequences of my sin. However, I am trusting in Jesus Christ as my Savior. I believe that His death and resurrection provided for my forgiveness. I trust in Jesus and Jesus alone as my personal Lord and

Savior. Thank you, Lord, for saving me and forgiving me! Amen!"

Afterward, we prayed together. My heart rejoiced. I was happy that Jonathan was finally making a change for the better. Maybe he wasn't such a bad guy after all.

When we returned home, Jonathan rested comfortably on the couch in the family room. I checked the mail and there was a package for me. I tore it open. It was the DVD set that Rayna had told me about.

"Hey, Cheyenne," I said as I walked into the family room holding the DVD case. She was sitting on the loveseat, flipping through the channels. Jonathan had fallen asleep. She turned her neck to look at me. "Rayna ordered this for me," I continued, "but I'd like for us to watch it together."

"Okay."

I placed the DVD in the player and pressed play. I sat down next to Cheyenne. We listened intently to the well-dressed, handsome preacher. He was charismatic and touched on a lot of good points about what to look for when selecting a mate. At the end of the DVD, I pressed the stop button.

"What did you think?" I asked.

She nodded her head. "It was good."

Since she wasn't going to initiate a conversation about the message, I decided to jump right in. "I agreed with what he said. I don't know if I told you this before, but Greg and I pulled our credit reports. We shared them with each other. He even let me review his tax returns so that I could see how much money he made." I smiled. "Honestly, I was glad he did. Not just because of how much he makes. I was relieved that he filed taxes. A lot of people don't."

"Really?"

"You'd be amazed at how many people are behind on their taxes." I adjusted my body so that I could sit on my foot. Now I was facing Cheyenne instead of looking at her from the side. "The thing I liked the most about that message was that the pastor didn't try to sugarcoat it."

"True." She nodded.

"I like the way he laid everything out. Some of the things that seemed like common sense obviously weren't that common. Like when he talked about making sure you see how your man reacts when he gets angry. Does he call you out of your name? Has he hit you?"

"Shoot, I wish Jonathan would hit me," she chuckled. "That would be the last time he'd ever hit anybody."

We both laughed and gave each other high fives.

"I feel you." I stopped laughing. "Nobody is perfect; we know that. I like the way the pastor pointed out finding out your man's issue before getting married. I was glad that he kept it real by pointing out his own issue."

"I know, right? Just by looking at him, you'd think his wife was the luckiest woman on earth. Her husband looks good, is successful, and makes plenty of bank."

"True. But like he said, he was selfish. What

I got out of the whole thing was that we should get to know as much as possible about our potential mate before getting married. No woman should even consider marrying a man who hasn't introduced her to his family and friends."

I looked over and saw that Jonathan was awake.

"Hi," Cheyenne said. "How are you feeling?"

"I'm all right," he replied.

I got up. "I'll leave you two alone."

I went upstairs and lay across my bed. I thought about my upcoming marriage. Greg and I were complete strangers before that fateful day of our first meeting. Now, we were best friends, and he already felt like family. It's amazing how love works. Two people from different backgrounds with different life experiences come together to form the ultimate union. From strangers to married . . . married strangers.

Coming Soon

When the Fairytale Ends

By Dwan Abrams

One

Turning thirty-five. What a milestone, Greg thought. Although he didn't feel any different than he had at twenty-five, somehow knowing that today was his 35th birthday made him feel a bit . . . old. He tried to shake the feeling and convince himself that age was a state of mind more so than a number, but when he went in the bathroom and caught a glimpse of his reflection in the mirror, that all changed.

He leaned in to take a closer look, hoping it was just the lighting. No such luck. There was a silver strand of hair sticking out of his temple. Swearing that gray hair hadn't been there the night before, he huffed as he searched for the tweezers to pluck the unruly strand. He found the tweezers and braced himself against the vanity as he pulled the wiry strand and stared at it. Frustrated, he then dropped it in the waste basket. He scratched his scalp and

picked up a hand-held mirror to check the rest
of his head. As far as he could tell, his hair was
still black. Sighing, he put the mirror down, realizing that aging was inevitable. The only exception was death, and he wasn't ready to die.
He considered shaving his head again instead of
the slightly faded Mohawk he was sporting. He
didn't have time to deal with that now, so he
washed his face, brushed his teeth, and took a
quick shower.

Changing into a ribbed crew neck shirt,
jeans, and boots, Greg looked forward to picking up the birthday gift that he had ordered for
himself. He had always dreamed of owning a
motorcycle and riding cross-country dressed in
leather. Seeing bikers ride on the interstate,
seemingly without a care in the world, made him
envious. Just like his father and older brother,
Neil, he had a fascination with bikes.

As a kid, he and his dad used to look through
biker publications and visit bike shops. He
never understood why his dad wouldn't indulge
himself and get a bike. It wasn't until Greg was
a senior in high school and begging for a bike as
a graduation gift that his dad confessed to him
that he had actually owned a bike for many
years before getting married. However, when
he met Greg's mom, at her urging, he gave up
his biker lifestyle in exchange for a wife and
kids. To keep peace in his relationship, he had-
n't ridden a bike since.

As far as Greg was concerned, that was his
dad's problem, not his. He had wanted a bike

more than anything and was crushed when his parents refused to get one for him. His mother went as far as to say she feared for his safety and didn't want him to buy one for as long as she was alive. As the youngest of three, Greg tried to be a good son and respect his mother's wishes. He placed the idea of owning a bike on the backburner. He did what his parents expected of him and went on to college at Morehouse College, majored in business, and graduated with honors. Shortly thereafter he landed a job selling insurance. He didn't mind wearing a suit and tie to work every day; it made him feel successful. What he regretted was that being so responsible quelled his free spirit. Having a successful career and making a good living appealed to him, but deep down inside, he yearned for the freedom that only riding on an open road could provide.

He had recently had a conversation with Neil, who had told him he purchased a bike. Greg was green with envy. Convinced that if Neil, a corporate lawyer with a wife and kid, could indulge, so could he. That was all the confirmation he needed. He immediately started researching bikes, and when he found the one he wanted, he couldn't wait to get it.

His mother was still alive, and he hoped the news of his latest purchase wouldn't change that. Unlike Neil, Greg lived in Georgia, and so did their mother. Keeping his motorcycle a secret from her the way Neil had wouldn't be that easy considering that she frequently visited him. He reminded himself that he was a grown man and that he didn't need his mother's approval.

His wife, Shania, walked into the bedroom and kissed him on the lips. She was the love of his life, and he hated doing anything that would let her down. They had gotten engaged during the Christmas holiday and initially planned on getting married three months later. When they found out that Valentine's Day fell on a Saturday, they changed their date. On Valentine's Day, he married his best friend and soul mate. He knew that she was The One, because he had prayed for God to send him a mate. The first time he laid eyes on Shania at the Corner Café in Buckhead, he knew there was something special about her.

On their wedding day, Greg thought she was the most beautiful woman he had ever seen. He couldn't wait to make her his wife and make love to her for the first time. Upon seeing her, he fell in love with her all over again.

Still dressed in her pajamas, Shania said, "Happy birthday!" With a smile plastered on her pouty lips, she continued. "I'm surprised you're dressed. Where are you going?"

Being deliberately aloof, he replied, "With Franklin."

His neighbor, Franklin, belonged to a bike club. He had already told Franklin that he was going to buy a bike and would need him to drop him off.

Shania placed a dainty hand on her round

hips. "Will you at least have time to eat the breakfast I prepared for you?"

He nodded, hoping that she wouldn't probe any deeper into where he was going. He pulled out his iPhone and scrolled until he found Franklin's number. He placed a call to Franklin, telling him to come over in thirty minutes. He then ended the call and followed Shania down the stairs. She led him into the breakfast area where they ate his favorite: Eggs Benedict, grits, and mixed fruit.

No sooner than he'd convinced himself he had nothing to feel guilty about, he wondered how he would explain his purchase to Shania. He had casually mentioned to her his love of motorcycles and that one day he wanted to own óne. She had responded in a manner similar to his mother. After that, he hadn't brought up the subject to her again.

He squeezed the bridge of his nose, trying to erase the image of a disappointed Shania from his brain. They had only been married three months, and they were still in the honeymoon stage. Greg hoped his decision to buy a bike without consulting her wouldn't change that. Life with Shania had been lovely, better than he could've ever imagined. The owner of a thriving catering business, Shania's culinary skills were beyond reproach; she kept a clean house, and enjoyed making love as much as he did.

A devilish grin graced his face when he thought about the awkwardness of their wedding night. Shania had saved herself for marriage.

Although Greg had felt like pounding his chest and shouting that he was the King of the World, he had been nervous about taking her virginity; he didn't want to hurt her. Once they got over that initial hurdle, their love life was more than gratifying.

Greg finished his breakfast and licked his lips. Shania cooked even better than his mother, and that was no easy feat in Greg's opinion. He checked his watch and Franklin would be arriving soon. He excused himself from the table and kissed Shania on the top of her head. He patted himself down, making sure that he had his wallet, and he did. Then he decided to go outside and wait for Franklin.

A look of wonder lust appeared on Greg's face the moment he saw the sparkly black BMW motorcycle with shiny chrome waiting for him. Time seemed to stand still. The muffled conversations of the people standing around him seemed to cease.

"That's top of the line right there," Franklin commented, rubbing his pointy beard.

Greg snapped out of his trance. "I know, right?" He chuckled.

"If you don't need me, I'll get at you later."

They gave each other daps and Greg thanked him for dropping him off. He then waved his hand, motioning for the sales rep to come over. Pointing to his dream bike, Greg explained that he was there to pick it up. The salesman grinned and complimented him on his choice. He took

Greg to his office where they finalized the paperwork. They shook hands, and Greg felt excited that his dream was finally coming true. The anticipation of riding his brand new bike made him feel like a teenager.

While waiting for the delivery of his keys, Greg thought about his wife. He wondered what he was going to say when he pulled up at the house on a motorcycle. He briefly considered telling Shania that he was the head of the household and that if he wanted a bike, he could have one. He smoothed his hand over his goatee and shook his head. That wouldn't work with her. Their relationship had been built on trust, mutual respect, and communication. There was no way he could get away with such a dismissive attitude.

Through the window, Greg looked out at the showroom floor. He saw his salesman approaching with a set of keys dangling from his hand. Greg stood up and met him at the door.

"These are for you," the salesman said, handing Greg the keys.

He clutched the keys in his hand like he had been given a precious gem and allowed his excitement to overshadow his previous thoughts.

The salesman continued. "Your ride is ready and waiting for you."

The corners of Greg's mouth curled upward as he shook the salesman's hand with his free hand. In need of a helmet, he went to a different section of the store and browsed the various helmets. A glossy black helmet with a red design caught his eye.

"I like that one too," a female voice said.

He turned his head and noticed Shannyn, the older sister of one of the students in his youth group, standing next to him.

Her glossy red lips formed a seductive smile as she spoke. "I didn't know you were in to motorcycles, Minister Greg Crinkle." She emphasized the word minister.

Hearing her call him "minister" took him by surprise, especially since he was the youth pastor, not the pastor of the church. She usually called him Greg, so he figured she was being facetious.

The way Shannyn ran her tongue over her white teeth made Greg have an inappropriate thought. Inside, he admonished the thought and forced himself to stop staring at her mouth.

"I've always had a thing for bikes." He placed the helmet on the counter and retrieved his wallet from his back pocket.

"And I've always had a thing for a man on a bike," she teased.

Greg slapped down a few bills to pay for his helmet. "It was nice seeing you again, Shannyn." He collected his change and picked up the helmet.

Grabbing the crook of his arm, Shannyn said, "How's Shania?"

Smiling politely, Greg replied, "She's great. I really need to get going." He looked down at his arm, indicating that she needed to let him go.

Shannyn released his arm. "Are you going to show me your bike?"

Sighing, Greg said, "Sure."

Once outside, he allowed himself to drink in the warm day in May. He showed off his new motorcycle, and Shannyn's eyes twinkled with delight. He wished that Shania would get that excited when she saw his bike.

"You're going to have to take me for a ride some time."

He pretended to clear his throat. He knew that Shania wasn't particularly fond of Shannyn. If he took Shannyn for a ride, it would prove to be his last voyage, because Shania would kill him.

"What brings you here today?" He attempted to change the subject.

Shannyn circled the bike and slightly bent over, giving Greg a full view of her dangerous curves. Her low cut shirt and tight jeans emphasized her hourglass figure.

"Oh, a friend of mine cracked his helmet, so I came up here to get him a new one."

He nodded. "Today's my birthday and Shania's waiting for me. I guess I'll see you at church on Sunday."

She stood upright with a slight bounce, causing her bosom to jiggle. "Happy birthday to you." Her tone was breathy. She walked over and hugged him.

Feeling uncomfortable and pushing her away, Greg thanked her and bid her adios. She left, and Greg redirected his attention to his bike. He took a few minutes to get better acquainted with Halle; that was the name he settled on for his bike. He then placed his body on top of the vehicle and shifted his weight on the seat. Taking a deep breath, he secured the helmet on his head, put the key in the ignition, and drove off. His heart pounded as he darted into traffic. He felt an adrenaline rush each time he shifted gears. To Greg, this was living. He had rented bikes numerous times in the past, but nothing compared to owning one. Hopefully his wife and mother would respect his decision. At that moment, though, nothing or no one could rob him of the joy he felt.

Rounding the corner into his Alpharetta sub-division, Greg slowed his pace. He passed by numerous brick houses with well-maintained lawns before pulling into his circular driveway and parking his bike. He paused for a moment, still getting used to the idea of living in such a massive house. The 6,000 square foot home once belonged to his wife's parents who died in an automobile accident nine years ago. They willed the house to Shania and her younger sister, Cheyenne.

Greg felt a tinge of sadness as he thought about his in-laws. He wished that he could have met them just one time so that he could thank them for the exceptional job they did raising Shania. He appreciated the spiritual foundation Shania's parents had given her. She had proven to be a woman of strong character, integrity, and faith by the way she stepped up to the plate at the tender age of twenty-two and raised her ten-year-old sister. That made him respect her even more.

Growing up on military bases, most of his childhood homes were a third the size of the estate standing before him. And the three-bedroom house he owned in Stone Mountain, and subsequently chose to rent out after the wedding, wasn't anywhere near as luxurious as Shania's. He found himself feeling as though he was living on an episode of *MTV Cribs*.

He removed his helmet and stepped down. As he tugged on his pant leg, he admired his new toy and smiled. He would've bent over and kissed her, but he didn't want to make a fool of himself. Instead, he patted her. He then turned his attention to his freshly cut lawn and figured that the lawn guy must've come by. The hedges were neatly trimmed with designer mulch lining the bushes. Fully bloomed and brightly colored purple hyacinths, yellow daffodils, pink zinnias, and white and red roses were in a flowerbed by the door. His home felt so inviting that he looked forward to coming there every day.

Sighing, he placed his key in the door and entered. He set his helmet on the floor next to the door. He called out to Shania, and she met him in the foyer. The way her face lit up when she saw him made him feel as though she was glad to see him. Her smile warmed his heart. She had a way of making him feel loved and appreciated. That alone endeared him to her.

He cleared his throat and grabbed her hand.

"I have something to show you." He paused.
"Close your eyes." He figured that if she could
feel his excitement about the bike, maybe she
could muster up some enthusiasm of her own.

She gave him an incredulous look before
closing her eyes and following his lead. He told
her not to peek as he guided her out the door.
When they reached the bike, he touched her
lower back and told her to open her eyes.

Shania opened her eyes and her jaw dropped.
"What's this?"

He could tell by the way her eyes blinked
rapidly and the way she snapped her neck that
she was less than thrilled. His heart sank.

"I just bought it," he explained.

She folded her arms across her chest. "I can
see that." She raised her voice. "Why did you
feel the need to get a motorcycle? Are you
going through an early mid-life crisis or something?"

Her words stung, and he found himself questioning his motives for wanting that bike at
this stage of his life. How did she know that a
part of him felt like he was getting old and
turning into his dad? Nothing against his pops,
because he had the utmost respect for him as a
man and a father. He was a retired Air Force
pilot and had provided a comfortable life for
Greg and the rest of his family. He also admired
his dad for being a devoted husband and family
man. As far as Greg was concerned, he couldn't
have asked for a better role model to teach him
how to be a man. Greg's point of contention
was that he never knew the biker side of his

dad. He only knew the disciplinarian and provider side. He refused to fall into that same trap. Before he and Shania started having children, Greg wanted to cross a few more items off his bucket list, like owning a bike.

"I-I," he stammered, unable to get his words out.

"Why would you make a major, and *dangerous*, purchase without consulting me?" She rolled her eyes. "How selfish and inconsiderate can you be?"

He clenched his jaw. He and Shania didn't usually argue, and he didn't like hearing Shania speak to him in such a harsh tone. He especially hated the disappointed look on her face.

She halted her hand. "The last thing I want to do is stand in the way of your happiness, but I wish you would've talked to me about this first." Her brownish-sable colored eyes stared into his light brown ones. She sighed. "You had to know that I wouldn't be okay with this. For Christ's sake, my parents have already been taken from me. If something bad happened to you . . ." Her voice trailed off.

He knew that Shania had taken her parents' death hard. Although he considered her to be a strong woman, he knew that she still had vulnerabilities. The more he had gotten to know her he realized that she had a fear of suddenly losing the people closest to her. He tried his best to give her emotional support and security by letting her know through his words and deeds that he was with her for the long haul.

"Baby, I'm sorry," Greg said. "It's just that

owning a motorcycle has been a lifelong dream of mine."

Shania softened her tone and continued. "Trust me; I'm not trying to crush your spirit." She unfolded her arms and placed them at her sides. "After you told me that Neil had gotten a motorcycle, I sensed in my spirit that something was going on with you." She turned her face away from his. "I love you; I just couldn't take if anything happened to you."

"I know, baby. Don't worry." He tried to sound sensitive to her concerns. "I'll be careful."

She bit her lower lip and lowered her head.

Greg stepped to the side so that he could look her in the face. Her eyes were filled with sadness. Just the thought of causing Shania pain hurt his heart. He reached out and grabbed her. With her head resting on his chest, he stroked her long, straight hair.

Trying to lighten the mood, Greg said, "Do you want me to take you for a ride?"

She broke away from him and smirked. "Yes," she replied, "but not that kind of ride."

Reading Group Discussion Questions

1. How did you feel about Rayna and her plight?

2. What was your initial impression of Bryce? Did your perception of him change? If so, what changed it?

3. Explain your reaction to Bryce's revelation about Fox?

4. What did you think about Aja?

5. Do you think that people who have affairs can still be good parents? Explain.

6. Which couple(s) do you think has/have the best chances of staying together? Why?

7. Who was your favorite character? Why?

8. Who was your least favorite character? Why?

9. Which character(s) could you personally identify with? In what way(s)?

10. How do you feel about running a background check and credit report on a potential mate?

11. When it comes to marriage, which do you feel is most important: love, sex, money, or being saved? Explain your answer.

12. What did you think about Shania's relationship with her sister?

13. Did you agree or disagree with Shania's feelings about Jonathan? Explain.

14. If you were in Sunni's shoes, how would you have handled the situation with Hunter, Aja, and Devin?

15. What advice would you have given to Cheyenne regarding her relationship with Jonathan?

Author Bio

Dwan Abrams is the author of *Divorcing the Devil*, *Only True Love Waits*, *The Scream Within* and "Favor" (a short story appearing in *The Midnight Clear* anthology). She's the founder, publisher, and editorial director of Nevaeh Publishing, a small press independent publishing house. She currently resides in a suburb of Atlanta with her family. She loves hearing from her readers via email at *dwanabrams1@aol.com*. Visit Dwan on the web at *www.dwanabrams.com*.

Urban Christian His Glory Book Club!

Established January 2007, *UC His Glory Book Club* is another way by which to introduce to the literary world, Urban Book's much-anticipated new imprint, **Urban Christian** and its authors. We are an online book club supporting Urban Christian authors by purchasing, reading, and providing written reviews of the authors' books that are read. *UC His Glory* welcomes both men and women of the literary world who have a passion for reading Christian based fiction.

UC His Glory is the brainchild of Joylynn Jossel, Author and Executive Editor of Urban Christian and Kendra Norman-Bellamy, Author and Copy Editor for Urban Christian. The book club will provide support, positive feedback, encouragement, and a forum whereby members can openly discuss and review the literary works of Urban Christian authors. In the future, we anticipate broadening our spectrum of services to include: online author chats, author spotlights, interviews with your favorite Urban Christian author(s), special online groups for *UC Book Club* members, ability to post reviews on the website and amazon.com, membership ID cards, *UC His Glory* Yahoo Group, and much more.

Even though there will be no membership fees attached to becoming a member of *UC His Glory Book Club*, we do expect our members to be active, committed, and to follow the guidelines of the Book Club.

UC His Glory members pledge to:

- Follow the guidelines of *UC His Glory Book Club*.
- Provide input, opinions, and reviews that build up, rather than tear down.
- Commit to purchasing, reading, and discussing featured book(s) of the month.
- Agree not to miss more than three consecutive online monthly meetings.
- Respect the Christian beliefs of *UC His Glory Book Club*.
- Believe that Jesus is the Christ, Son of the Living God

We look forward to the online fellowship.

Many Blessings to You!

Shelia E Lipsey
President
UC His Glory Book Club

**Visit the official Urban Christian Book Club website at *www.uchisglorybookclub.net*